TWELVE GIRLS IN THE GARDEN

TWELVE GIRLS IN THE GARDEN

Shane Martin

WILLIAM MORROW & COMPANY
New York

This book is entirely a work of fiction.
No relationship to actual persons or
incidents is intended, inferred, or implied.

for
Colin and Ursula
—for fun.

CONTENTS

one: LONDON

꘎꘎꘎

I

IT WAS A COMBINATION OF CIRCUMSTANCES, none conclusive in itself, which led Professor Ronald Challis to walk along the Thames from Pimlico to Chelsea, and began the queer chain of events that ended, some two months later, on a rocky and desolate island in the Aegean.

The day had been surprisingly mild for late October in London: the Thames on this particular evening was the river of Turner rather than of Whistler. The smoke had not yet begun to settle, and the sunset could still produce fire and gold and not just that luminous grey darkness that threatened smog.

This unexpected phenomenon of rare light and magical warmth had unsettled the professor in a somewhat paradoxical way, so that instead of succumbing to the charms of his surroundings, he found himself divided between a nostalgia for the more robust and flamboyant coloring of fall in his native New England, and a biting regret that the demands of scholarship had dragged him from the sunburnt rocks of Greece, where he had recently completed an active and pleasant eighteen months of digging. It was ironic that the results of this activity now confined him, and had for the past six weeks confined him, to a round of lonely and cheerless commuting between the monstrous black classical façade of the British Museum and the peeling stucco of the small bachelor flat he occupied in a tall and rather unprepossessing building at 93 St. George's Square.

Partly also there was the desire to escape, if only briefly, from the jungle of ormolu, restored French furniture, assorted mid-Victorian objects, ornate chandeliers, and nineteenth-century mezzotints which his landlord, Mr. Valentine, a friendly and attentive man who subscribed to *The Connoisseur*, had encouraged to proliferate in the apartment in the hospitable but misguided belief that he was making it snug as well as artistic.

And finally there was this curious and unaccountable fact that for no reason at all he had found himself thinking about Erica and John Barrington: thinking of them quite vividly, although he had not seen Erica for three years, and Barrington had been dead for even longer. And he had been unable to resist the impulse to walk along the Chelsea Embankment merely to look at the house again. In this impulse there was nothing of morbidity, for the professor was not a morbid man: perhaps, being an archaeologist, he sensed that some greater assurance of permanent values might be found in stone and mortar than could ever be extracted from reflections on the flux of human relationships.

In this he was to find himself quite wrong.

Well-wrapped against the impending river chill, he walked briskly along the gleaming riverside, past the huge block of Dolphin Square, past the churning grandeur of the Battersea Power Station across the river, past the swinging curve of the bridge that Whistler had loved, to the small Georgian house around the corner in Tite Street.

Outwardly the house seemed little changed. The paint work of the door had been refreshed, and the knocker was gleamingly polished, but the windows were dark and blank. The house clearly had acquired new ownership since he had seen it last; just as obviously, it was for the moment unoccupied. The corner window nearest the river was suddenly illuminated from outside by the final gold glinting of the setting sun, although the rest of the street and all the houses were steeped in the gathering dusk.

Now, to a man whose entire adult life has been devoted to the

probing of whole extinct civilizations, curiosity is the most natural
instinct in the world. Professor Challis had exhumed and dissected
cities, empires, kings, tyrants, and courtesans: there was to him
no such thing as privacy. It was therefore the compulsion of this
innate and almost childlike curiosity that led him to walk slowly
across to the single glowing window and, because he was an
uncommonly short man, to lift himself to the tips of his toes so
he might peer inside. It did not occur to him that he should first
take the precaution of seeing that he was not observed in this
act of blatant prying; nor was he particularly put out when he
heard a deep voice from the darkness behind him saying:

"Yes? Is there anything special you're looking for?"

He turned with a shy, quick smile to find himself confronted
by a man who studied him suspiciously from across the street.
He was a very big man, and the loose drape of his thick tweed
overcoat seemed to accentuate rather than conceal the thrust of
his muscles, the strong bulging solidity of the body beneath. He
was hatless and, although his hair had begun to thin at the fore-
head, clearly not beyond his middle thirties, and handsome in a
heavy, overmasculine way. He spoke with an accent which, while
distinctly American, suggested a parentage that had moved across
the Atlantic not more than a generation before.

It was the accent which interested Professor Challis most. The
fact of having been caught red-handed in an act of inexcusable
inquisitiveness was of negligible importance. The menacing
strength of the looming figure in the dusk did not concern him in
the least, although the professor was precisely five feet five inches
in height and had never in his entire sixty-six years turned a scale
at more than one hundred and twenty-six pounds. His own ancestors had crossed the Atlantic to Massachusetts in the brig
Jupiter in 1754; of his own life, more than half had been spent in
Europe, mostly in the classical digging grounds of the Mediterranean. He spoke in what people call a "cosmopolitan" accent.

Yet there was something queerly interesting and coincidental
in his being addressed in American accents from the gathering

Chelsea dusk outside the house where John Barrington, himself an American, had lived and died.

"I was trying to get a peep inside," he said cheerfully. "The light is flat across the glass, unfortunately. I couldn't see a thing."

"Why?" The man's voice was expressionless. "Why do you want to see inside?"

"Curiosity," answered Professor Challis simply, and chuckled softly. "I knew a man who lived here once."

"You did?" The man seemed to consider the statement carefully, standing huge and still and monolithic in the darkness. "Well, I live here now," he said finally, with a sort of flat emphasis, as if all the past history of the house might be wiped away by the remark. "If you want to look inside, you can come in," he added grudgingly.

"I should very much like to." The professor's sense of curiosity found it easy to forgive the ungraciousness of the invitation. "My name is Challis," he added. "Professor Ronald Challis." He held out his hand.

The big man stared at it unforgivingly and hesitated a moment. "Flett," he said gruffly. "Brandon Flett." He shook hands perfunctorily and took a thin black leather holder from his pocket, flipping the keys out and scowling down at them as he searched for the right one. "Professor of what?" he asked, without looking up.

"Classical studies is the official designation." The professor smiled. "Archaeology explains it better."

Flett grunted, turned the key in the lock, pushed the door, reached a thick arm around to flick the hall switch, and motioned the professor inside.

"Polly will be here in half an hour or so," he said. But whether this remark was addressed to his visitor or was merely to remind himself of the fact was not specified. He began to take off his coat without further explanation.

Professor Challis had the curious feeling of disorientation that comes from returning to a house that one has known in the past with a reasonable familiarity but that in the interim has passed into other hands and become imbued with a different personality. The rooms seemed out-of-shape and lopsided, the levels wrong: he had the queer impression that the whole house had been twisted around on an axis so that it had come to face in an entirely different direction. He could no longer remember upon which wall Barrington had kept his Hokusais, nor whether this same staircase had been there, leading to the upstairs drawing room.

"This man you knew who lived here," said Flett, "his name was Grasset?"

"Oh, no, not at all. His name was Barrington. John Barrington." He smiled at his grudging host. "It's more than three years since I was here, remember."

"Paul Grasset was the man who had the place before me," said Flett flatly. "He got it from somebody whose name I forget, but that wasn't it. Not Barrington." He gestured to the professor to precede him upstairs.

"Barrington's widow lived here a few months," the professor explained helpfully. "She is Lady Peart now. Lady Granville Peart. She did not keep the house long, but maybe—"

"I don't remember names." Flett waved a dismissive hand. "That doesn't mean anything to me, either." He ushered his companion into the drawing room and walked across to a big cocktail cabinet built into that corner of the room where, Professor Challis remembered, John Barrington had kept an old Venetian chest and a Flemish madonna in carved wood. Without asking the professor what he would have, Flett poured two deep whiskeys into tall glasses, siphoned in soda, brought one across to the professor, and took the other with him to a deep armchair. He sat heavily, his arms resting along his thick thighs, his thick fingers slowly twirling the highball glass. Everything about the man, the professor reflected, was thick and settled, like an all-American quarterback who has finally come to rest with fluid on the knee.

The professor liked surprising people, so he smiled quickly and said, "This is the room where Barrington died. He shot himself one night when his wife was away."

This information had no visible effect on Flett. He nodded slightly and grunted and lifted his glass rather churlishly to the professor and said, "Here's to you." This done, he relapsed again into his weighty pensiveness. Covertly studying him, Professor Challis found himself forming the impression that the man, in spite of his heavy and forbidding stolidity, was uneasy about something—or afraid.

If it was either, probably it would be revealed in time; meanwhile the professor patiently turned his attention to an examination of the room he had once known so well. It had lost the collector's character which Barrington had imparted to it—the earlier owner would have frowned at the leather armchairs and cast the cocktail cabinet from the house—but it had by no means moved all the way to the purely utilitarian or mundane.

The big studio windows that gave on to the walled garden, now concealed in darkness, still remained to give an atmosphere that could only be described as "artistic": an atmosphere now raffishly emphasized by the half-dozen expressionist paintings on the walls, some queer pieces of semiabstract sculpture, and in the far corner a Scandinavian-looking drawing desk, a weird contraption of laminated wood and thin rods of tubular steel, above which hung the dull metal cowls of two modern work lamps. In the open fireplace, like some inexplicable intrusion from Upper Tooting, was one of those electric heaters with a spinning gadget inside which is unreasonably supposed to suggest that a log fire is smoldering. Above the chimney piece was a remarkably fine portrait in oils of a young woman in tight black trousers and a striped shirt, seated on a high stool in a pose of stiff and calculated arrogance.

At first glance he had thought the portrait to be a representation of Erica—with what queer persistence these personalities of a dead time haunted their old environment—and even now, although he was aware that it was a picture of some other woman, and a picture, moreover, that he had never set eyes on before, the resemblance remained sharply embedded in his thoughts. The same *quality* of beauty perhaps . . . something in the pose and set of the small dark head. . . .

"Do you know who she is?" Flett asked softly.

Professor Challis turned quickly to find the big man regarding him with a still, watchful intensity. He had moved forward on the armchair and his fingers were splayed heavily across his knees.

"I beg your pardon?"

"That girl in the picture," Flett said patiently. "Do you know who she is?"

"I am afraid I don't. For a moment I thought—"

"There are twelve girls in the garden," said Flett, "but she's the only one of them who's up here, too. That's what makes Jenny kind of special."

"Jenny?" The professor glanced at his companion's drink, but he had scarcely touched it.

"I guess that isn't her name. It's just what I call her. Jenny." He frowned. "I don't know who she is, either. I thought maybe the picture was here when you knew this fellow Barrington, although I guess it wouldn't have been, since she's in the garden, too. I just thought maybe you'd know who she was, that's all." He placed his glass carefully on the side table and rose. "Finish your drink," he said, "and come with me. I'll show you something interesting."

He led the way downstairs, going ahead along a narrow corridor and through a kitchen which had a culinary still life of Braque's on the wall; a door at the far end opened onto an untidy, shedlike room which had clearly once been a sculptor's workshop. The wooden clay bins along one side were overlaid now with a fine chalky dust, and on the central wooden pedestal was an abandoned figurine in white clay that had gone hard. The legs and torso were beautifully modeled, flowing upward and ending in rough blobs of clay and the grotesque twists of armature wires. Professor Challis formed the impression that it was not so much unfinished as destroyed: the upper part seemed to have been torn off violently while the clay was still wet. In the corner of the room a wooden manikin lolled absurdly on top of another heap of dusty armatures.

"This is the way Grasset left it," said Flett moodily. "It looks a mess now, although he was pretty smart about tidiness."

"He was a sculptor then?"

Flett nodded. "A fine one, too, when he wanted to be. He was French. The sort of Frenchman who doesn't belong to any country in the world except the one he's working in. But sometimes he wasn't so good because he was after women, and he didn't care whether he was working or not. When he came to London, you wouldn't know whether he was coming to see Butler's sculpture, or Epstein's, or whether it was to meet some woman at the Savoy."

"You met him here? Or in France?"

"In the States. He came over there every so often to exhibit. He had quite a following in New York."

"And what happened to him?"

"God knows," said Flett. He walked across to a light switch and flicked it. Through the flat rectangle of the window the light jumped green and gold against the blackness, as the garden outside was illuminated. From a nail beside the switch Flett took a big key and unlocked the garden door. As he led the professor outside, he had to bend his head a little to pass beneath the lintel.

"There," he said. "This is what I wanted you to see."

Like the house itself, the walled garden had acquired a character quite different from the picture that lingered in the professor's memory from three years before. Remembrance identified a detail here and there: the texture of the pale bricks in the corner of the wall, the shape of the lily pond, the dry scratchy pattern of the withered vines, the gaunt branches of leafless fruit trees. But what remained were the merest atoms of familiarity in a picture that was almost totally strange.

An ornate stone pergola had been built against the wall facing the house, with a curved fan of steps running up to it from the lily pond. On either side of the pergola were two arched stone niches, and there were four identical niches spaced along each of the other two walls. In each of the twelve niches stood the statue of a girl, a little more than half life-size. Some were nude, some half-draped, all seemed vaguely classical in pose until you looked more closely, when you saw that they were not classical at all. And no two were alike.

In the distance a bell pealed faintly.

Flett said, "Ah, that'll be Polly." For a moment he stood beside the professor, impersonally surveying the garden, then he grunted and without another word went inside.

Professor Challis walked across to the nearest of the twelve girls in the garden.

All the statues had been cast in rough concrete and treated with paint and acids to simulate old bronze. For what seemed to be a long time he walked around the garden examining them. It was likely that Grasset had modeled them, for each one of them had the same skilled competence of workmanship which he had observed in the broken little figurine in the workshop, yet none was without flaws. In one, a magnificently modeled hand would be in sharp contrast to the almost crude workmanship displayed in the folds of drapery, or a shoulder, or the curve of a thigh; in another, the head would appear to be slightly out of scale with the rest of the figure. (Closely examining one, Professor Challis suspected that a different head had been substituted before the figure finally had been cast.) In each of the twelve works was this same contradiction of a brilliant virtuosity and a supreme carelessness; it was only in the heads that one found no evidence whatever of creative shortcomings or skimped workmanship. Clearly, they were distinct portraits, all of women who must have been uncommonly beautiful, all different in character and personality, all imbued with some warmth and life and vitality which still seemed latent even in the cold immobility of the rough concrete. The girl with the arrogant face whose portrait hung in the drawing room was personified in the second statue to the left of the pergola: the similarity between the painting and the sculpture was striking enough to suggest that both had been done by the same artist.

Was all this, the professor wondered whimsically, Grasset's gallery of conquests? Flett had more than hinted that the sculptor was something of a philanderer. Did he mount his trophies in these niches in the garden wall as a hunter might put the horns of an elk in his hallway or an eland's head above the sideboard?

"Very intriguing," he said aloud. It was a habit he had acquired during his excavations in lonely places; frequently, when he was solitary, he would chatter to himself for hours. But suddenly he was inhibited by the sound of his own voice in the quiet garden, by the figures of the twelve golden girls spaced around him.

He could hear the murmur of voices from inside the house, the clink of glass. Once, glancing up, he saw two figures silhouetted in the bright oblong of the studio window. They were looking down, watching him. Flett seemed in no great hurry to return to him. Or had he been dismissed altogether? Was he expected to find some back gate leading out of the garden through which he was quietly to take his leave, to disappear into the anonymous Chelsea night?

Again he walked slowly around the garden, carefully examining each of the statues in turn, and he was engrossed in a study of the one in which he suspected the head had been replaced, when he heard the soft voice behind him.

"You mustn't let Ben's enigma worry you too much," she said, and even as Professor Challis turned to look at her, he was intrigued by her pronunciation of "enigma." Her voice was soft and precise, and, but for that one word, it would not have been so easy to judge her extraction as foreign.

She was a slim and singularly attractive girl, wearing a red handkerchief knotted at the neck of a black fisherman's-knit jersey, and bluejeans rolled up a turn or two above soft moccasins. Her black hair was cropped short. In the deliberately smart casualness of her clothing as much as in her air of assurance and of a half-suppressed quality of vitality and intelligence, there was something one associated with those new forms of young life which move around art classes and schools of drama and youth hostels on the Continent.

"Ben?" said Professor Challis.

"Brandon." She gave him a quick smile. "It's an awful name. We call him Ben."

"Mr. Flett, you mean? Yes, I see." He studied her for a moment, then turned slowly toward one of the statues in the niches.

"Yes," she said calmly, and for a moment a fleeting melancholy seemed to touch her eyes, and then she smiled again. "That's me over there. It was done a few years ago. If you'd like to come up now," she said, "we've made some coffee."

In the drawing room Flett was attending to the percolator. With the arrival of the girl his manner seemed to have softened a little; the professor realized for the first time that for all the man's weight and heaviness he could probably move quickly and even gracefully. He even grinned as he said, "This is Polly Sorelle, but I guess you introduced yourselves in the garden." He had fine teeth.

The professor turned to the girl, seated now on the rug by the fireplace, her feet crossed, her small pointed chin cupped in her hands. "You are Greek, aren't you?" he asked.

She glanced at him quickly, hesitated an instant, and said, "Yes."

"Then Polly, of course, is Polyxéna."

"Priam's loveliest daughter, sacrificed to the shade of Achilles," said Flett surprisingly. "That's why we call her Polly."

"How could you tell I was Greek?" she asked, alert with interest.

"The way you pronounced 'enigma.' You gave it the Greek accent."

"What enigma?" Flett turned to them. In his big hands the balanced coffee cups looked absurdly fragile.

"Your girls in the garden," said Polly. "And *her*." She tilted her head toward the portrait above the chimney piece, and, as she did so, Professor Challis caught the same fleeting resemblance which at first had made him think of Erica. Erica, Polly, the unknown girl in the portrait: between the three of them there was no true likeness you could put your finger on, and yet there was some queer, elusive resemblance, a sort of fugitive quality that all three of them shared. And both Erica and Polly were Greek. . . .

"It wasn't only the accent, of course," he said, "because in fact you have almost no accent at all. You remind me a little of someone I knew once. Oddly enough, she often came to this house, and she was Greek, too." He paused and glanced at the portrait. "I would be inclined to think that she is Greek also," he said.

"Ah, that's interesting," said Flett, frowning. "That's *very* interesting." But he made no attempt to explain in what way it was interesting. Handing the professor his coffee, he said, "You know Greece then?"

Professor Challis smiled to himself. How healthy and chastening it was to move in the company of the young. Half a lifetime's work in Greece, the discovery of the Gournian Treasury, a distinguished professorship and an impressive number of honorary doctorates, enough excavated material to fill a good-size museum, and a series of monographs which the Royal Society had designated as the greatest single contribution to knowledge of the preclassical past since Evans—and these two young and evidently intelligent people had never even heard of him!

"Yes, I know it pretty well," he said dryly. "I have been working there for the past eighteen months. I plan to return there about mid-November."

Flett looked at him for a moment before speaking. "I never finished what I was saying about Grasset, did I?"

"You never really began," reproved the professor mildly. "I asked you what had happened to him and you said, 'God knows.'"

"Well, that's it. He disappeared."

"You mean—"

"I mean just that. Disappeared. Vanished. He had a show of his work booked for the Galerie Rive Droite, in Paris. He came back from New York, as far as London anyway, about two weeks before, planning to be there for the opening, and that's the last anybody saw of him."

"And when was this?"

"A little over six months ago. In May."

"I keep telling Ben," Polly put in, "that people just *can't* disappear like that, not these days, not with passports, and all the—"

"Well, maybe they can't, but that's the way it happened, isn't it?"

Polly nodded her head patiently. "What I was going to say, if you'll let me, is that people can't disappear like that unless they *want* to."

"How could he have *wanted* to, with that show coming up in Paris?" Flett protested. "All the topnotchers would have been there. Did you know Picasso had promised to come? Can't you see, it was the biggest thing that ever happened to him, the crux of his whole career. Particularly coming on top of the success he'd had in New York. You want to tell me all this adds up to a good reason for wanting to disappear from the face of the earth? Not Paul Grasset, no, sir!"

"You didn't see him when he came back here to London?" asked the professor quietly.

"No." Flett shook his head. "I was with him in New York ten days or so before he sailed. We were making arrangements about the house."

"The house?"

"This house. We'd been negotiating about it for some little time. I'd known Grasset two or three years; we were rather friendly. He wanted to settle down in Paris, and I wanted to study architecture here in London, so we made a deal about the house. Did you know Whistler lived here once? Just before he went broke over that business with Ruskin. That's what they say, anyway."

"You had to pay a year's rent in advance, don't forget," Polly said insistently, disregarding Whistler. "I've often thought since that if somebody was planning to disappear, that would be a nice lump sum to have."

"Naturally," agreed Flett dryly. "Except that he'd gone through it all before he got back here. The way he lived in New York, and then crossing in a suite on the *Queen Elizabeth*, there wouldn't have been cab fare left by the time he got to Southampton."

"You have made some attempt, I take it, to try to unravel the mystery of his disappearance?" asked the professor.

"I didn't arrive in London until a month or so after he'd come back. By the time I began to think that something was wrong,

I was in the house anyway, so I stayed on. Since then I've been trying to figure out what happened."

"When Grasset returned from New York he was not seen by anybody? He left no messages? Nothing like that?"

"Nothing." Flett shrugged and turned away, then hunched his broad shoulders over the coffeepot. "Nothing except those damned girls of his in the garden. I keep coming back to them, as if they could tell me what happened."

"But one of them is here," the professor said, turning toward Polly Sorelle with a smile. But she looked away quickly.

Flett put down the coffeepot. "Polly doesn't know anything about it," he said, with a vague suggestion of accusation in his voice, and he seemed to address the statement to her, rather than to the professor. "Grasset did that head years ago, in Paris," he said. "The last time Polly saw him was six months before he went to the States. That's right, isn't it, Polly?"

"Yes," she said.

"Well, there are eleven other statues," said the professor. "Are you able to identify any of the—er—of the other models?"

Flett smiled briefly. "I can pick out one or two of them. Not all. My guess is that nobody ever had a full tally of Paul Grasset's women. One of them is a Swedish girl called Freda Lindstrom. She used to model for him in Paris, but she's been in London for quite a while now. Another was an Indian girl who worked in a dealer's shop in the rue Bonaparte while she was getting through the Sorbonne. Her name I don't recall, and wouldn't be able to pronounce even if I could."

"And Giji," suggested Polly.

"And Giji, certainly," said Flett. He repeated the name with the flat intonation of a man marking off an item in an inventory. Was it no more than imagination on the professor's part that the big man's eyes for an instant seemed to harbor a sort of defensive bitterness?

"Who is Giji?" the professor asked interestedly.

Flett shrugged, and it was left to Polly to reply. "Oh, she's just a woman in Montmartre," she said, and in the simple statement, with all its paucity of information, there was a peculiar depth of meaning, as if the natural sense of charity in her nature was being deliberately asserted over a feeling of disgust. It was curious that throughout all this discussion about the girls in the garden, about the twelve statues that comprised Paul Grasset's gallery, one was aware of the quality of things unspoken, of meanings hinted at but never expressed, of thoughts that came half-formed, and disappeared before they could be rounded off and shaped. Polly, as if vaguely aware of the inconclusive nature of her remark, added, "Everyone knows Giji."

Professor Challis nodded agreeably. "And then, of course," he said brightly, "there is our mysterious young lady in the portrait here." He glanced at Flett and turned his attention to the oil painting on the wall. From the high stool above the chimney piece, Jenny looked down at them, young, aloof, and arrogant. "You seem to feel that there is some rather special significance to this one," he said.

Flett stared at the picture thoughtfully. "It's a hunch, that's all," he said slowly. "I just have a feeling she's the one who has the answer to it all."

2

PROFESSOR CHALLIS' heart sank a little at the door of the apartment house, because there was a faint smell of French polish in the air, and when the hallway smelt of French polish, it meant that Mr. Valentine was renovating another *objet d'art* and would waylay him to admire it. There was a singular danger in this, because if he expressed only meager admiration, Mr. Valentine would be hurt, and if he displayed enthusiasm, the fearful object —and all Mr. Valentine's objects were in some degree fearful— would inevitably be earmarked for the professor's already cluttered quarters.

He took the thick gold watch from his vest pocket and saw that it was almost midnight, which was very late even for his land-lord's French polishing. Perhaps he could creep in stealthily and evade the man, and so preserve the warmth and excitement which the night's unexpected adventure had given him. It was for this very reason of preserving the pleasure that he had taken so long to come home, walking up to Sloane Square and all the way to the Albert Hall before turning back toward Pimlico. It would be a great shame if it were all to be dissipated in the smell of shellac.

As he went cautiously across the hallway, the side door opened, and there was Mr. Valentine beaming at him, his arms red to the elbows and a stained polishing pad in his hand.

"Ah, I've been waiting up for you, Professor," he said jovially. "There's a telephone message I have to give you." He smiled archly. "From a girl."

"A *girl?*"

"Name of Polly. That's what she said. She gave another name, too, but I'm afraid I didn't catch it. I kept asking her to spell it out but she said just say Polly, he'll know."

"Oh, yes," said Professor Challis patiently. For a moment he wondered how she had known his telephone number, and then he remembered that at Flett's request he had left one of his cards with them.

"The message is—" Mr. Valentine adjusted his glasses and frowned down at a slip of paper. "The message is that if you can manage it, she would like you to meet her in the saloon bar of the Woburn Arms, that's a public house in Bloomsbury quite close to the museum. . . . Yes, at the Woburn Arms, five-forty-five to-morrow." He ducked his head inside the room, where at least twenty clocks of various shapes and sizes were ticking, took a random sight at the nearest of the four grandfather clocks, grinned at the professor and corrected himself. "Five-forty-five *today*," he said. "It's three minutes past midnight."

"Five-forty-five," said the professor. "The Woburn Arms. Yes, thank you very much, Mr. Valentine."

The landlord tossed his polishing pad into the air and caught it deftly. "Did I show you my rosewood inkstand?" he asked.

"Would you mind very much if it was tomorrow?" said the professor wearily. "I have an awful headache."

The professor was a methodical man—the science of archaeology, like the practice of criminal detection, has room only for the methodical man—so that on the following morning he began his day exactly as he would have begun it had he not visited the house in Tite Street the evening before, nor had the definite intuition that this day was to produce something that would be unexpected and might quite possibly even be strange.

He took his hot bath and shaved himself while he was in the tub, did four minutes of yogi breathing by the open window, and brewed himself two cups of thick Turkish coffee over the small, spluttering gas ring in the corner of the room. It was typical of his landlord's preoccupation with refinement over function that, while the room boasted not one but three crystal chandeliers, it had no facilities for cooking, apart from this single antiquated gas ring. This shortcoming would have worried most men far more than it worried Professor Challis. He liked his coffee black, thick, gritty, and Turkish, and to achieve this end always carried with him a long-handled copper coffee jug which had been given him by the owner of a *kafenéion* in Piraeus. With this simple device he was quite capable of brewing coffee to his liking over a couple of charcoal embers: the gas ring was luxury itself.

While he drank his coffee, he opened and read a letter from a German colleague giving a somewhat cautious account of excavations on the island of Samos, glanced down the personal column of *The Times*, consulted his appointment book, and revised two pages in proof of a paper he was contributing to one of the more erudite quarterlies. At exactly nine o'clock he left the house, walked briskly down the embankment and along the river to the Tate Gallery, where he hailed a No. 88 bus which took him to Oxford Circus. From there he strode purposefully to the British Museum, where for some time he was preoccupied with the classification of certain Minoan seals. At precisely eleven o'clock he interrupted his normal program by going to the reading room, where he made a careful examination of the catalogue and had an attendant fetch him four books concerned with European sculpture. These he studied diligently for an hour and a quarter. At half-past twelve he was in Soho, at a corner table in the Restaurant Bourgogne, ordering a Crème Dame Blanche, Gâteau de Foie Lyonnais, and a half-bottle of Pouilly-Fuissé.

It was not until then that he began to give serious consideration to the matter of Polly, Flett, the twelve girls in the garden, the portrait of Jenny, and the strange disappearance of the sculptor Paul Grasset.

What extraordinary complexities life provided in its chance encounters, he reflected. He had gone to the house in Tite Street expecting perhaps to finger again the tenuous substance of an old experience. He had then never heard of Brandon Flett nor of the Greek girl Polyxéna—there was something queer about that relationship: they had a familiarity, yet there was some intangible element of conflict between them—and the name of Paul Grasset had meant nothing to him whatsoever. As for the Swedish model called Freda Lindstrom, and the anonymous Indian girl from the rue Bonaparte, and the equally anonymous girl in the portrait whom Flett called Jenny. . . . And Giji!

Yet these were the people who now possessed his thoughts to the degree where his own direct experience with the house in Tite Street had receded into some misty hinterland as remote as the world of the Minoan seals which he had spent much of the morning studying. Erica and John Barrington and the problems of their life had all passed together out of consequence. It was the same stage, but the scenery was different. A new company had taken over.

Would Flett consider him presumptuous, he wondered, if he asked for a photograph of the portrait above the chimney piece?

His guess that the girl was Greek was little more than a shot at random; but Athens was not a large city and within it the sophisticated world was a fairly compact minority. If the girl was Greek, it was a reasonable assumption that she would be known in Athens, at least in the world of students and artists and the

theater. With a photograph of the portrait to show people, identification of the girl might not be all that troublesome.

And what then? And how would it concern the vanished
sculptor? Or the twelve girls in the garden?

Professor Challis turned his attention to the Pouilly-Fuissé. At
the Woburn Arms, no doubt, Miss Polly would be able to throw
a little more light on the subject.

3

"THERE ARE certain things," said Professor Challis, "which for no
logical reason at all can never be entertained as valid suppositions. You could never possibly trust, for example, a marriage
manual written by a man with a hyphenated name. I don't know
why this should be. There is no reason or logic in it—it just waives
validity."

"You don't accept the theory that he might have been murdered?" said Polly.

"Oh, that I neither accept nor reject. Obviously anybody who
has been missing for six months may have been the victim of foul
play. What I am saying is that I think your friend Flett knows
more about the disappearance than he is prepared to disclose. I
have no logical reason for assuming this—well, no more than what
Flett himself would call a hunch—but unlike the case of the man
with a hyphenated name, it does not, to me at least, lack validity.
Merely as a supposition, of course; something to go on for a start."

He smiled across at the girl. She was drinking lager from a very
tall thin tumbler faintly dewed on the outer surface of the glass
—how like the English to drink their beer lukewarm all through
summer and to begin icing it now that the winter was setting in!
Her dark eyes were fixed on him with an earnest concentration
which he considered rather flattering, but which the two young
men at the bar who kept casting covert glances at the girl obviously found most mystifying. The professor could understand

both the covert glances and the mystification. He was well enough aware of his own queer appearance (a profile of him published in an American magazine had once likened him to a cross between a cassowary and a small Adélie penguin halfway through its moult!), and Polly was very attractive indeed.

The bluejeans, he was glad to see, had been dispensed with. A French fisherman's shirt of thin horizontal stripes, red and white, worn beneath a severe charcoal-grey suit, was her only concession now to the world where colors were bright, Bechet was as big a word as Bach, everyone read Strindberg, and nobody had ever heard of Professor Ronald Challis, Ph.D.; that and a bunch of heavy Italian silver jewelry at her wrist. She wore no covering over the short jagged crop of her hair. She had small, neat hands, and her figure was striking enough not only to keep the eyes of the two men at the bar turning toward her, but to evoke admiration even in the mind of an aging professor of classical studies.

"I formed the impression," he said, "that Flett is very anxious to find Grasset."

"Yes, he is." She nodded.

"Why?"

"Well, I think they were friendly in America." She shrugged. "And I suppose having his house and all. . . ."

"You don't have the feeling that there is more to it than that? Some deeper, more insistent reason?"

"I . . . I don't know," she said doubtfully. "He is not a very communicative man about some things."

"Quite," said the professor, and decided to let the matter rest there for the moment. He suspected that Polly, like Flett, might know rather more than she was prepared to disclose. He folded his hands and gave his attention to his surroundings.

The saloon bar was richly mid-Victorian, ornately decorated with those panels of engraved glass which give so much warmth and charm to the smaller London pubs, and in the glittering mirrors that surrounded them he could see his own reflection many times repeated. Had he paid as much attention to this picture as he gave to his study of his young companion, he would have seen a personality just as striking in appearance as Polly, but in a totally different way. He would have seen a thin face, pink and pointed, that looked rather like the face of an elderly pixie, a face with quick, bird-bright eyes surmounted by a shock of thin white hair that seemed as if it had been spun from thistledown. He would have seen this, had familiarity not blunted him to the oddness of the picture, and had his attention not been divided between the charming girl who sat across from him at the small round table and the man in the corner who had been watching them ever since Polly had entered the saloon bar.

He was a swarthy, neatly dressed man, small in build, and for half an hour he had been sitting there staring at them, his hands cupped around his pint of bitter. Not once in all that time had he touched his drink.

The bar was away from the shopping crowds of Oxford Street, and obviously the sort of people who came here were distinctly from an intellectual level higher than one would expect to find, say, a little nearer the Tottenham Court Road—students and people who had business at the British Museum, booksellers and art dealers, young men and girls from London University, B.B.C. men, and odd, ascetic-looking wraiths, carrying straps of books, who must have wandered in from the graveyard of the Bloomsbury Set. The man in the corner fitted in well enough with this queerly introspective clientele, yet there was something in the quiet patience of his eyes, injured and melancholy, that set him quite apart. That, and the particular quality of his watchfulness.

Beneath the rim of the table, Professor Challis rubbed his hands together happily.

"Does Flett know about this talk we're having?" he asked.

"No. I left last night very soon after you did," she said. "I phoned from a public telephone near Harrod's."

"You didn't wish him to know you wanted to discuss the matter with me?"

She shook her head, and after a moment he said, "Don't look for the moment, but there's a man over there in the corner who keeps watching you. Do you know him?"

She lifted the glass of lager and sipped it, with a casual glance toward the corner. When her eyes met the professor's again, they were vaguely puzzled. "I don't know," she said. "His face is familiar in a way, but I just don't know. I seem to have seen him somewhere, or met him, but I just can't remember." A slight frown touched her face.

"It doesn't matter then," said the professor cheerfully. "Let us talk about Paul Grasset. There is a great deal more, you understand, that I want to know about him. In a way, his personality is the core of the whole matter. This morning I was looking at some books on sculpture—I am very good on the archaic periods, you see, but not particularly *au fait* with modern work—and I came to the conclusion that Grasset's talent was of an uncommonly high order."

"He was very clever," she said. "He had a tremendous technical brilliance."

"Which may have offset the fact that his weakness lay in a lack of originality," the professor suggested.

"Perhaps. I don't know enough about it to say."

"But you sat for him. That example in the garden is an excellent piece of portraiture."

"It was three or four years ago when I sat for him. In Paris. It was just when he was beginning to be successful. He only did the head. . . . I don't know where he got the figure from. He must have done that later."

Professor Challis smiled. "That is a trick almost as old as sculpture, Miss Sorelle. In ancient Rome they used to use replaceable heads on almost all the statues. The Emperor Hadrian once had four hundred and seventy-two portrait heads of himself sent out to be fixed onto existing trunks." He chuckled. "How well did you know Grasset?" he said.

The unexpectedness of the question seemed to take her by surprise, so that she hesitated for a moment before answering. "I didn't really know him," she said. "He was not an easy person to get to know."

"Well, what sort of a person was he?"

"That is a question I can't really answer." She was staring down at the table. There was a little pool of beer spilt on the green rubber top, and with her forefinger she was tracing it out into whorls and circles.

"But surely if you knew him, and sat for him, you could not fail to gain some sort of impression, even superficial, and—"

"That is what I am trying to explain." She looked up quickly. "I said before he was not easy to get to know. He was very quick and . . . and volatile. You could never seem to talk to him for more than a minute or two before he would be darting off to somebody else. It was impossible to pin him down."

"But he *was* pinned down." The professor smiled. "Quite often, it seems, if the girls in the garden can be taken as reasonable evidence. You are simply an early head fitted onto another torso—perhaps a later vintage or one from stock, like the Emperor Hadrian—but what about the others? Flett seems to think Grasset was promiscuous. Do you think the same?"

She shrugged. "It's what everybody seemed to think. I don't know. You must remember that he was a sculptor by profession; he would naturally use many women for his models. It doesn't necessarily follow that he was some sort of Bluebeard."

"All the women in that gallery of girls, present company not excepted, are exceedingly beautiful. Superficially, at any rate, this would seem to indicate that the man had considerable charm."

"He had very great personal charm," she said. "He was a very attractive man in many ways."

"Have you noticed that we keep talking of him in the past tense?"

"It's difficult not to."

"Quite. I notice you qualify his attractiveness, too. You said, 'in many ways.' In other ways he was not so attractive, then?"

"Oh, I suppose he had his weaknesses, like anybody else. He was vain, obsessively vain. He liked success and public esteem, and like a good many other people there were times when he was not altogether scrupulous in his methods of attaining them. Fanlec used to say of him that he was incapable of moral distinctions.

. . ." She paused and quickly added, "Although he didn't really say it as if he were condemning him."

"Fanlec? Who is Fanlec?"

"He was his agent in Paris. This time the past tense is correct, because he's dead now."

"I see. When you say moral distinctions, I take it you are not thinking solely of his relationships with women." She did not reply. He sensed that the interrogation was beginning to irritate her slightly, but he had no intention of abandoning it. He was anxious to probe for the reason behind her defensiveness of the missing man, which, he suspected, would also explain why she had been so anxious to talk to him without Flett being present. Clearly, she was just as eager as Flett to find the missing sculptor —and equally reluctant to explain why. With a girl so beautiful and a man whose evident charm had both direct and indirect testimony, the supposition that immediately sprang to one's mind was the existence of some romantic attachment between her and the Frenchman who had vanished into thin air. If this, then, was the supposition to be explored, obviously the most sensitive spot to probe was the man's relationships with other women. "I come back to Flett's insistence that Grasset was a philanderer," he said evenly. "And on that score—"

"Well, perhaps he was," she said, with scarcely concealed impatience. This time he *had* touched her on the raw. "Flett knew him a good deal better than I did. And I suppose men know more about that sort of thing than women. I imagine they'd talk about it."

"I don't believe they *talk* about it," said the professor. "Well, not as a general rule. But they do *know*—yes, that's true."

They were silent for a moment or two, then Polly said abruptly, "Are you doing anything tonight?"

"I?" He chuckled at the suggestion, and shook his head.

"Do you think you could bear a studio party? To go with me to a studio party? In Chelsea."

"But I don't—"

"You could take me somewhere to dinner first," she cut in with a curious urgency. "Or we could just have a snack here, some of that cold pie over there." She glanced toward the bar, where a wedge of meat, pale-pink, mottled, and encased in a thick grey pastry, languished sadly beneath a cracked plastic cupola.

Professor Challis studied it for a fascinated moment and shuddered. "Shall we save that for a time of final madness?" he suggested. "If I am to take you to a party, I shall need much more fortifying than that. And, besides, I know a very pleasant little place not far from here where we shall be able to find a bottle of excellent Samian wine." He rubbed his hands briskly together. "And now, having settled that, just *why* do you want to take an old man like me to this party?"

"There is someone I want you to meet," she said. "Somebody who knew Paul Grasset. Who knew him well, I mean—much better than I did."

"One of the other girls in the garden?" He made the suggestion jokingly, and her reply, after a brief hesitation, rather took him aback.

"Yes," she said. "Freda Lindstrom."

"Ah," said the professor, retrieving the situation. "I had hoped for Giji."

As they left the saloon bar, Polly seemed preoccupied and did not even notice the swarthy man who still sat patiently in the corner. But the professor stared deliberately at him. His gaze was returned quite steadily. When they went through the door, the man was still watching them.

4

AS HE HAD EXPECTED, the studio was in a mews, on the third floor of a long, narrow building that looked like a converted warehouse. On the dark and narrow stairway it smelt pungently of linoleum polish and stewed cabbage, on the landings of aniseed and old tea leaves. In spite of brightly painted doors and cupboards and a few valiantly struggling pots of indoor ivy, the studio had a sad and cheerless appearance, as if it had finally realized that art dwelt outside the perimeter of society.

By the time the professor and Polly arrived, more than twenty people were already there, caught in the listless gyrations of a party's beginning. None could be identified as host or hostess, although this appeared not to matter. The women, to the professor's startled eyes, appeared to be dressed-up rather than dressed: the *dernier cri* seemed to be very large gypsy earrings and very tight, masculine-looking trousers. Several of the men, perhaps in response to this challenge, had beards. It was ironic to reflect on the thought that English anthropologists spent so much time traveling to the islands of Melanesia, when this fertile field of tribal research lay at their very doorsteps.

Nonetheless, the company on the whole was both more intelligent and far kindlier than the professor had expected. Indeed, for the first half hour he found himself distinctly, and not unenjoyably, the center of attraction. A huge bearded man with a green corduroy coat and compassionate doglike eyes, whom everyone addressed as Bimbo, informed him that Miss Lindstrom had not yet arrived but was imminently expected.

As a concession to the professor's field of interest, there was an earnest discussion on the Oedipus myth and much running to and fro to find an olive for his Martini. This, in spite of his protests, firstly that he did not care for a cocktail after a dinner which had included a Samian wine, and then, when this was overruled, that he did not really want an olive in it. Finally the olive triumphantly was found but as it proved to be a very old one, and tasteless, Professor Challis was obliged to keep it in the bottom of his glass by dint of sipping at the liquor with scarcely parted lips, like a man with an ulcerated mouth.

Having ushered him into the studio and vaguely introduced him, Polly had deserted him altogether, and for a long time she was seated on the floor at the far end of the room engrossed in earnest conversation with a young man of such tragic features that one could not help feeling that only some terrible affliction prevented him from mingling with the other guests.

In time the discussion on Oedipus—which had proved to be quite beyond the professor's depth—moved inevitably to the poetry of Ezra Pound, the pack cheerfully followed this topic to the table where the gin was being poured, and Professor Challis found himself seated on a low padded bench next to the man called Bimbo.

"Are you a poet also?" he asked, feeling that the question was demanded of him, since it had been Bimbo who had dragged in Ezra Pound.

"Quite," said Bimbo moodily. "At heart, that is. All of us are, I imagine, where there is any sensitivity left. In practice, however, I am a sculptor. Regrettably I haven't any commissions—" He darted a quick glance of inquiry at the professor, saw no commissions there, and looked away. "—and therefore my bread is buttered by teaching French and Spanish at the Berlitz School." He studied the professor with commiserating spaniel eyes and rather surprisingly added, "I should keep falcons if I had my choice."

"It would be nice to keep falcons," the professor agreed. And added, "If you are a sculptor, perhaps you know a French artist named Grasset?"

"Poor Pip," said Bimbo. "I have never kept falcons, in fact, but once I had a myna bird." His eyes mournfully intercepted the question. "We called him Pip. Not the bird. Grasset." He twirled his gin glass morosely and said, "He was assassinated, you know. One night on the Orient Express, in a second-class *wagon-lit*, steaming out of Belgrade."

The professor turned to him in astonishment. "But . . . but I had no idea! I thought—"

Bimbo nodded and rubbed his beard with the back of his hand. "Men in black hats," he said. "With zithers. The motive, of course, was political, although there were other rumors. With Grasset there were always rumors."

"I had been led to believe he had disappeared, that it was all a complete mystery."

"I detest mysteries," said Bimbo impatiently. "Mysteries are for idle minds. If there is a mystery, I simply provide my own solution and let it go at that. So far as Grasset is concerned, the chaps with black hats and zithers seem to me perfectly reasonable. There are others who hint at a *crime passionnel*, which I find altogether too vulgar to consider." He licked the tip of his finger and began to run it around and around the rim of his tumbler to make the glass sing. "Do *you* know what happened to Grasset?" he asked suddenly.

"No."

"Nor do I. Nor does anybody." He sighed heavily. "People move on and we rummage in the residue they leave behind. Grasset left quite a lot of residue, one way and another. That house of his, those sculptures, an absolute litter of women. And Flett. I understand you've met Flett."

"Yes."

"An oafish and charmless fellow. He worries about Grasset, you know. It preys on his mind. I think he disapproves of things being untidy." He paused and bent his ear to the glass, and said, "And then there is a dealer in Paddington with the quite absurd name of Joákimos who is saddled with thirty-nine pieces of sculpture that should have gone to some gallery in Paris. More untidiness, you see. To say nothing of poor, dear Polly. Just look at her up there being slowly ground into a fine powder by the inexorable cant of that horrible little squirt Beamish! As I say, to this day poor Polly is repining her lost love."

"What lost love?"

"Why, Paul Grasset, of course. She was crazy about him. Surely you knew *that*. You came here with Polly, didn't you?"

"Yes, but if this is true—"

"True?" Bimbo smiled wearily. "And what is truth? It was what Pilate said, remember. In your calling, Professor, naturally you must seek it indefatigably. You are a dealer in the verities of death, in the things that have established their final actualities long, long ago. But in the moil and mull of the living, in the flux and clot of human relationships, where are we to seek? Take my own case. I never have the slightest idea when I am telling the truth or when I am conjuring images merely for my own satisfaction. But does it matter? Whichever it is, I have the same measure of satisfaction. Or dissatisfaction. This, I suppose, is the poet within me." He glanced up and frowned. "Ah, here comes a little more of the residue."

A brightly blonde woman with a shapely figure that was on the verge of becoming considerable had appeared in the doorway, had paused for a moment as if settling herself into a frame, and was now advancing toward them. She said, "Darling Bimbo!" to the bearded man and, "But aren't you adorable, whoever you are!" to the professor, in a flat and distinctly Scandinavian accent and with a vacuity of expression that was majestically disconcerting.

"This is Professor Challis," said Bimbo, "and he is an American archaeologist who has been digging in Greece." He spoke very slowly and patiently, as if he were trying to impress a difficult fact into the mind of a rather dull child. "He has for no accountable reason found his way into this hotbed of inanity, and we must treat him with great consideration until he is able to make his escape."

Bimbo had evidently taken it for granted that everybody would know who the blonde lady was, and indeed the professor was not in any doubt that this was the long-awaited Freda Lindstrom, although between this tired Valkyrie and any of the statues in the garden in Tite Street he could see no resemblance at all. While he was thinking this, she had taken both his hands in hers and was saying, "But, darling, who *found* you? And *where?* What a pet you are! What a heavenly pet!"

In spite of the fervor of her words, they seemed to emerge from a great golden vacuum. The glittering blondeness was built around her like an encasement. She had pale golden skin and pale shining hair, and her breasts were great gilded globes that threatened at any moment to burst from the startling low neckline of the gold lamé cocktail dress she was wearing. And yet all the goldness and the glitter created a sense of emptiness. Perhaps it was the eyes that looked at him so vacantly: eyes that were a pale golden-brown of a quality so thin and faraway that looking into them was like looking into two honeypots that have been emptied of all but the merest film of nectar.

"The professor," said Bimbo carefully, "is Polly's discovery. He is interested in the raising of falcons. He is also interested in an old friend of yours, whom at one time he knew. Paul Grasset." Bimbo had at last succeeded in drawing sound from the rim of his tumbler and he was leaning back with an expression of happy concentration while his circling finger tip lifted the low, throbbing hum to a higher pitch.

"Poor Greg," said Miss Lindstrom.

"Greg?" The professor's eyes were bright with inquiry, his thin pointed face with its shock of loose white hair tilted a little to one side. He looked like some queer, crested bird.

"We called him Greg," she said.

"Pip, actually," Bimbo corrected her. "Not that it matters."

"I get confused," said Miss Lindstrom. She had relinquished both the professor's hands and any further interest in him. Her empty glance was moving slowly around the room.

It was *all* becoming rather too confusing, the professor reflected. Brandon was called Ben, and Polyxéna was called Polly, and Grasset was called Pip or Greg (depending on how confused you were), and doubtless Bimbo had a different name altogether which he used on checks—always supposing he had the occasion to write them—and then there was Giji. . . .

"Has Kurt not come yet?" said Miss Lindstrom, with a faint tremor of something which in a more emotionally expressive person might have been anger. "He told me he would be here before nine."

"Kurt will come," said Bimbo, a relaxed smile on his face as he listened to the whining of the glass. "Kurt will always come. In the meantime, the professor is anxious to ask you some questions about Grasset."

"I shall die if I don't have a drink," said Miss Lindstrom, and sauntered away toward the bar like a figure moving out of a Rubens painting.

"It is a very queer thing," said Bimbo musingly, "but they will never talk about him. Still, there is no harm in your trying."

Professor Challis nodded, and followed the golden woman to the bar. The sound of Bimbo's glass lingered in his ears like the squeaking of a demented insect.

"Why are you so interested in Paul Grasset?" asked Miss Lindstrom boredly, her almost vacuous attention on the door through which, presumably, the tardy Kurt would ultimately make his entrance.

"I am interested in writing a short appreciation of Grasset's work for a periodical in America," the professor lied cheerfully. "I should very much like to include in it a brief sketch of the man's character and personality."

Miss Lindstrom sniffed. "I was his favorite model," she said. "I would only sit for him on rainy days."

"Yes," said the professor encouragingly.

"So perhaps my opinion of him is influenced by the mood of the weather. All that rain. In Paris . . . and in London."

"I suppose it would have an influence, yes."

"Men have been pursuing me since I was twelve," she said, with melancholy irrelevance. "Even at school in Jonkoping. . . . It would startle you if I told you some of the things that have happened to me."

The professor made a murmuring sound to convey his sympathy: the amorous confessions of Miss Lindstrom may have startled him but would hardly have surprised him. She was the sort of woman who would absorb erotic experience as a sponge would absorb water, and she would have the same degree of elasticity about it.

"And Grasset?" he prompted gently.

"When he disappeared, no tears were shed by me," she said, speaking for the first time almost with a trace of emotion. "Nor by anyone else, I imagine. He was the most despicable man I have ever known—and I have known some *very* unpleasant men.

You would be surprised at some of the stories I could tell you about men." She passed her glass to the professor. "This gin is very weak. Would you fill it up for me like a darling."

Professor Challis did as he was told, brought the glass back to her, and said, "In what way was he despicable?" It was essential to keep her on the single subject of Grasset, to check her obvious desire to explore the multitudinous sins and shortcomings of the many men who had solicited, and doubtless enjoyed, her opulent Nordic favors.

"He was cruel, selfish, egotistical to an almost insane degree. He never cared who suffered so long as he got on. He had the idea the world owed him a living and he intended to collect the debt with interest. That was Paul Grasset." It was only the definition of the words she used that conveyed anything of contempt or resentment: her intonation was as unemotional and colorless as if she were discussing the weather.

"Yet I understand he was a man of great charm," said the professor wonderingly.

"Yes. So was the devil, I believe. It was because of that charm of his that he was able to tread on everybody. Everybody he touched he spoilt or ruined. Everybody except me. I'd learnt too much about men by the time he got to me." A slight smile touched her full, rich mouth, and then a glint of something else passed like a cloud across the honeyed emptiness of her eyes. "Ah, here is Kurt now," she said softly. "You could have asked others about Grasset," she said wearily, as if the subject had been exhausted of its interest. "You could have asked Claude Fanlec, except that it was Grasset who drove him to suicide. You could ask Bimbo. Or the Sorelle girl. They knew him. They suffered."

"Just one more question," said the professor quickly, because obviously Miss Lindstrom's attention had strayed to the small, hairy, Levantine-looking man with thick spectacles who was standing in the doorway divesting himself of his raincoat—a man so small and dark and insectine that, despite his preoccupation with the subject of Paul Grasset, the professor could not help thinking that in association with the expansive golden ripeness of

Freda Lindstrom the man called Kurt would look rather like a gnat hovering over a summer wheatfield. "When did you last see Paul Grasset?" he said.

"I can't remember," said Miss Lindstrom disinterestedly and moved off toward the doorway like a wrathful Hera descending from Olympus to scold some errant mortal.

It must have been half an hour later before the professor was able to detach Polly from the young man with the tragic demeanor who, it seemed, had gone some way toward grinding her into the fine powder that Bimbo had suggested. She looked strained and tired and unhappy. In that half hour he had had time to reflect on what Miss Lindstrom had told him, for all the guests were now quite preoccupied by their analyses of their own egos and paid no attention to him whatsoever; and he was not at all sure that there was the slightest value in anything the Swedish woman had said.

"I don't know that I have got anywhere at all with Miss Lindstrom," he said to Polly, when at last they were alone together in a neglected corner of the studio. "Her picture of Grasset is not a very pleasant one. She seems to have regarded him as some sort of monstrous ogre, and—"

"She talks like that about every man who has ever touched her," said Polly impatiently, then added with an air of weariness, "Oh, let's skip it all. I know. It's all such a waste of time, and so silly. I am sorry I dragged you into it. You— You've been very sweet, and all it means is that I have been wasting your time, too." Looking into her pale, exhausted face he was surprised to see that she seemed very close to tears. She reached out her hand and her fingers lightly touched his wrist, as if in some way this might convey her apology. "Look," she said, "if you want to go now, we can get you a cab. You must find this all so tedious and stupid. Bimbo can go down with you and get you a cab." She hesitated and seemed about to say something more, but then she shook her head quickly and smiled at him, a smile that was rather sad and childlike. "I think we'll skip it all, don't you?" she said with a feigned lightness, and turned away to find Bimbo.

There was a cab cruising slowly at the end of the mews and a whistle could have hailed it, but Bimbo completely disregarded it and said, "Walk down with me to the King's Road."

In his duffel coat, with the hood pulled up around his bearded face, he was a gigantic figure, and he walked with long, loose strides so that the professor, who barely came up to his shoulder, was obliged to trot alongside him like a terrier.

The big man said nothing while they went down to the King's Road—which was just as well, for if he had spoken, Professor Challis would have been far too breathless to frame a reply—but they had hardly turned into the brightly lit street with its red buses and flooding traffic before he said, "Let's go in here and take a coffee."

The coffee lounge was like any one of a dozen others in the vicinity: heavy oak tables, Windsor chairs, a few low candle-power lights behind secretive shades, and a tiny muted radio whispering in the corner. It was turned to the Third Programme, and a man with a very cultured voice was examining the legend of Gilgamesh in terms of surviving cuneiform tablets. Except for the proprietor, a languid, rather effete young man in grey flannels who looked as if he himself could have written a radio script equally erudite, the coffee lounge was empty. Bimbo threw himself and his duffel coat into a Windsor chair, ordered the coffee, locked his fingers beneath his beard, and stared hard at Professor Challis.

"All right," he said. "Now let's talk about Paul Grasset."

Professor Challis nodded quickly, but said nothing. There was something suddenly compelling about the other man, as if the energetic walk through the night had sloughed off all the rather ridiculous trappings which had clung around him in the studio.

"Unless you're particularly interested in Paul Grasset," he said seriously, "I think it's rather a waste of time to go around asking questions about him. *Are* you particularly interested?"

"I am rather intrigued, yes."

"Being intrigued isn't quite the same thing as being interested."

"Well, if you want me to put it that way, yes, I am interested."

"Why?"

"I like piecing things together. Unlike you, I very much enjoy mysteries. It is my profession, in a sense. One finds a fragment here and a fragment there and, provided the fragments are intriguing enough, one has the wish to fit all the odd pieces together and assemble the whole picture."

The bearded man grunted. "Polly asked you to help her find Paul Grasset, is that it?"

"In fact, she didn't." Professor Challis smiled. "I had the feeling that she intended to, but she never got around to it. I gather she feels now that I should forget all about it."

"I think that's wise. On the whole, very wise."

"Oh, I have no intention of taking her advice," remarked the professor imperturbably. "Once one's curiosity is aroused . . ." He allowed the sentence to end in a bland smile. "And I assure you that I find the subject of Paul Grasset very stimulating indeed to my curiosity. I find the subject, shall we say, exceedingly piquant." He paused for a moment, then asked, "Who was Claude Fanlec?"

Bimbo lit a cigarette, allowed the match to burn down until the flame had almost reached his finger tips before blowing it out. "Who told you about Fanlec?"

"Miss Sorelle mentioned him this evening. So did Miss Lindstrom. According to her, Grasset drove this man Fanlec to his death."

"Fanlec committed suicide."

"Quite. That is what she told me. She also told me that Grasset had been responsible for a good deal of suffering on the part of other people. In point of fact, she quoted you as an example. And Miss Sorelle."

"She was talking a lot of humbug," said Bimbo quietly. His elbows were on the table, his clenched fists pushed into his beard, his eyes fixed on the professor's with a penetrating intensity, as if he might see into the thoughts moving within the old man's brain. "I've nothing against Paul Grasset," he said. And added meaningly, "In fact, I liked him enough to wish that people wouldn't meddle in his affairs."

"That's what makes it so intriguing," said the professor pleasantly. "All the opinions you get on the man differ from each other. One person vilifies him, another defends him. What sort of person was he?—Or *is* he?"

"He's all right. As I've already said, I've nothing against him."

"You're not even envious of him?"

"Envious? Why should I be envious?"

"You are both sculptors, he a notably successful one and you—forgive me, but it is by your own admission—not particularly so. I had always understood that artists—" He broke off. The bearded man was laughing softly, and then he stopped and put his hands flat down on the table.

"Let's talk about something else, shall we?" Bimbo suggested.

"You still haven't answered my question about Fanlec."

"Fanlec wasn't important," Bimbo said impatiently. "And he's dead, anyway. The answer to your question—let's get this over and done with—is that he was a dealer in Paris. He handled Paul's shows and sales. If he hadn't shot himself, maybe he could have explained the mystery, or some of it, anyway. But he killed himself, and that's that. It was nothing to do with Paul. What Freda Lindstrom told you about him I don't know, but it was probably her usual nonsense. She's generally quite happy to talk about Fanlec, provided she can be nasty and venomous. She didn't like him."

"Did he—er—pursue her, too?"

"I think he was one of the few who didn't," said Bimbo, with a faint, dry smile. "I suppose that's the point, really." Crisply he stubbed the cigarette in his saucer. "I understand you intend returning to Greece quite soon, Professor," he said.

"In three weeks' time." The professor smiled, accepting the abrupt termination of the subject they had been discussing. "I should be in Athens by the twenty-eighth."

"You may run into Polly again. She goes back shortly."

"To Athens?"

"That's where her family is. They own ships." He grinned, as if there was something deeply amusing in the fact of people owning ships, and the professor had the impression that Bimbo would be an exceedingly good-looking young man, if he would only remove his absurd beard. "Indeed," he continued cheerfully, "it's not inconceivable that you may see me again, also. I've always had a yen to visit Greece. I suppose it comes from the infective quality of all that poetry." His grin was suddenly self-mocking and vaguely impudent.

"I should be delighted if you did," said Professor Challis with grave courtesy. "You can always find my whereabouts through the American School."

"Of course, it depends on what can be teed up," Bimbo went on thoughtfully. "A teaching job at one of the institutes perhaps. Berlitz could help in that, I suppose. These things depend on what strings can be pulled, you know."

"If I can be of any help at all. . . ."

"Oh, I shouldn't think it will be necessary," said Bimbo. "Thanks all the same." He put a half-crown on the table and began to fasten the wooden toggles of his duffel coat. "Shall we grab that cab for you now?" he suggested.

Outside the leaves stirred soggily on the damp sidewalk as the wind sighed up from the river.

A Putney bus, blood-red in the lamplight, wallowed past them, panting out exhaust fumes sideways in a foggy breath. From the corner movie house the people were emerging, blinking their way back into the humdrum unreality of existence.

Professor Challis, watching the cab circling in toward the curb, said, "In the event you do come to Athens, it might be a sound idea to have your name." He smiled. "At the moment, you see, I know you only as—er—as Bimbo."

"Grasset," said the bearded man, opening the cab door for him. "I thought you knew. Charles Grasset."

5

HAD PROFESSOR CHALLIS not been an archaeologist by profession, he might have felt singularly let down in the days that followed.

The movement from a promising beginning to an anticlimactic hiatus was something he had frequently experienced during excavations: the gradual decay of that feeling that one was within reach of something new and exciting. Promise was one thing, but between it and either failure or fulfillment lay the banks of dreary clay and mud that had to be probed and explored and shoveled aside, the days of humdrum digging into nothing, the days when the promise itself seemed misleading and futile, an *ignis fatuus* leading one on and on into matters without meaning.

Yet when he considered the matter that had begun so unexpectedly in Tite Street, he was obliged to confess to himself that these professional consolations gave only scant comfort.

After the party at Chelsea, he had confidently expected to hear again from Polly, but she had made no further attempt to see him or to call him, and, being ignorant of her address, he had no way of getting in touch with her.

The big man Bimbo, after so startlingly declaring his name, had strode off down the King's Road and into a mysterious, enveloping darkness from which he had not since emerged.

Twice the professor had attempted to telephone Brandon Flett with the object of requesting a photographic copy of the portrait of the girl in the striped shirt. The phone was not answered, and one evening when he walked again to the house in Tite Street he found the place in darkness, a darkness of shuttered windows and an atmosphere of brooding emptiness.

It was upon his return from this abortive excursion that he sat down and wrote to a colleague in the Académie française, requesting certain information on Paul Grasset. Toward the end of the week a letter arrived from Paris which read:

My dear Challis:

You must know, of course, that your inquiry concerning the sculptor Grasset is rather outside the scope of my field. I passed the matter over to young Challon, who has some little knowledge of these rather decadent Bohemian circles. He tells me Grasset was a young man of considerable talent but evidently of rather wayward disposition. I should say his disappearance has been accepted with calm resignation

—even with considerable relief—by his immediate circle of cronies. It seems that those who do not regard it as a good riddance suspect that his absence merely means that he is, as they put it, "up to something."

Grasset's parents came of mercantile stock, passably comfortable, in Cherbourg. Both are now deceased. There were three brothers, of whom your man was the second. The elder brother is a magistrate in the Cameroons. The youngest left France some years ago to further his fortunes elsewhere. Challon thinks his name was Charles, but can't be sure. You specifically request that I make no inquiries from the Sûreté, although I am sure they must have a section concerned with missing persons, and doubtless you appreciate that this injunction renders the task more difficult than it otherwise might have been. Grasset evidently had the reputation of being something of a libertine. Challon has some improper but vague story involving a banker's wife in Toulon, and one gathers that there is quite a history of promiscuity. On the other hand there is unanimity of opinion that his work was uncommonly good.

So far as Fanlec is concerned, the attached clipping from *Paris Soir* of May 13th may be of some interest. I vaguely recall the matter of the Rocamadour Reliefs. If memory serves me, I believe a petition of some sort was hawked around the Sorbonne. I understood Fanlec was what you might call a decayed nobleman, a descendant of the Duc de Fanlec, whom you will remember Mirabeau attacked in that famous series of letters. Beyond this there is little help I can give you, although I shall have Challon obtain for you a transcript of the inquest evidence, if such a thing is available, and whatever other press clippings seem relevant to the case.

I see by the last *Journal* that that imbecile Cartwright is at it again, printing more of his taradiddle on that Minoan-Philistine nonsense. It is high time he was thoroughly discredited. I am astonished you do not publish a paper in contradiction. The fellow makes my blood boil. My very best regards.

—Jacques Monfreid.

The newspaper clipping enclosed with the letter was an item of no more than a few paragraphs which appeared to have been culled from a rather obscure position on an inside page. It stated that Claude François Fanlec, aged thirty-seven, dealer, of Nantes, had died by his own hand on Dieppe Pier while the balance of his mind was disturbed, according to a coroner's finding in that city. He was unmarried and had no relatives. Evidently the reporter had not been aware of the dead man's patrician blood, for the fact that this was the end of an old aristocratic line was not mentioned. The item did say, however, that bankruptcy proceedings had been pending against Fanlec and that his shop in the rue St.-Julien had been disposed of to pay off sundry creditors. It was the culminating paragraph which Professor Challis found most interesting:

Fanlec was responsible for the discovery in 1948 of the so-called Rocamadour Reliefs, an early medieval church group of eighteen small figures in sandstone, part of a Romanesque frieze depicting pilgrims adoring the Virgin of Rocamadour. In spite of protests by French antiquarians and churchmen, these priceless fragments were disposed of by Fanlec to the New York collector, Curtis J. Grantheim, Jr., for a sum reputed to have been in the vicinity of forty million francs. At present they are housed in the Grantheim Collection on Long Island.

Altogether it did not really add very much, and with this the matter seemed to end. Professor Challis, with his own professional problems to occupy him—Monfreid was right, of course, and Cartwright's ridiculous hypotheses had to be challenged—made a very valiant attempt to purge his mind of this quite irrelevant matter of Paul Grasset. Yet even as he worked on the letter, which he confidently expected would topple Cartwright into the dust of discredited scholarship, little things continued to niggle at him, to disturb him, challenging his reason and logic. It was like some queer, twisted puppet show of silent, miming figures, known and unknown, which kept tiptoeing in and out of his consciousness—Brandon Flett, Polly Sorelle, Paul Grasset, Bimbo, Giji, Claude Fanlec, Freda Lindstrom, Jenny . . . even Mirabeau was there, and that noble Duc de Fanlec who had died nearly two centuries before. . . . It was no wonder, therefore, that his paper in refutation of Cartwright was less effective than it should have been. Cartwright lived to write another day.

London, in any case, was by mid-November clamped in a windless, freezing grip: the balmy October evening which had taken him to Tite Street had been as false in its promise as the story he had found there. Crossing St. James's Park, the spires of Whitehall seemed like pinnacles of ice against a sky implacably dull and black, like the surface of a wiped slate after the wet shine has faded. The pulped mulch of yellow leaves had been swept away, the cold seeped up from the unprotected ground, over the Battersea and Lambeth factories the smoke hung sulphurous, sullen, heavy, and lit with yellow bruises, across the parks the bare trees were blinded giants stumbling through miasma.

Professor Challis sat in his room listening to the hiss of the kettle on the gas ring and he dreamed of blue skies coldly glittering and the thin dark pencils of the cypresses against them, of the rough tumbling shine of the Mediterranean, of the sun brilliant on white rocks.

On the morning of November 17 he began to pack his bags. When this was done he took a leisurely luncheon at the Restaurant Bourgogne—Coquilles à la Flamberge, a broccoli vinaigrette, soft Camembert, and the half-bottle of Moselle from Trarbach which he had been promising himself for a fortnight—walked up to the New Bond Street underground and took a tube to the Marble Arch, where he plunged valiantly into the dusky, neon-striped maelstrom of the Edgware Road. ONLY THIRTY-ONE SHOPPING DAYS TO CHRISTMAS! the fiery letters hissed. Professor Challis ignored this taunt and bustled bravely along through the panic-stricken crowd to Praed Street. A sultry wind was blowing out from the door of the A.B.C. café on the corner, a sirocco from some strange desert smelling of stewing tea, wet rubber, and Swiss rolls. A man emerged swinging a bottle of stout in a string bag. Around the vivid oblongs of the candy-shop windows the crowds were gathered. In Praed Street, near a large and unprepossessing building which looked as if it might house the lower echelon of some obscure government department, a long line of grey-faced women in headscarves and thick snowboots waited patiently for some unspecified boon. A hundred yards further to the west, in a small cul-de-sac between a cycle repair shop and a hardware store, he found the shop of Joákimos the dealer.

In no way was it particularly different from any other second-hand dealer's shop that lies outside the orbit of fashionable patronage. It had that dubious air of muddle and secrecy, with a flavor of ignorant stockpiling, that might lead one quite mistakenly to believe in the possibility of discovering a rare Memlinc or a genuine van Eyck or, at worst, a quite good Byzantine icon underneath its coating of discolored varnish and grime. It followed the usual custom of displaying in its windows and on the pavement outside only the tawdriest of trash—cumbersome pieces of furniture which were either blatantly spavined or suspiciously wormy; chamber pots of impressive size and florid *décor* but quite lacking in handles; chipped saucers filled with wedding rings, synthetic gems, old coins, and unmatched earrings; cases of medals concerned with forgotten gallantries in campaigns against Kaffir, Boer, and Afridi; mid-Victorian specimen cabinets choked either with geological fragments or brittle moths and insects; a tray of surgical instruments that looked as if they must have been used by Crippen; miscellaneous articles of *chinoiserie* brought from Foochow in that free-enterprising period when taste had declined in inverse ratio to the prosperity of the English tea trade; a varied but rather damaged selection of Spode, Staffordshire, and Rockingham; the usual china dog and Negro boy; a stuffed owl, solemnly dusty; and a group of hideously colored plaster statuettes of girls in the cloche hats, shingles, and alluring postures of the twenties.

The whole goat's-nest, Professor Challis suspected, was to mislead the gullible into supposing that since no human being who had not been certified could possibly wish to buy anything from a display so ghastly, it followed that the real treasures must be inside, secreted in some glittering Ali Baba's cavern to which only the cognoscenti had the key.

The professor had a momentary image of his landlord, Mr. Valentine, rummaging around inside, and he shuddered a little as he pushed into the narrow entrance past two coal scuttles, a frond of hanging Japanese samurai swords, a death mask of Beethoven in plaster of Paris, and a portion of a ship's figurehead.

The girl inside, a thin creature with adenoids and suspicious eyes, seemed put out at being obliged to rise from a cane chair in a dark corner, where she appeared to have been knitting a wind-sock for a small airfield, and even more aggrieved when her caller asked if he might see Mr. Joákimos personally.

"'E don't see *nobody*," she said emphatically, and sniffed. "Not wivout an appointment."

"Perhaps in my case he might make an exception." The professor smiled pleasantly. "I am from America, you see. And I must leave for Greece this evening. It's rather important. Possibly if you took in my card. . . ."

The girl studied the card morosely, sniffed again, and said slyly, "I not e'en sure 'e's in." Or rather, that was the sense of the message she conveyed, for the professor found himself reflecting how curious it was that there was a whole race of linguists in London who scarcely needed to use consonants at all. He waited. The girl sniffed, peered at the card once more, and said, "I see wot 'e says."

With this she shuffled across to a door between two enormous mahogany bookcases—she was wearing large bedroom slippers of pink satin decorated with what appeared to be the remnants of a very old feather boa—entered, without knocking, a room of which the professor had the merest glimpse, and closed the door softly behind her. He could hear voices but could not make out what was being said.

He seated himself in a wicker chair and examined the interior of the shop. As he had suspected, the material inside was rather better than the rubbish on public show outside; this was still not to say it was particularly appealing. There was an odd painting or two that merited a second glance, a few quite reasonable chairs, some pleasant ivory chessmen. Otherwise the room was void of interest. It remained very difficult indeed to reconcile the place with the sculpture of Paul Grasset.

The thin girl emerged, her face sulky and her catarrh bothering her more than ever. This time she left the door ajar.

"In yer go," she said grudgingly, and returned to her wind-sock.

6

Professor Challis' first impression of Joákimos was that he did not see anybody because he was physically incapable of any movement whatsoever. The huge figure sat behind a large desk, and in both his pear-shaped contours and facial expression he looked very like one of those Japanese trick dolls, enormously enlarged, which when rolled over always springs back to an upright position.

The similarity was made even more striking by the completely bald skull which, being rather pointed on top and sagging away into massive dewlaps, gave the impression of being a smaller and glossier pear balanced upon the larger; by the thick lips pursed into a chiseled politeness and the rather Oriental-looking eyes fixed expressionlessly on the professor as he entered; by a faint gloss on the sallow skin that made it appear like celluloid; by the complete absence of eyebrows above the unblinking eyes; and by the small, almost feminine hands that toyed with the thick glass paperweight on the blotter before him.

He blinked and glanced down at the card lying beside the paperweight as if to refresh his memory—when he blinked his eyes had that fleshy, flicking, shuttered look that you see in a hen's eyes—and said, "Please do sit down, Professor Challis." His voice was gentle and cultured, and only very faintly flavored with the memory of some remote Near East beginning. His fingers caressed the oblong paperweight.

"Thank you," said the professor, and took the offered seat beside the desk. "I am sorry to intrude upon you like this, but I shall be leaving London by the evening boat train, and—"

"Please." Joákimos smiled. It was a bland smile, queer and dreamy. "It is a great privilege for me, Professor. I am acquainted with your work, particularly on the Minoan cultures. I am, you might say, an admirer."

"That is very kind of you."

"But I am afraid in my poor establishment you will find nothing of great interest to you," said Joákimos. "Here there is not much consideration for anything earlier than Regency. Indeed, even that is giving way to mid-Victorian, even Edwardian. Now, in my branch at Izmir I dare say we could rummage out an object or two to hold your attention, but there is no call for that sort of thing here. We cater for a passing trade, for the renovated attics, not for the museums or the intelligent collector."

His small, plump fingers stroked the curved edges of the paper-weight. There was printing embedded inside the glass that said, TADGPOLE, CLIPHANGER, SONS, & Co. Ltd., Process Engravers, 26a Fetter Lane, E.C.4. Whose sons? Professor Challis wondered; Tadgpole's or Cliphanger's or both? At school the young Tadg-poles would be called "Tadpole," of course, but what would they call the little Cliphangers?

"Actually what I wanted to talk to you about, Mr. Joákimos, was something rather outside my own field," he began. "I have become very interested in a sculptor called Paul Grasset."

"Ah, yes. In the man or in his work?"

"In both, really."

"Poor Grasset," said Joákimos, and the hen's eyes blinked slowly across the desk.

"I was informed you were in possession of some of the more recent of his works."

"Yes, that was perfectly true."

"Was?"

Joákimos nodded. "We have them no longer. We acted as his agent in London, and we gathered together a collection of his pieces, some from here and some from New York, which we pro-posed to send over to Paris for an exhibition. Ultimately they were disposed of. After his death there was an interest in Grasset's work —it frequently happens that way—but it was a very brief interest, no more than a few weeks, and I accepted an offer from another dealer, who felt he could handle them more advantageously than I."

"I don't quite understand what you mean when you say 'after Grasset's death,'" said the professor. "I knew he had rather mysteriously disappeared. I had never heard it suggested that he had died."

Joákimos favored him again with the bland, dreamy smile. "In a sense," he said, "I am talking figuratively. He is dead, shall we say, *artistically*. Well, of course, for all we know he may be dead in actuality. It is now many months since we have heard anything of him."

"I believe him to be alive," said the professor. "In a way it is because of this belief that I had the wish to come to see you."

"Indeed. I do hope you are right, Professor Challis. There are quite a number of things outstanding with Grasset which have been left hanging in the air because of the unaccountable mystery of his disappearance. If you can find him, I for one would be most grateful."

"I think I can find him," said the professor calmly.

"You do? How interesting. Where, may I ask?"

"I'm not sure. But I am leaving for Greece tonight and I have a feeling that some inquiries there might not be unprofitable."

"Ah, I detect a scholar's interest in this." The fat man smiled benevolently. "You think that because of Grasset's great interest in the archaic periods of Greek sculpture, he may have fled there, seeking inspiration?"

"Partly that, I suppose," admitted the professor. "Partly also because other people who seem to be interested in finding the man appear to be moving off in that direction." There was no point in explaining to Joákimos that it was also partly because of the intuition he had about the painting of the girl in the striped shirt, the girl whom Flett called Jenny.

"If you do find him, you must promise to let me know, Professor Challis. Why, it may even mean that I was unwise to dispose of that collection of his which I was holding. A letter of advice, or better still a cable, would be of great advantage to me."

"I shall let you know, yes." Professor Challis placed his finger tips together and glanced around the room. It had a quality of austerity in striking contrast to the clutter outside. It was sparsely furnished, but the pieces were good. On the walls were four fine English landscapes: one could have been a Constable and another a Cotman. The rest of the room was taken up with books in old leather bindings which looked as if they had been an auctioned lot from a nobleman's estate. There was no sculpture in the room, Grasset's or anybody else's. "This dealer who purchased the Grassets," Professor Challis said thoughtfully, "I was wondering if his name was Fanlec."

"Fanlec?" Joákimos closed his eyes as he repeated the name musingly. "Fanlec?" He shook his head and smiled, but the professor did not fail to observe that for the first time his fingers were quite still on the paperweight. "Good heavens, no," he said, and opened his eyes. "Poor Fanlec was dead by the time we were obliged to dispose of the pieces. And even had he lived, I am sure *he* would not have taken the collection. He and Grasset had had a difference, I understand."

"But surely Fanlec was his agent in Paris?"

"Not at the end. They had severed their association. They were no longer good friends." He paused and smiled. "So you knew Fanlec then?"

"Not as well as I should have liked to," said the professor, with the reflection that once you had begun, it was not all that difficult to become a master of the half-truth, or even of the barefaced lie.

"A man of great culture and intelligence," said Joákimos, "but with a business sense that was deplorable. Yet, in a way, Grasset owed much to him." He sighed, "Well, it is the way it goes, I suppose." He put the paperweight aside, as if it had fulfilled its purpose, and said, "If you would take my tip, Professor, I should, as a dealer, rather advise against investing in Grasset's work, if that was your intention. As I explained, there was a heightened interest after his disappearance, but it was brief and it has long since waned. His work, as you probably know, always made a compelling first impression, it had a quality of life and excitement and technical virtuosity, but it does not—er—it does not *carry*. In a year or two all Grasset's pieces will be as dead as the man himself." He favored the discarded paperweight with a slow, dreamy smile. The professor wondered why he was still anxious to assure him that Grasset was dead. Joákimos glanced up quickly. "I say this only in the way of advice, you understand," he amended.

"You are very kind. Actually, it was not so much his exhibition pieces I was interested in as some work he had done in his studio in Tite Street. I was shown them several weeks ago when I was visiting the present tenant of the house, a Mr. Flett. A number of sculptures of young women that—"

"Ah, the girls in the garden, yes." Joákimos smiled. "But I regret to say that this work also is now quite out of reach. Had Flett accepted our offer, no doubt we could have helped you, but at the last moment, a few days before his departure, he decided to have all the pieces destroyed."

"Destroyed?" Professor Challis looked at him sharply. "But I was not aware that Flett had left the house."

"Some ten days ago." Joákimos nodded. "We made a very reasonable offer for the girls—we were confident of disposing of them here and there as garden statuary: there is a call for that sort of thing—but at the last moment . . ." He shrugged and smiled resignedly.

What was the setup, the professor wondered, where the moment a man disappeared everyone was apparently at liberty to dispose of his property and effects? "Has Mr. Flett gone back to America?" he asked.

"Well, that was what I would have presumed. He simply told us he was giving up the house and leaving the country."

"I see." The professor was thoughtful for a moment, then looked up with a quick smile and said, "You've been most kind to put me on the right track about Grasset."

"Oh, come now, I've done nothing." The smile of Joákimos was expansive. "If at any time we can be of the least service to you, Professor Challis, we must count it a privilege. As I pointed out, I consider myself an admirer." The smile flicked off as he glanced quickly toward the door. "Ah, here is Mr. Roach now," he said.

Turning, the professor could not quite control his start of surprise.

In the doorway was a small, swarthy man with a gun in his hand. He was dressed with that neat, inoffensive reticence that bespeaks a bank cashier or an articled clerk. There was something startlingly quiet and still about him: a mild, quiet man in repose with a gun in his hand. The same man who nearly three weeks before had sat at the corner table of the Woburn Arms, in the saloon bar, watching Polly and the professor.

"Do come in, Mr. Roach," said Joákimos. "Professor Challis is just leaving." He made the introductions and said, in explanation, "Mr. Roach is my partner and valuer."

The professor observed that the gun in Roach's hand was not a threatening weapon. It was an old, stub-barreled pistol with a broken hammer, just a gun from a dusty cabinet in a secondhand dealer's shop. Yet in spite of the harmless aspect of the relic, in spite of the quiet man's neat and inoffensive demeanor, the professor had a feeling, queer and inexplicable and vaguely sinister, that this was not the first time Roach had walked into a room with a gun in his hand—a different sort of gun.

two: SIMPLON-ORIENT

≫⫷

I

Almost at the very point where the Simplon-Orient Express begins to shed its glamor as a snake discards its old skin, Professor Challis realized that the man known as Bimbo was also on the train—in the second-class and without his beard.

This discovery he found very cheering. Until then he had resigned himself to a tedious four and a half days of inescapable travel-confinement.

He was prepared to accept this, because it gave him time to sleep and read, and because he had an acute distaste for the alternatives: airplanes he regarded as unsafe, and he had no relish for the slow and uncomfortable crossing of the wintry Bay of Biscay in a steamer. At the same time, he had always found the Orient Express rather disappointing. In the Jazz Age he had been too old and already too academic to succumb to the alluring fictions of Maurice Dekobra: nonetheless, he had always felt that on any train that undertook to freight humanity between Occident and Orient on every day of the week save Thursday, it was feasible to expect that something exciting would happen. Nothing ever did.

Yet each time he traveled the hope would spring anew, and beneath the great glass canopy of the Gare de Lyon he would feel that this time something *must* happen. The great, gleaming locomotive hissed and snorted restlessly, trolleys were trundled along the low platform embowered in Parisian flowers and baskets of big peaches, importunate messenger boys waved telegrams, Thomas Cook men inclined their knowing and competent heads, groups coalesced and split around the polished steps, and Professor Challis was always acutely sensitive to the secret allure of strange women and to the sinister possibilities of men. . . .

Yet in the restaurant car the evening before, sweeping through the lush, moonlit French countryside, disappointment had come again. For all his pleasure in the musky bouquet of an excellent Margaux and his natural enjoyment of overheard conversations, he had been able to eavesdrop only on some dreary discussions concerned with taxation, stomach ulcers, the unsporting behavior of an Italian cyclist in the *Tour-de-France,* the disheartening performance of a horse called Cobra Jade at Chantilly, and the deplorable state of the trade in export mustard.

The men who at the Gare de Lyon had seemed so much like secret agents and remittance men and dope smugglers and worse had become no more than tired traveling salesmen moving on fruitless enterprises. Their eyes were bruised not by sin but by business, and they had a melancholy way of burping over their coffees. And even to a man of advancing years, who might be expected to be excessively impressionable, the women had lost their secret allure. In between discussing infant illnesses with exhaustive monotony, their tongues probed the recesses of their teeth for overlooked scraps of food.

Consequently, Professor Challis was greatly cheered to see, as the train began to move slowly out of Milan Station, the big figure of Bimbo Grasset sprinting from the newsstand to a second-class carriage, a copy of *Oggi* in his hand and his duffel coat flapping behind him. It was the duffel coat rather than the face that struck the first chord of recognition, for without his beard the man galloping down the platform bore almost no resemblance to the professor's companion in the King's Road coffeehouse. The professor remembered having thought that Bimbo would be quite good-looking were he to remove his beard, and this proved to be the case, although he looked much younger and far tougher.

At Venice, while some of the more handsome carriages were being shunted away, he walked slowly down what remained of the train in search of Bimbo. It was clear that winter travel across the width of Europe offered little appeal; even the second-class was practically empty. It would stay that way through Trieste and as far as Sezana, on the Yugoslavian frontier, and from then on it would be packed with thick-booted Slavs and Croats and Serbs who would sing jolly songs and drink *slivovitz* all the way across their country, perhaps to stop themselves looking at the shaggy pigs rooting in the mud and the barren desolation of the wilderness around them.

He could not find Bimbo in any of the carriages, and ultimately, as he was beginning to fear that he had left the train, he discovered him in the station bar, hunched in his duffel coat over a glass of vermouth and a saucer of black olives. He looked morose and lonely, which may have accounted for the warmth of his greeting when he saw the professor.

"Hello, *hello!*" he said. "I expected you'd have flown down." He shook hands with a heartiness that the old man found gratifying enough but distinctly painful.

"No, I always go by train," said Professor Challis. "Somehow there are always papers that I have never got around to finishing, and details that have to be put in order. This way, one gets a little time." He smiled.

"A bloody lot of time," said Bimbo.

"You're going right through to Athens?"

"Yes."

"You're fixed with a job then?"

"Well, up to a point."

"And Polly?"

"She's there already. She flew." Bimbo selected an olive and studied it frowningly.

"I see." The professor caught the waiter's eye, ordered a Dubonnet, and waited. He had an idea that with Bimbo you just sat back and waited.

"She sent me a cable on Saturday," Bimbo went on, "so I thought I might just as well trot down there anyway."

"Of course," said the professor. Traveling from one end of Europe to the other, second-class, and in midwinter, and he spoke of it as if it were a walk across the park. At the same time, the casualness was in his words and not his attitude. He seemed nervous and preoccupied. He kept jabbing with his forefinger at the pits of the olives he had eaten until he had them all neatly arranged in a little glistening cairn in the middle of the saucer.

"What is the real reason for your journey?" the professor asked quietly. "To take a job? To see Polly? Or to find your brother?"

The man's fingers stopped pushing the olive pits about and began to drum out some rhythm on the table top: the rhythm not of music but of some inner agitation. The professor remembered other fingers he had watched—Polly's fingers tracing patterns in the spilt beer on a table top, Joákimos' caressing the glass paperweight, Roach's cupped around a pint of bitter. . . .

Bimbo looked up suddenly and the chestnut eyes fixed to a sharp, stubborn focus as they met the professor's. When he spoke, it was with the air of a man who had come to a decision with himself. "Maybe it would be better if you saw this cable anyway," he said, and began to rummage in an inside pocket. From a battered pigskin wallet he extracted a folded cable form and passed it across the table. The professor unfolded it and read:

> PAUL DEFINITELY SEEN HERE SOME MONTHS AGO
> STOP FLETT ARRIVED YESTERDAY GRANDE BRE-
> TAGNE STOP SUSPECT THEY KNOW STOP LOVE
> —POLLY.

Professor Challis read the message twice, very carefully, and then neatly folded the paper back into its creases and returned it to Bimbo.

"The Paul is Paul Grasset?" he said.

"Yes."

"And he is your brother?"

For a fraction of a second the other man seemed to hesitate, and then nodded and said, "He is, yes."

"And the *they* whom Polly seems to suspect . . . Flett, do you think? Or Joákimos? Or—"

Bimbo glanced at him sharply. "Who told you about Joákimos?" he asked suspiciously.

"You did." The professor smiled and rubbed his hands together cheerfully. "Look," he said, "I think I can stand another Dubonnet. Would you care for the other half of that vermouth?" Bimbo, still studying him guardedly, shook his head slowly. The professor leaned back while the waiter poured the *apéritif,* and when this was done, he stared at Bimbo with bright, earnest eyes and said, "I wanted to ask you—because it does come within your field—I wanted to ask whether you had ever heard of some sculptures, some medieval church carvings, known as the Rocamadour Reliefs?"

Bimbo turned slowly and beckoned to the waiter. "I will have that other vermouth, I believe," he said quietly. "Yes," he added, "I have heard of them."

"They are fakes, aren't they?" asked the professor casually.

His companion sipped his drink and glanced meaningly at the restaurant clock. "I think we'd better drink these up and get back to the train," he said. "Otherwise we might miss it."

"That would be a pity. Just as I am beginning to really enjoy the trip. They do ring a bell, you know. I was wondering—you must tell me if I'm being a nuisance—I was wondering if you would have any objection to my joining you in your carriage as far as Trieste. I have a dull crowd with me."

Bimbo shrugged. "I supposed since we've started this thing," he said, "we might as well talk it out."

"I quite agree. We're going to be three more days together on this train. We can spend all the time in evasions, or we can employ it much more profitably."

Walking back along the platform, the professor caught a glimpse of the flat causeway running to the low shoreline of Italy, scrubby-looking and dreary across the rain-stippled water, and he could see through the steel station girders past the bustling bedlam of porters and peddlers to the slaty, decrepit mass of unlovely buildings in the drizzle. He murmured to himself, "Once did she hold the gorgeous East in fee. . . ." It was difficult to imagine that the Palace of the Doges lay beyond the Cinzano and Necchi advertisements and the streamlined garishness of the automobile garage; difficult to believe in the reality of old, pale buildings of stone rising from the Grand Canal, or the pigeons fluttering above the Piazza San Marco, or the market boats clotted around the Rialto like colors that had run. . . . He was musing contentedly on this problem of the protective coloring that humanity places around its achievements, when he saw the man hurrying up the platform in their direction. Quickly and neatly, he took Bimbo by the sleeve of his coat and jerked him in behind the newsstand.

The man strode past without seeing them. He was a short, neat man in a gabardine raincoat, and in his hand was an overnight bag from which fluttered a luggage tag marked British European Airways. He kept glancing at the ticket in his hand to check the number of his sleeping berth. A porter hurried behind him trundling two small suitcases on a rubber-tired trolley.

"What the hell is all this about?" Bimbo growled.

"I didn't want that man to see us, that's all," the professor explained. "I know him."

They both stared toward the man in the gabardine raincoat, and there was a faintly puzzled look in Bimbo's eyes, as if he were trying to remember something he had mislaid. The man had checked his ticket with the conductor and was climbing into the first-class carriage which carried the sign "Thessaloniki-Athenes" beside the door.

"Ah, we are to be neighbors, I see," said the professor.

"Who is he?" asked Bimbo, his eyes still perplexed.

"I thought you might have known. That's Roach. He's right-hand man to Joákimos. He must have flown down from London to pick up the train here."

"Roach." Bimbo repeated the name thoughtfully, and shook his head slowly. "The name doesn't mean anything to me, but I have a feeling I know him . . . that I've met him before. A long time ago. In Paris, I think." He shook his head again, as if to dismiss the problem, and asked, "Why do you think he flew down here to pick up the train?"

Professor Challis shrugged. "Possibly because I called on him yesterday just before I left London. Or perhaps it's nothing to do with that at all. They have a branch of their business at Izmir, I understand. He could be going there. Although, in that event, one would expect him to be in an Istanbul carriage."

"The more we are together the merrier we'll be," said Bimbo, but there was not much jollity in the way he said it, and it was obvious that something else was still nagging at him.

2

IN SPITE OF harder seat cushions and a sense of less opulent surroundings, Professor Challis found the second-class carriage far more enjoyable than his own plush and private little world of the first-class had been . . . so enjoyable, indeed, that he stayed on with Bimbo even when the train steamed out of Trieste.

They had talked together about a great many things, and now they were silent and a little preoccupied as the train climbed up through the bare, eroded cliffs above the blue bay. Two big tankers were being built on the slipways across the gulf: there was something absurdly toylike in the scaffolding surrounding them and the slow-moving gantries that trundled back and forth above the forming decks. Both hulls had been painted with red lead, and in the grey, sunless afternoon, rinsed pale and clear by the showers of rain which still clung to the hills in the south, the color glowed with that curious incandescence that the Mediterranean light always imparts to reds. And then the train turned on a slow curve for the upgrade, and the bay was hidden, and suddenly they were in a landscape forlorn and twisted and desolate, with deep fissures scarring the cliffs and queer pinnacles of black rock and stunted trees, and the rainwater trickling down brown and ocherous gullies.

"I remember who he is now," said Bimbo suddenly, starting up from where he had been half-dozing in the corner, head cocked sideways against the window pad, the copy of *Oggi* lying neglected in his lap. "That chap who got on the train at Venice."

"You mean Roach?"

"Yes, but that wasn't his name. It was something like that, but—" He formed the name carefully with his lips and frowned. "Just a minute, I'll remember it," he said, and closed his eyes.

The Orient Express, with two locomotives coupled to the sinuous curve of carriages, curled slowly upward through the dismal landscape. Professor Challis folded his small hands in his lap and allowed his eyes to wander restfully over the simple appointments of the carriage while he waited—the usual colored picture of the Matterhorn, the water trembling in the squat carafe racked above Bimbo's head, the pale varnish and woven cord of the luggage cradle. . . .

Bimbo opened his chestnut eyes lazily and said, as if to himself, "Rakmet—" then repeated it again, quite loudly, "Rakmet. Yes, that was it—Rakmet!"

"Roach's name, you mean, was Rakmet?"

"Yes. It was in Paris, just at the end of the war, when I met him first. He'd come from the Lebanon or Syria, somewhere out that way . . . yes, from Beirut, that was it. He was studying art, and I got to know him vaguely because he was interested in sculpture. I seem to remember he wasn't bad, either, although that was ten years ago. . . . Maybe he wasn't as good as I recall. What he *did* have was an extraordinary knowledge of art. He used to write articles . . . books, too, I think."

"Did you know him well?" the professor asked interestedly.

"No, not really. I didn't like him all that much. He was moody and conceited and he had that sort of Oriental shell that was difficult to penetrate. He was older than I, too, and rather patronizing. Paul knew him better. In fact—" He seemed about to say something, but broke off suddenly and looked out the window.

"In fact . . ." the professor prompted gently.

But when Bimbo turned again, it was obvious that another thought had supplanted whatever he had checked himself from expressing. "Is it possible that he would be going to Athens, do you think, to look for Paul, too?"

"Why not? Assuming he has some reason to do so. It is significant that when I met him yesterday, although he knew I was leaving in the evening for Athens, he did not inform me that he intended making the same journey—which, after all, would be a normal civility of conversation. I might add that earlier I had informed Joákimos of my belief that Paul Grasset might be in Greece, and also that there were other interested parties who appeared to be activated by the same feeling." He shrugged. "One can put two and two together. But then one must assume a *reason* for Roach's making the journey."

"There might be a reason," said Bimbo slowly. "If somebody was jealous of Paul, and hated him, somebody suffering from a sense of injury and persecution, and if that somebody was in a position to reveal something that could harm his persecutor irreparably—would that give you the reason you seek?"

"It would if it were true," said the professor with a smile. "But, as you explained to me that night of the party in Chelsea, what is truth? This may be just another of those images you told me you conjure up for your own satisfaction."

A wry smile touched Bimbo's mouth. "If it's an image," he said, "it isn't one that will give me much satisfaction." He paused. "Maybe it's time I told you the story of Paul Grasset," he said slowly.

"I think you'll find me a very good listener."

"It isn't the portrait of the artist as a young man, or the portrait of the young man as an artist. It's the portrait of the artist as a bastard. Do you mind that?"

"It's your story," said the professor contentedly, and settled himself into a more comfortable position.

"The main trouble about Paul was that he always had an obsession about success," Bimbo began. "He had to be a success with everything he did and with everybody with whom he came in contact . . . at games and in his work, with people, with women. . . ."

Professor Challis, as he listened, was able to assemble in his mind a clear picture of the stolid, respectable, middle-class family in the dull Cherbourg house in a dull Cherbourg street from which the Grasset brothers had unaccountably emerged; of the bourgeois and bullying elder brother Victor who had taken himself off to a civil service post in the Cameroons and had never since written to his family; of the brilliant and mercurial Paul, handsome and selfish, playing with his shy younger brother Charles in the marble- and granite-littered workyard of their uncle René, who had carved heavily respectable tombstones and monuments for the heavily respectable Cherbourg deceased; of the incredible technical brilliance with which, before he had reached his teens, Paul could cut and chisel stone; of the gradual development of a skill less technically brilliant but more painstaking in Charles, alternately suffering and worshipping under the impatient, cocksure tutelage of his clever brother; and of the bitter disappointment that fell upon the good-natured stonemason uncle when Paul finished school and came of age to go to work in the stonecutting yard, and instead turned his back on it without an expression of gratitude or a word of explanation, and went off to Paris. The uncle and the stoneyard had served their purpose. He had used them: they could be discarded without compunction. . . .

"What was your relationship with him when you were children?" the professor asked.

"With Paul? Much the same as it was later, except that when we were young, we were forced into a closer unity because of Victor. He was nine years older than Paul, and a bully. He hated Paul for his good looks and his cleverness— Oh, Paul didn't make it any easier, let's face it—and it was harder for him to throw his weight about when there were two of us together."

"Paul was your protector, then?"

"That's what I believed at the time. Now I'm not so sure that

Paul wasn't using me to protect himself. He could goad Victor farther when there were two of us to contend with." He smiled dryly. "He was queer and unpredictable even as a child. He had an extraordinary charm, and he knew it, and he would carry it to the very limit of tolerance, and then smile and turn his back on you. I idolized him and I hated him—and sometimes I was so jealous of him that in bed I had to bite the knuckles of my hand until the blood came, to stop myself from weeping. And then he would do something quite unexpected and wonderful and touching—like giving you his pocket money, or buying you some gift which you had secretly coveted, or taking the blame for some mistake which you had made—and then he would become a god again."

"And afterwards, in Paris?"

"He'd been there four years when I went, and it was he who arranged for me to go there to study, but he had his own circle of friends, most of them older than I, and it wasn't easy to take up again the things that had been shared by us in Cherbourg. Besides that, he was beginning to be successful, and he wasn't really interested in anybody he couldn't use to further that success. And then I began to discover *why* he had to use people. You see, he had an almost fantastic technical brilliance, but he had no true originality.

"I remember he was having a little one-man show in a gallery just off the Boul' Mich' at about this time, and when I went along, I was astonished to see that three of the exhibits were developed from studies which *I* had made. The real point is, I suppose, that they were beautifully realized—much better than I could have done—and . . . this is a funny thing . . . I left the gallery treading on air, feeling more flattered than I'd ever been in my life."

Bimbo smiled to himself, and for a long interval he was silent. Then he continued, "It took me a little time to realize that I wasn't the only one. He was quite capable of taking the ideas of anyone he came across and presenting them to the public first. Some were angry, some were hurt, some didn't seem to mind. If anyone complained, he simply pointed out that he had presented the ideas much more skillfully than their original authors could have done—which was true enough, as far as it went—and that they should be suitably grateful. The queer thing is that he always got away with it: he was still able to ride that personal charm of his to the limits of tolerance."

"But surely some of these people he victimized and duped must have shown their resentment."

"Some did. Rakmet was one—the man you call Roach. He suffered. I don't remember the details now, but I do remember that he tried to raise a rumpus about it—it was something to do with a contest for a memorial medallion—but Paul was too clever for him and twisted the thing around so that Rakmet looked a damn fool. He left Paris soon after, and I never saw him again until today."

"What effect did all this have on you, worshipping your brother as you had?"

"Well, one was disappointed and hurt. One stopped being an idolator. It wasn't easy to stomach the fact that somehow in all your relationships with your own brother you were being subtly cheated—that to further his own projects he would unscrupulously use anything you had, your loyalty, your admiration, your ideas, your friends, even your women. And added to that, of course, there was the other bitter pill to swallow, that for all his lack of originality he was a better sculptor than I could hope to be in a lifetime. Anyway, it was about this time that I went away from France—first to Spain, then across to the United States. I was there three years, then back to Lisbon and Madrid, finally London. I didn't see very much of Paul in all that time."

"He showed his work in New York, didn't he?"

"Yes, he had three exhibitions there."

"Successful?"

"For sculpture, very."

"While you were in New York?"

"I was there for his last show."

"Did you see him then?"

There was a slight pause before Bimbo answered. "I saw him at the opening, of course. But there was quite a crowd there and it wasn't much more than a smile and a handshake and a how-do-you-do. Paul had his hands full. It was one of those openings —tubs of orchids and two Hollywood stars, critics drinking the best Scotch, even a brace of millionaire collectors." He permitted himself a dry smile. "It was Paul's—"

"One of the millionaires was not Grantheim, by any chance?" the professor interrupted.

"Yes, Grantheim was there." Bimbo nodded slowly. "Why do you ask?"

"Because he was the man who bought the Rocamadour Reliefs."

"Ah, we're back to *that* again."

"I have a feeling it's something we'll have to keep on coming back to." Professor Challis smiled pleasantly. "But I'm sorry. I interrupted. You were saying . . ."

"Oh, there's nothing more to it. That's all."

"You mean to say that the only time you saw your brother in New York was this one brief handshake in a crowded gallery?"

"We circulated around at different levels. It suited me. Paul was a great success. I wasn't. I saw him again, yes, but he didn't see me. I had been along to the gallery to take a second look at the show, and I met two artists I knew and they insisted on dragging me along to a party. It was up along the Hudson, at Croton, and it was a big, crazy party. Lots of people. People tangled up together and all over each other. Possibly you don't know that sort of a party. If you're very drunk it's wonderful, and if you're sober, as I was, it's like being pitchforked into an illustration by Doré. Incidentally, our friend Flett was there. That was the first time I ever saw him, but I didn't get around to meeting him, or speaking to him. I didn't even speak to my own brother. As usual, there was a bunch of women around him, and he was going on rather. He was pretty much under the weather, so I just quietly moved out after a while. The air was wonderfully fresh along the river." He paused and frowned. "Perhaps I should have just gone up and said hello to him or something. That was the last time I saw him."

"When you say he was 'going on rather,' what exactly do you mean?"

"Well—going on, that's all," said Bimbo awkwardly. "How else do you put it?"

"That is what I am trying to find out," the professor said mildly. "If you could put it some other way, perhaps I would understand what you mean."

His companion smiled slightly. "Well, in Paul's case it was vanity. He had a rather special devotion to his own cleverness. He liked to show off. If there were women about and he'd had a little to drink, he liked to show off very much indeed. That was what I meant by going on. Trying to impress everybody with how clever he was."

"But he *was* clever."

"Exceedingly."

"Too much so, perhaps?"

"Perhaps," said Bimbo noncommittally.

"You mentioned Flett's presence at the party. How does he come into it, do you think?"

"Paul liked people he could use, or thought he might be able to use. I suppose Flett was one of them. I don't know his background, but he was some sort of protégé of that chap you mentioned, Grantheim, and I imagine in Paul's view Grantheim would always be a very promising prospect."

"A multimillionaire collector, particularly if he happens to be American, can't help but be a promising prospect to a European. You didn't meet Flett at the party, but you got to know him later?"

"In London. When he took over the house. I never got to know him well."

"Yet Polly gave me the impression of being on terms of—well, of some familiarity with him."

This remark appeared to have a particular effect on the other man. He squirmed in his seat, frowned down at his thumbnail, then turned his head away and stared out the window. The bleak landscape slid by, ruddy rocks and black craters, pitted like the surface of the moon.

"That's Polly's business," he said finally.

Professor Challis realized that his remark had brought the discussion to a point of some delicacy. One could not be sure that Bimbo had been telling the truth when he had said that Polly was still in love with the missing sculptor: it could just as easily have been part of that absurd fantasy of Bimbo's which had included the assassination of Paul Grasset at the hands of the men in black hats, with zithers. On the other hand, it was not difficult to believe that Bimbo himself was very much in love with the girl. If, then, his first story was true, his position was extremely invidious, for his task was to find a brother of whom he was already envious, and who had treated him badly over a long period of years, so that this brother could be romantically reunited with the girl whom Bimbo himself loved. If Flett also was interested in the girl, the matter became even more complicated.

But supposing Bimbo's story was a fiction, and Polly did not love Paul Grasset: then one was forced to look for some other explanation of the girl's obviously genuine anxiety that the missing sculptor should be located. If there was no romantic association to be considered, if she was not exercised by a sense of filial responsibility—which clearly still lingered in Bimbo's conscience in spite of all the psychological abuses he must have suffered at his elder brother's hands—then one would be obliged to theorize that her concern must be for somebody else who was or had been associated with Paul Grasset. . . .

His ruminations had brought the professor to the point where he was aware that it might be more circumspect to leave this rather delicate matter in abeyance for the time being. Moreover, there was a danger that in digressing into the more abstract channels of amatory behavior the thread he was pursuing would be lost. Deliberately he changed the subject.

"To buy a house in Chelsea," he said musingly, as if he were speaking his thoughts aloud, "in that part of Chelsea and that sort of house, must cost quite a lot of money. Did your brother have that sort of money?"

"I've no idea what sort of money he had," said Bimbo gruffly, as if he had not quite forgiven the professor for having brought Polly into the discussion.

"He seems to have had the reputation of being a lavish spender. Did he have private means?"

Bimbo shook his head. "When my father died, the family business at Cherbourg was sold, but the money went to Victor. Paul and I got a little. Not much. My share took me across to the States."

"In Paris, Paul presumably kept some sort of studio?"

"A small one on the Left Bank, across from Notre Dame. He'd had it from the time he was a student. It wouldn't have cost him much more than two thousand francs a month."

"Yes, but to buy the house in Tite Street might have cost him ten or twelve thousand pounds, possibly even more."

"I suppose it would have, yes."

"Could he have made that much money out of his sculpture, to buy that house, I mean, *and* to enjoy the particular sort of life he favored?"

Bimbo shrugged. "Does Epstein?" he said.

"Then the money came from somewhere else." Professor Challis leant his white head back, experienced the hard shudder of the padding against his skull, and bent forward again, locking his fingers together. "And in my opinion that leads us around and back again to two things—the Rocamadour Reliefs and the late M. Claude Fanlec." He waited, but Bimbo was quite silent, watching him. "I find myself thinking a good deal about this man Fanlec," the professor went on slowly. "Did you know him?"

"I met him once or twice in Paris. I wouldn't say I knew him very well. Like Paul, he was circulating in an atmosphere a little too rarefied for me."

"But he was closely associated with your brother?"

"He was a dealer. Paul was a successful artist. He handled Paul's work."

"Was he a good dealer?"

"I suppose so. He had a very good knowledge of art, and I think he loved it. He could be a contemptuous, arrogant bastard, but he seemed to be all right with those people he favored. He was just too proud and too lordly for me."

"Quite young, was he not, for that calling? As I understand it, he was only in his late thirties at the time of his death."

"What's so odd about that? There were any number of bright young men who emerged at the end of the war in that intellectual world around Paris. Fanlec was one of them. He had good family background and he'd done some clever work for the allied military governments, in France and Italy and Germany, tracing stolen works of art and so on, and then for a while he was with UNESCO, I think, and after that he set himself up as a dealer."

"Was there ever any suggestion that he might have been involved in enterprises that were—well, on the dubious side, shall we say? Shady art deals, that sort of thing?"

The younger man shrugged, his eyes still watchful and guarded. "He was an art dealer," he said. "There are always stories about art dealers. I dare say he wasn't very different from most other dealers in Paris."

"Or London?"

"Quite," said Bimbo agreeably. "Or London."

"Joákimos, for example?"

"There wasn't much resemblance between Fanlec and Joákimos. Why, is he supposed to be a shady dealer, too?"

"He keeps a shop which, if it isn't a front for something else, is the queerest shop I have seen in many a long day. And he keeps this man Roach, too." He paused. "It is possible," he said, "that your brother was tangled up with a couple of very odd dealers."

"It is possible," retorted Bimbo, "that artists usually are." He smiled dryly and looked out the window again.

"What is also possible, however," said the professor quietly, "is that Claude Fanlec did not commit suicide on the end of Dieppe Pier, but that he was murdered. A man whose body is found floating in the water with a bullet wound in the head may have taken his own life. Equally, he may have been the victim of a murderer."

Bimbo turned and looked at him slowly and said, "The coroner seems to have thought otherwise. In any case, what are you attempting to deduce?"

"At the moment I am not attempting to deduce anything. I am simply exploring a possible theory that your brother might have murdered Claude Fanlec—which could, after all, account for his sudden flight into concealment. It is significant, I think, that the death of Fanlec and the disappearance of your brother happened at the same time. They had had what Joákimos called 'a difference.'" He shrugged.

"Go on," said Bimbo.

"In my profession," said the professor, "there is a system we often have to work on which involves the establishment of an initial hypothesis. We may have discovered a section of crumbled wall, some fragments of pottery, a heap of charred ash, a bronze arrowhead, a coin or two. The fragments are scattered and seem to be unrelated. The levels are confusing. The gaps to be filled in seem impossibly blank. What we try to do is to establish a working hypothesis and try to build the pieces around it. If the picture begins to fit together, we press on with it."

"And if it doesn't?"

"If it doesn't, we discard it altogether and look around for something different."

"I shot an arrow into the air, it fell to earth I knew not where," Bimbo quoted softly.

"Precisely. Chance comes into it. It is an elastic combination of expert knowledge, pure chance, luck, deduction, and the ability to master jigsaw puzzles." He paused and coughed. "Now, on the basis of this rather hit-or-miss system, would you like to hear my theory on your brother's disappearance?"

"I would, yes."

"In 1948, when the Rocamadour Reliefs were discovered by Claude Fanlec, your brother was a young sculptor of rather remarkable gifts. His virtuosity lay in three things—an extraordinary knowledge of stonecutting, a phenomenal technical brilliance, and an uncanny capacity for reproduction. He was a man who already had significant weaknesses as well as significant skills. He liked to live expansively and to throw money about. He was uncommonly obsessed by his own cleverness. He was unscrupulous in the

methods he was prepared to use to achieve success. He was the
sort of young man who would always consider himself not to be
bound by the rules that applied to ordinary people. Polly told me
that Fanlec had once said he was the sort of person who was
quite incapable of moral distinctions. . . ." He broke off and
smiled. "Is this sufficiently accurate as a basic character sketch?"

"Go on," said Bimbo patiently.

"Very well. My theory is that your brother—perhaps deliberately, perhaps as an exercise in his craft, perhaps even as a piece
of blatant showing-off—devised a very skillful and elaborate piece
of sculpture which was later to be known as the Rocamadour
Reliefs and which was to fetch an extraordinarily high price from
a New York collector. With sandstone it is very easy by artificial
means to simulate centuries of aging, and in any case no form of
art forgery is as difficult as it seems. There are more Corots and
Cezannes and Renoirs in American private collections than the
painters ever painted in their lifetimes. The Sûreté will always
give you the figures of the thousands of art fakes which have made
the journey across the Atlantic during this century. And very en-
tertaining figures they are." He paused, but his companion had
nothing to say.

"So far as sculpture is concerned," the professor continued, "any
authoritative handbook will tell you where to be on your guard
for fakes—Ancient Egyptian, Etruscan, my own Minoan period,
T'ang horses, Tanagra figurines. Faking the Romanesque was, I
agree, rather an innovation: it is not a period that generally falls
within what one may term the orthodox fields of forgery. An example, shall we say, of your brother's cleverness.

"Now, what I suggest is that, as a result of this, your brother
found himself deeply entangled with M. Fanlec, a very clever
young man of about his own age who had set himself up about
this time as an art dealer in Paris—a highly competitive field in
which, presumably, a new man would not be at all averse to figur-
ing in an important artistic coup guaranteed to give him some
very gratifying publicity and to establish his reputation almost
overnight. In return, your brother found himself with a good deal

of money to spend. A one-third share of Fanlec's check from Curtis Grantheim would have quite comfortably bought that house in Tite Street. The London house, in any event, would have been a good base for future operations, and your brother may have carried out other—er—commissions of which we are not at present aware. It is possible that he had by this time established an arrangement with Joákimos not dissimilar to the arrangement he had had with Fanlec. He began to make regular visits to New York—to show his work, but also perhaps to study the possibilities of the more profitable market in what we shall euphemistically call genuine antiquities. He was—"

"If I remember your words correctly," Bimbo interrupted quietly, "your equation involved expert knowledge as well as pure chance and the ability to do jigsaw puzzles. I've no idea what expert knowledge you have of stonecutting, but I happen to be a sculptor of sorts. However brilliant a man might be, faking medieval stonework is not as easy as you appear to think. What makes you think Paul was capable of doing it?"

"He was perfectly capable of doing it."

"Yes, but how do you know?"

"I know because I took the opportunity of making a very careful study of those girls of his in the garden. When I first looked at them, I was intrigued by something queer about them. There was a fugitive sense of resemblance in each statue, as if one had seen something very like it before. It wasn't in the heads—that was his fun, his gallery of conquests, a sort of public overflowing of his vanity; but below these detachable conceits was something different, something more revealing. The following day I studied some references in the British Museum, and I began to see light. All the figures incorporated little details of other sculptors' works, superbly executed—a Donatello hand, a Rodin foot, exquisite little details drawn from artists as far apart as Verrocchio and Maillol and Houdon and Bernini. Now, in this extraordinary detail there was no point at all, unless they were exercises for the sculptor's own self-admiration, or practice for some—er—some future project along the lines of the Rocamadour Reliefs."

"It's a rather sweeping accusation merely on the basis of a check with some books in a museum library," said Bimbo.

"One would need a more expert opinion, I agree. I am only telling you my own suppositions and theories. And, in fact, we may never be able to get that expert opinion. Joákimos told me yesterday that the girls in the garden had been destroyed. Destroyed by Flett."

"Destroyed? But why?"

"I believe it is called the concealment of vital evidence. I cannot be sure, of course, that Joákimos was telling me the truth, any more than he was telling me the truth when he said he was ignorant of the present whereabouts of the remainder of your brother's work. I remember thinking at the time that it seemed strange that everybody was at liberty to sell, discard, or destroy your brother's property at will, merely because he had disappeared. So I wrote a letter in Paris yesterday to my landlord in London—he lives not far from Tite Street—suggesting that he might try to peek over the garden wall to see if the girls are still there."

Bimbo studied him for a moment with a sort of wary respect. "All right. Well, let's hear the rest of it."

"The rest of it takes us into what Polly calls the enigma." He gave the word Polly's pronunciation and smiled. "Quite suddenly your brother disappears. At the height of his success, and with everything apparently in his favor, he disposes of his house, returns from America, leaves a whole collection of his sculpture with our friend Joákimos, defects on an important showing of his work in Paris, and vanishes into thin air. Now, why should he do that, would you think?"

"This is your hypothesis, Professor," said Bimbo.

The old man chuckled. "Oh, it's nothing but guesswork now. From what we have assembled so far, and what we know of your brother, we could find a number of plausible reasons for his disappearance. He may have murdered Fanlec and run for cover. He may be hidden away somewhere turning out counterfeit antiques like an Egyptian bazaar broker. He may have fled the fury of a

spurned woman or the malice of a jealous husband. He may
have suspected the imminent exposure of his fake or fakes and
deemed discretion the better part of valor. He may have gone
chasing off after some other girl." He paused and added meaningly, "Or, like Fanlec, he may be dead."

Bimbo stared at him.

"You see, we are shooting not one but a number of arrows into
the air," said the professor. "And in the meantime I believe we
are coming into Sezana."

The muted whistle of the locomotive drifted down to them, and
the rattling hum of the wheels began to slacken. They were
running across a flat, brown plain scattered with low, poor-looking
farms. The land was soggy with rain. Two oxen pulled a flat cart
along a rutted road of clay. Hairy pigs and rather thin-looking
sheep huddled beneath the dripping pepper trees. Threatening
clouds drifted like tattered streamers above the dismal landscape.

"Are you going back to your compartment now?" asked Bimbo.

Professor Challis had a sudden picture of Roach standing in the
Paddington doorway with the broken old horse pistol in his hand.

"I shall go back when we get to the station," he said. "We
usually have to wait there for hours while they search the train.
That's if I'm not in the way here," he added apologetically.

"Not at all," said Bimbo politely.

3

MOST FRONTIER TOWNS have an infinite capacity to depress one,
but about Sezana there is an air of grim hopelessness—or there
was on this particular day—which by four in the afternoon had
plunged Bimbo into a daze of bored misery. Unable to read and
incapable of making conversation, interrupted by soldiers or customs officials every time he attempted to doze, he was left with
nothing to occupy his mind but the thoughts that Professor Challis
had placed there and the dreary scene beyond the rain-stippled

window—the flat and monotonous plain of mud which on every
hand invaded right to the cement edges of the frontier post; the
churned yellow quagmire of the solitary road which curled away
to some unimaginable destination; the extraordinary number of
black pigs which snuffled and rooted beneath the pepper trees.
Bimbo had never before seen pigs covered with a sort of greasy
wool, curling in the rain, and they had long, pointed snouts and
high, lean hams, and to him they looked as if they had emerged
from some medieval woodcut.

It was a question of either looking at the pigs or looking at the
soldiers—he classified them all as soldiers because, although there
were customs inspectors and policemen mixed up with the frontier guards, they all wore the same sort of ill-cut blue-grey uniforms and they all carried rifles or revolvers or submachine guns—
and it was not really much of a choice. Huddled beneath the
dripping trees, they had the look of a beleaguered garrison which
is prevented only by apathy from raising the white flag of sur-
render.

The locomotive snorted away to get water. A restaurant coach
was shunted along a siding. A swineherd in a brown cape trudged
through the mud to count the pigs suspiciously and plodded away
again. Water dribbled from the mouth of a stone faucet in the
guise of a laughing man. Posses of customs men made sporadic
searching forays along the train. Men hurried backward and forward through the rain carrying sheaves of documents. An officer,
who looked as if he might use scent, made a stern parade of the
length of the train, to inspect the heavily armed soldiery which
guarded the door of every coach to see that no passenger left his
place. Everybody seemed to be saluting everybody else.

Bimbo closed his eyes and tried to think of Polly.

Professor Challis, nibbling at the remnants of a packet of stale
salami sandwiches which his companion had bought in Venice,
swallowed with some difficulty, then spoke. "If you ever make this
trip again and you do want to smuggle something, you must
remember to hide it beneath the mattress of your sleeping berth,
or under the pillow. They look everywhere else, but they never

look at the beds. It's the one safe place for contraband. It's handy to know."

"Thank you," said Bimbo drowsily, registering the thought that, in the first place, wild horses could never drag him on such a journey again, and, in the second place, his compartment had no beds.

"These sandwiches of yours, you know, really are very stale indeed." The professor studied the scraps of dried bread unhappily. "Still," he went on, brightening, "once we get started again, we shall be able to have some proper food. From now on, there will be only the one restaurant car on, and that's for the whole train, so it's my suggestion we get along there as soon as we begin to move. The food will be quite good and the wine ghastly."

"That's fine," said Bimbo absently.

"I imagine Roach will go there, too."

"I suppose so."

"That might make it interesting."

Bimbo grunted.

It was not until four hours after their arrival at Sezana—it was now quite dark—that the Orient Express let out a tormented shriek and began to slide slowly through the wet night in the general direction of Belgrade. Professor Challis jumped to his feet immediately, rubbed his hands briskly together, and trotted off down the corridor in search of the restaurant car. Yawning heavily, Bimbo followed.

The restaurant car was six coaches along, and Roach was already there, in the corner seat at the far end of the car. There was a coffee cup on the table before him, and he was engrossed in a copy of the *Illustrated London News*. He did not look up as they entered. Professor Challis hesitated a moment, attracted by the thought of walking straight down to him and saying, "Why, hello, Mr. Roach; you do remember Grasset, don't you?" On second thought, since they had not been observed, he decided it would perhaps be more judicious to keep it that way. He and Bimbo took the table by the door and sat side by side with their backs turned to Roach.

It was surprising how peculiar it seemed, sitting like that with his back turned to Joákimos' partner.

Professor Challis picked up the handwritten menu sheet, glanced at it for a moment, and said, "Roach—or Rakmet, if you want to call him that—would hardly be going down to look for your brother just because of some injury or slight or plagiarism he suffered ten years ago. There would have to be some other reason." He gave his attention to the menu, but he was aware that Bimbo was watching him fixedly. "Ah!" The professor smiled happily and rubbed his hands together. "They have a *moussaka*, I see. You should try it, that is if you're not too allergic to cinnamon or caraway seed."

As he had predicted, the food was good, and plentiful into the bargain, and by the time they had eaten—they each choked down one glass of *slivovitz* rather than gamble on the wine—the restaurant car was full, and quite a number of people were crowded into the doorway waiting for seats as they were vacated.

Leaving the car, Professor Challis paused at the door and looked back. Through the drift of cigarette smoke he could still see Roach, engrossed in his magazine, oblivious to those who were waiting.

"I guess I might as well go back to my own coach now," he said, and smiled. "Perhaps you want to sleep. I'm sure I do."

Bimbo followed him down the swaying corridor for a few yards and then said, "You're sure you'll be all right?"

The professor turned to him in surprise. "All right?" he repeated. "Why, of course. Why shouldn't I be?"

"Well, I don't know," said Bimbo lamely. "I just wondered, that's all."

"It is very kind of you, but I'm sure I shall be perfectly all right." The professor smiled again and pointed to the toilet. "If you'd like to go past," he said, "I want to go in here." He pressed himself back against the quivering window, his arms flung wide in that attitude of flattened crucifixion which in the corridors of transcontinental trains is the only polite way of allowing somebody to pass.

"Well, good night." Bimbo seemed about to say something more, thought better of it, nodded, and walked away.

"Good night." Like some queer insect pinned against its frame, Professor Challis remained in his curious, transfixed attitude while he watched Bimbo's huge figure lurch down the swaying corridor, watched him until he disappeared through the doorway leading to the next coach.

Then he lowered his arms slowly to his side and smiled to himself and turned and walked back along the corridor toward the restaurant car.

4

WITHOUT GETTING OUT OF BED and looking at the thick gold watch in the pocket of his waistcoat, there was no way of knowing what time it was.

Through the two-inch crack of window where he had rolled the screen back he could see the plunging blur of the landscape. There was now bright moonlight and the rain had ceased, although torn rags of cloud still swirled from the peaks of a distant range of hills. Thick black shapes would come jumping up and falling away, clumps of trees probably, growing in scattered coppices close beside the railroad track, and often in the weird jump and flicker of black and silver the pale range of hills would be obscured, and sometimes the leaping black shapes blotted out even the moon itself. The combination of moonlight and the nervous hurry of the train created in the professor's mind, still fogged with sleep, the illusion that while he had been sleeping all normal terrestrial landscapes had been left behind and the night had moved itself into a world of old steel engravings, illustrations to a Gothic tale. It was hard to believe that when the sky lightened they would be steaming into Belgrade.

He tensed himself beneath the bed coverings and waited to hear the tiny sound again. Or, coming out of sleep into this world of unreality, had he merely imagined the sound? Less a sound, really, than a feeling, an animal instinct that something ominous was abroad in the night. . . .

He lay quite still and waited.

In a moment or two it came again, and this time there was no doubt of it: a faint click and the slow scratch of metal in friction. It was something embedded in all the other sounds of the train: the clattering rhythm of the wheels, the creak of woodwork and the soft groan of couplings, the singing rush of air along the windows, the distant frantic panting of the locomotive, occasionally the eerie wail of the whistle. Yet this was something quite distinct and unrelated. Without any doubt whatever, somebody was trying the handle of the door of his compartment.

Professor Challis lifted himself from the pillow, coughed loudly twice, and switched on the light. There was no sound from beyond the door.

He put his feet into slippers, threw his overcoat around his shoulders, opened the door, and stepped cautiously into the dim corridor. Outside only a single bulb was burning, and the screens had been drawn across all the windows. The hurry of the train was something locked outside the shuddering, dusky tunnel, something violent that howled and snarled and hammered at the shutters. Along the line of sleeping compartments the closed doors seemed as secretive as ancient sealed tombs.

At the far end of the coach there was a figure motionless in the shadows. As the professor began to walk slowly toward it, he saw that the side door of the coach had been opened and fastened back on its hook, and that the man who stood beside it staring out into the rushing flood of darkness, the man still wearing his gabardine raincoat, was Roach.

The professor walked toward him with a quickened step, smiling as he approached. "Why, Mr. Roach," he said warmly, "I had no idea our acquaintance was to be so soon renewed." He held out his hand.

Roach peered at him from the shadows, gave a start of surprised recognition, and smiled as he took the offered hand.

The man's acting was of mixed quality, the professor reflected. The way he had watched his approach, with an admirable combination of doubt and wariness, had been very well done, but the start of surprise had been no better than high-school histrionics.

"My dear Professor Challis," said Roach. "I had no idea you were on the train."

"Actually, I saw you earlier, in the restaurant car," said the professor, "but there was such a crowd, and people were waiting for seats. I went back a little later, but you'd gone." A rush of wind gusted in the open door. He shivered and pulled his overcoat more tightly around his shoulders. "Aren't you cold, standing here?" he asked.

"I found my berth unbearably stuffy. I felt I had to get some air." Roach smiled. "Do you know, I have never yet really mastered the art of sleeping on a train."

The man's voice was in keeping with his manner and appearance: it was very quiet and uninflected—the voice of Roach rather than of Rakmet, of London rather than Beirut. Indeed, there was something a little disconcerting in its absolute ordinariness. With his swarthy complexion and dark, patient eyes, one would have expected him to talk at the very least like a Welshman.

"You're going where?" asked the professor. "Athens? Istanbul?"

"Athens. There are some things to be looked at, part of a shipowner's estate, and a collection or two that interests us, then Samos and Chios, and a week or so in Smyrna. I must admit I am not at all sorry to be getting away from London at this time of the year."

It all sounded so matter-of-fact and reasonable, yet the professor found himself trying to read latent subtleties into the man's words. He could see Joákimos seated at the big desk in the inner room of the sleazy little shop in Paddington, running his fingers across the glass paperweight, and saying, "There is a collection or two in Athens, but there is no call for that sort of thing here." Why did Roach use the old name of Smyrna, and not Izmir, as his partner did? Why fly to Venice just to catch this particular train, when a plane on another schedule could have taken him, in only a few more hours, all the way to Athens? And was it Roach who had been trying the handle of his door?

"You must get in touch with me in Athens," said the professor pleasantly. "I shall be staying at the Grande Bretagne." He had never stayed at the Grande Bretagne—he disliked four-star hotels and had always preferred a small, friendly hotel near the more plebeian Plateia Omonia kept by the widowed daughter of an old man who had helped Schleimann dig at Mycenae—but he had suddenly remembered what Polly had said in her cable, that Brandon Flett was staying at the Grande Bretagne. "Or you can usually find me through the American School," he added. "If you can spare the time and you are interested, I know two or three dealers around the *plaka* who have some worthwhile material. If there is any call for that sort of thing, that is."

"That is very kind of you, Professor. I shall certainly try to avail myself of the offer."

He spoke rather absently, however, as if his real thoughts were concerned with something altogether different, and his eyes seemed to look past the professor, out to the cold rush of the night beyond the open door. Professor Challis half-turned. Between the side of the train and the telegraph poles blinking past, there appeared to exist a tangible world of black and silver movement, but behind it was the void, an utter emptiness in which no light gleamed.

"Oh, yes," said the professor, as if he had suddenly remembered something. "There was something I had in mind to ask you. It was one reason, indeed, why I was looking for you in the restaurant car earlier. It concerns a dealer friend of mine in Paris, whom possibly you might have known. Dead now, poor fellow. Fanlec was his name. Claude Fanlec."

He looked at Roach directly. He seemed to have moved around a little and was now standing rather more behind him, as if to get a little shelter from the blast gusting in the open door, and his hands were thrust deeply into the patch pockets of his raincoat. Professor Challis had a queer, premonitory feeling, almost of fear, as he waited for Roach's reply.

"I was acquainted with him, yes," said Roach at last. "He was not one of our affiliates in France, but we had dealings with him from time to time."

"You were not associated with him at the time of the sale of the Rocamadour Reliefs?"

"We were not. Why do you ask?"

"I have become rather interested in the works. I have been spending some time in New York and London in the last few years on a study of comparative sculpture. . . . It was this that gave me an interest in Paul Grasset—possibly Mr. Joákimos acquainted you with my reasons for calling on him." He smiled. "What I set out to do in the first place was to try to find a linking factor in various schools of sculpture—the Archaic Apollo and the Jain Saints, the sculpture of Byzantium and the early Romanesque developments in southern France—that sort of thing. As often happens, one thing led to another, and in the course of my inquiries I began to form the opinion that the Rocamadour carvings were not what they purported to be; that they were, in short, not genuine works of their period."

"How interesting," said Roach quietly. "I myself never had the privilege of seeing the reliefs."

"Fanlec was a reputable dealer and an honorable man. I feel sure he could not have known." He sighed. "Ah well, a sad ending to the poor fellow's story, I'm afraid."

Roach nodded. His face was quiet and patient.

"I read an item in *Paris Soir* on the inquest," the professor continued. "It seems they brought in a clear finding of suicide. Suicide while of unsound mind. I confess I should have thought an open finding would have been nearer the mark."

"Yes?" Roach nodded. "I saw no reports."

"My theory, of course," said the professor simply, "is that he was murdered. After all, there is nothing in the world simpler to fake than a suicide, a suicide by shooting, when the conditions are as they appeared to be in Fanlec's case."

"I am afraid I don't quite follow, Professor."

"Well, you have a victim who is faced by the imminence of

proceedings against him in bankruptcy—an almost classic motive
for suicide. He is alone in a provincial town where he is a total
stranger, which presents you with an almost classic setting. Now
all you need is for his murderer to be someone who is sufficiently
acquainted with him to be able to lure him privately to the end
of a deserted pier at night—a mistress, a colleague perhaps, a
partner. . . ."

"I confess I had never thought of it that way," Roach said
quietly. "We simply heard that he had had rather complicated
business worries—he had a good many irons in the fire, you know
—and had taken his life at Dieppe in a moment of depression."
He smiled slightly. "I must admit, Professor, that I find your murder theory much more fascinating."

"Oh, I am full of theories," said Professor Challis brightly, but
even as he spoke he was aware, with a sudden unreasoning clutch
of panic, that Roach had moved a little more to one side. There
was nothing of menace in the quiet eyes watching from the
swarthy face, nothing threatening in the relaxed, attentive demeanor of the man. Yet he had only to take a step forward and
push, and Professor Challis had nothing behind him but the open
door of the coach and the wild rush of the night and the dark
desolation that created an infinity of menace all around them.

He could feel the sting of the wind on the back of his neck,
a cold plucking and tugging at his long white mane of hair: there
was some sort of queer, insistent rhythm to it, as if it were a physi-
cal manifestation of that visual thing he had seen through the
window—the plunge and fall of the black clumps of trees swinging
by.

Roach had only to take his hands from the pockets of his raincoat and move half a step forward, and it could all be over with
one neat, quiet push; and then all he had to do was to pull the
communication cord and explain to the conductor about the silly
old man who had found the compartment too stuffy and had insisted on opening the coach door to get a breath of fresh air. . . .

The man's eyes, quiet and patient, seemed to commiserate with him as he began to withdraw his hands from the pockets of his coat.

He clenched his fists and put them to his mouth and blew on them as if he were suddenly aware of the cold. Professor Challis could feel his own overcoat flapping and tugging at his thighs, and in his mind began to stir that dreamlike feeling, atavistic and lonely, that one is beginning to fall into a bottomless pit.

Roach lowered his hands slowly and sighed.

The movement came as Professor Challis attempted to dodge away, feeling the violent pull and drag of the air behind him; but it was a movement totally unexpected, a violence that was huge and threatening, something that came whirling out of the dark shadows to swing Roach around with a muffled gasp that seemed an extension of the sigh. A fist cracked against bone with the sound of a mallet rapping on a wood block. Roach was reeling away and falling beneath a black, overhanging figure. The professor felt a tired weakness take possession of his legs as his fingers groped vainly for the safety bar beside the door, and then a great fist was laid upon his shoulders and he was flung bodily to the floor.

"You bloody old fool!" said Bimbo angrily. "You really *are* a bloody old fool!" He pushed the professor against the corridor partition, and turned away to bend over the unconscious figure of Roach, crumpled on the floor, a thin trickle of blood just beginning to dribble from the corner of his mouth.

"Laid him out," Bimbo said unnecessarily, but with a certain intonation of satisfaction, and then he turned to the professor and frowned. "It's a wonder I could hit him at all," he said irritably, "perched in that blasted lavatory for three-quarters of an hour, all cramped up!"

"You mean . . . you mean you've been there all the time?"

"The whole bloody night, off and on. I had a feeling something like this might happen. So I kept coming down this way every now and then to see that all was well. That's when I saw this fellow fooling around at the door of your compartment. So I decided to wait around and see what happened. The trouble was he came back up this end, and there was nothing for me to do but jump into the lavatory." His mouth twitched, and suddenly he was grinning. "I must apologize for calling you a silly old fool, but in a way you were, you know. I suppose you realize that he was about to toss you out that open door!"

"Oh, come now, you are being melodramatic." The professor summoned a smile, but his lips were pale and he felt rather sick in the stomach and his knees ached intolerably.

But Bimbo had gone down on one knee beside the fallen Roach and was rummaging in his pockets. From the raincoat he took a gun, a small, flat automatic, and rose slowly with it in his hand and said, "Your friend Roach carries one of these, I see."

"I've never known him to be without one," retorted the professor, with a brave attempt at levity. He wished he could stop the trembling of his fingers.

Bimbo took the gun and hurled it out into the clattering darkness and then he thumbed up the hook and kicked the door shut. "All right," he said, "now let's go to your compartment." He frowned down at the crumpled figure on the floor. Roach was breathing heavily and his fingers were jerking spasmodically. The trickle of blood had stopped before it had reached his chin. "He'll come around in a minute or so. Let's leave him to find his own bed. Have you anything to drink in your room?"

"Brandy," said the professor. "Medicinal brandy," he added primly.

Bimbo grinned. "What could be nicer?" he said.

In the compartment Bimbo took the professor's flask, emptied three-fourths of it into the water glass, drained it at a gulp, poured out what remained of the cognac and handed it across to the professor.

"The trouble with you is you won't listen to what I tell you," he said, curling his big body at one end of the rumpled bed. "And so you go around shooting those damned arrows of yours into the air like some crazy William Tell—except that you never hit the apple."

"What I was—"

"You listen to me," growled Bimbo. "You've talked enough in the last half hour. Do you remember my telling you this afternoon that there could be a very good reason for Roach to go looking for Paul?"

"Of course I remember. I said—"

"Never mind what *you* said. You were clever enough to see that some slight he suffered ten years ago at Paul's hands in Paris didn't constitute sufficient reason. There had to be something else, that's what you said."

"Exactly."

"All right. You also say the Rocamadour Reliefs are fakes; that they were faked by Paul. If that's true—and I don't deny that it *could* be true—then it explains a whole lot. It might even explain Flett, but we'll leave him out of it for the moment. What you evidently didn't understand when you were shooting those arrows of yours at Roach was this: that after he left Paris he continued his writings as an art expert, and within eighteen months he had landed a very comfortable and lucrative position as an expert adviser on European antiquities to an American millionaire—an American millionaire named Curtis Grantheim. It was on his advice, presumably, that the Rocamadour Reliefs were purchased." He took a deep breath before continuing. "Okay, let's take that as a starting point and go on from there."

"You mean that—"

"I mean that if the sculptures were forgeries, there were three people who almost certainly knew—Fanlec, Roach, and my brother. That's a lively little setup for all sorts of possibilities—possibilities like blackmail."

"Or murder," the professor suggested softly.

"Or murder, yes."

three: ATHENS

I

PROFESSOR CHALLIS FOUND IT uncommonly pleasant sitting at the small iron coffee table with half an hour to kill, watching the Athenian taxis circling lethally around Constitution Square, savoring on this last day of November a sun that rode in a sky of unsmirched blue and laid a band of real heat across his shoulders.

They had put the tables out around the palms in the square, carefully arranged as if a brass band would appear at any moment, men in gold uniforms with velvet frogs and plumed hussar's hats, come to play Sousa marches and arrangements from Strauss and excerpts from *Cavalleria Rusticana*. There were ripe oranges growing in the trees. The fruit, overlarge and improbably golden, had the unreal look of having been tied there in a very judicious arrangement among the dark-green leaves, as a cunning touch for the attraction of tourists.

Had everything been arranged like this, he wondered, by some very shrewd and talented stage director, employed by the government for the purpose of drawing currency into the country through the traveler's checks of strangers? The two *Evzones* in their dark-blue, skirted winter uniforms, formally guarding the Tomb of the Unknown Soldier in a slow, stately ballet; the blue enameled backdrop of the sky above rocky Hymettus; the bright kiosks flaunting shiny icons and tasseled beads and the magazines of all the world; the neat, attractive girls hurrying past with a crisp, sophisticated clatter of high heels on marble flags (how many other cities in the world, he wondered, were paved with marble?); the men with the baskets of pistachio nuts, the vendors of striped blankets, the shuffling mendicants hung with mountains of tawny sponges; the smell of coffee in the sunshine. . . .

And if he tilted his chair back only a little, he could see, blocking the distant end of a crowded street, the pearly sticks of the Parthenon surmounting the majestic rock of the Acropolis: perfection poised eternally above the tumult.

Professor Challis reluctantly withdrew his gaze from this satisfying spectacle, took up his pen again and completed the letter to his London landlord, Mr. Valentine, with a note on the weather and the observation that the garish vulgarity of modern Athens, in contrast to the superb beauty of its setting, simply proved an old contention of his, that cities were destroyed when they grew bigger than the ability of their people to walk around them comfortably on a warm day. (He was aware that Mr. Valentine kept his letters and showed them to friends whom he met each Sunday evening over a pint of stout at the King's Head and Eight Bells.) He concluded the letter with a reminder about the inquiry he had made earlier, and the hope that the London weather had been tolerably kind, and the November fogs not as unpleasant as usual.

This done, he lifted a finger for the waiter—being American and democratic, he had never been able to adopt the Turkish custom of clapping his hands for service—tilted his chair back again so that the Acropolis came within the range of his vision, smiled contentedly, and waited for Polly.

Somehow he had a distinct feeling about Polly which, in a younger man, might well have been construed as a romantic excitement. Certainly this feeling had all the thought components that rightly should have been concerned with a tryst of lovers. Would she come? Would she be punctual or, womanlike, provocatively late? What would she be wearing? How would she greet him? These and similar questions, however, were not derived from a glandular or sentimental attitude toward the girl's impending arrival: they were partly the lazy mental processes of an old man idling in the sun, and they were partly a feeling that it was Polly more than anybody else who could supplement those parts in the Paul Grasset story that might make the mystery understandable.

They had learnt upon their arrival that she was visiting friends on Ydra, and Bimbo had taken the ship down to meet her and bring her back. No doubt he would have talked to her and explained the necessity for absolute frankness. After the rather startling incident with Roach on the train, Bimbo had made it clear that his own wish to lay all his cards on the table was qualified by the fact that there were certain aspects of the story which had to be told, if she were willing, by Polly—and by Polly alone. On this point he had been adamant.

The professor allowed his thoughts to drift from Polly and Bimbo to the man Roach. Where had he gone? After what had happened on the train outside Belgrade, they had not seen him again until their arrival at Athens, and even then it had been only a passing glimpse of the man struggling to get his baggage into a taxi outside Larissa Station. Evidently on the train he had taken all his subsequent meals in his compartment; several times they had seen the waiter from the restaurant car swaying up the corridor with covered trays of food.

Staying at the Grande Bretagne had also been abortive, so far as Brandon Flett was concerned. He was staying at the hotel— yes, this the booking clerk confirmed, jabbing an informative finger at the key hook numbered 223—but it appeared that he was away most of the time. "He is not an easy man to catch," said the booking clerk. "He comes and goes. Mostly he goes." He had suggested leaving a message. Twice the professor had tried to telephone Flett's room, but nobody had answered the call; a note he had scribbled remained two days in the rack, and then disappeared, but it elicited no reply.

Professor Challis stirred the sherbet, sipped at it, pursed his mouth, and waited for Polly.

He could see her coming across the square for quite some time before she saw him. She had a quick, light walk and an air of youthful audacity that took the eye, and he saw the men turning to look after her as she passed, and being Mediterraneans they had no need to dissemble the admiration in their eyes. She was, as usual, hatless, wearing a suit of tan wool with a yellow sweater, and a sprig of narcissus in her buttonhole. Narcissus in November! It was no wonder, the professor reflected, that the Greeks had once worshipped the earth. Seeing Polly coming toward him, walking with the resilient springiness of life and with the whole of the day wrapped around her, it was no wonder they had worshipped a lot of things! At the curb she caught sight of him, and her face lit up and she waved to him across the traffic.

"But I thought you'd be with Mr. Grasset," he said, moving the chair for her. "I understood he was coming back with you."

"He did." She smiled as she took the seat. "It's so nice to see you again," she said. "He did come back with me, but we worked it out together coming up on the boat, and he—well, *we* felt it might be better if you and I had a talk first, just the two of us. And then—that is, if you've nothing else arranged—we thought the three of us could have dinner together this evening."

"Thank you, that would be fine. Will you have something here? Coffee? Something stronger?"

She glanced at his glass of sherbet and smiled. "Nothing really." She placed one of her gloves on top of the other, arranged them carefully so that the finger tips were even, and said, "If it's all the same to you, I think we had better have this talk. Bimbo told me what happened on the train. That was the man who was staring at us in the Woburn Arms, you know. I didn't realize—"

"Yes, I know. Where would you like to talk? Here?"

"Not here, no. Somewhere quiet, I think."

"Come then. It's a lovely day, and I have just been sitting here, looking at it." He glanced along the crowded tunnel of the street to the serene red rock at the far end. "We can get a No. 16 bus and be there in five minutes."

The bus dropped them near a clump of eucalypts, beneath which a group of marble cutters were chipping stone seats for the theater of Herodus Atticus, and they walked together in silence up the broad, curving roadway that led to the Acropolis.

On the summit a cool wind blew in from Piraeus, and there were not more than half a dozen tourists wandering among the ruins. A few anemones, like drops of blood, were already visible in the long yellow grasses that tossed among the tumbled stones. They found a seat, sun-warm and sheltered from the breeze, at the edge of the Erectheum, with their backs to the porch of the Caryatides and their eyes on the mellow, apricot-flushed grandeur of the Parthenon.

Athens had dropped away below them, a great wen of diseased flesh soiled by the smoke of the Piraeus factory belt; it had for the moment less significance than the wind stirring in the long grasses.

It was curious to think that the matter they had come here to discuss spread its tentacles far beyond the Attic plain: to a Paddington junk shop off Praed Street, to a Georgian house in Chelsea, to a millionaire's mansion on Long Island, to Dieppe Pier and a shop on the rue Saint-Julien, to the yard of a monumental mason in Cherbourg, to places where lives had impinged upon each other in London and Paris and New York, to whatever lay in the past of this singularly attractive girl who sat silently beside him on a fallen pediment of marble in the soft warmth of the Grecian sun. . . .

"I suppose you would like me to begin at the beginning," she said at last.

"In the long run, I always think it simplifies matters if you do," he said quietly.

"Except that in these things it's not always so easy to find a beginning, that's the trouble."

"Well, one can say that about most things. If one could always be sure of clearly working out where a thing began, it wouldn't be all that difficult to predict the ending fairly accurately. We can always fill in the middle parts ourselves. What happens, unfortunately, is that by the time we are prepared to look back for beginnings, they have all run together and become confused."

She nodded, and after a thoughtful silence said, "I think Bimbo told you I was in love with his brother Paul, didn't he?"

"Yes, he did." The professor smiled. "I was inclined to take it as one of his jokes."

"But it wasn't really a joke," she said.

He turned and looked at her. "But surely when I questioned you about him, you gave the impression that you knew him only slightly, that he was—" He broke off and waited, aware that she had something more to say.

"I *was* in love with him, it's quite true," she said quietly. "You have to understand that, because it leads to the rest of it. Oh, it was just a silly, romantic thing, I suppose. He didn't really care about me at all, but—" She stopped abruptly and turned her head away, and again he waited for her to continue. He sensed that Bimbo might have been very forceful in his insistence on her being frank with him.

Two sea gulls brought in on the wind from Piraeus had settled on the Parthenon pediment, where they were irreverently squabbling.

"Anyway, that's not the beginning of it at all," she said, and smiled shyly. There was something in her expression which he found very young and endearingly naïve, something almost childlike, so that it seemed appropriate that she should say, "It really begins when I was just a schoolgirl. In Switzerland, at a little place outside Zurich. . . ."

2

"JUST A SCHOOLGIRL," the professor realized, was a rather misleading phrase, for the little place outside Zurich had been a very smart finishing school for wealthy young ladies, and suitable for the final social and cultural polish of a girl of seventeen whose father's fleet of oil tankers—under various charters and, to avoid taxation, flying the flags of such disparate nations as Panama and

Liberia, to say nothing of Paraguay and Honduras—sailed the oceans of all the world.

Seeing Polly now, at the age of twenty-three, it was not difficult for the old man, knowing something of the early beauty and nubility of Greek girls, to appreciate that Polly at the Swiss finishing school would have presented a picture far different from the average conception of a plaits-pimples-and-pinafores schoolgirl.

It had been the sort of school which, influenced by the excellent fine-art reproductions truthfully facsimiled in the printing houses of nearby Zurich, could rightly feel that a young woman's education was incomplete without a sound working knowledge of Europe's creative and cultural heritage. And since the fees were singularly high, and what were called "Creative Project Excursions" were added as extras onto the annual bill—and invariably paid for without the blink of an eye by parents addicted to the expensive spoiling of their young—the pursuit of this cultural heritage twice a year took the form of elaborate forays to Oberammergau, to the Salzburg Festival, to the Gothic masterpieces of Chartres, Rheims, Bruges, and Strasbourg. These costly jaunts—chartered parlor coaches, ample pocket money, four- or, at the very least, three-star hotels—were conducted by the headmaster of the school, a certain Dr. Malcolm Marlowe, who had come to Switzerland from Oxford many years before because of chronic bronchial ailments and who was, fittingly enough, the author of a three-volume work entitled *Europe's Heritage of Culture*. From seats of medieval distinction with which, in his opinion, no scholar was more familiar, he winnowed the appropriate doses of culture for the thirty-two privileged young ladies who sat demurely in the airfoam seats of the chartered parlor coach.

The excursion with which Polly's story was concerned, however, was slightly off Dr. Marlowe's heavily beaten track. It had arisen as a result of a churlish attack by a Brussels book reviewer on the third of Dr. Marlowe's volumes, the charge being that the author had deliberately turned his back on the most interesting taproot of European culture.

The thirty-two young ladies were accordingly bundled into the parlor coach and whisked off to the Vezere Valley to see the strange works of their remote ancestors, the Reindeer Men, with a climactic visit to the prehistoric masterpieces in the painted cave at Lascaux, which were described with mellifluous and possessive pleasure by Dr. Marlowe as "the Chartres of prehistory" without the slightest acknowledgement to the good Abbé Breuil, who had originated the phrase.

It was while staying overnight at Montignac, for a second and final morning visit to the famous cave, that Polly's first adult adventure began. There not being even a three-star hotel in the little riverside village, Dr. Marlowe had been obliged to quarter his girls in the best inn available. While this establishment was both clean and comfortable, it was not altogether easy to obtain that measure of seclusion and privacy which can be taken for granted in the higher strata of the *Guide Michelin.*

Staying at the same hotel on this particular evening had been a good-looking and extremely intelligent young man who modestly described himself as an art student from Paris, and who quickly succeeded in captivating Dr. Marlowe both with his personal charm and his remarkably deep knowledge of the Romanesque sculpture and architecture which is to that section of France what Gothic is to the north.

Under the benevolent and appreciative eye of Dr. Marlowe, the young man was therefore permitted a much greater liberty of intrusion into the party of sheltered young ladies than otherwise would have been permitted. Since he was then aged twenty-eight and possessed of very great charm, as well as being handsome and intelligent, he had no difficulty in also captivating the young ladies of Dr. Marlowe's school, without any necessity of referring to the development and decay of the Romanesque in medieval architecture.

These were the circumstances, then, in which Polly had first met Paul Grasset. She was seventeen, he was twenty-eight, spring was stirring in the valleys, and Dr. Marlowe, heavy with the claret that the young man had so generously insisted on buying, retired early to his room on the pretext of sifting the Abbé Breuil's researches in preparation for his morning lecture to his young charges.

The moon was full when Polly and Paul Grasset walked slowly together along the riverbank to see the apricot trees in blossom.

3

"AND AFTERWARDS?" said Professor Challis gently.

"Oh, it was the usual schoolgirl thing. I kept a diary and wrote down everything I thought, and I used to send long letters to him once a week. He replied to the first two, and he wrote occasionally afterwards, but he was back in Paris then, and the intervals between his letters grew longer and then they stopped coming altogether. I think I must have grown up a little by then, because when he stopped writing it was almost a relief; at least it didn't hurt half so much as when he'd taken two days longer to answer a letter than he should have. And in any case, I left the school a year later."

"You returned to Greece then?"

Polly nodded. "I did for a time. But Daddy was away in New York establishing a new branch of the company, so it really became a choice of going to live with an aunt on Rhodes or joining my sister in Paris. I have no mother, you see. She died in the occupation."

"And this sister—she is older than you? I take it she is, since she was living in Paris, alone presumably, while you were still at school."

"Five years older. Her name is Helen." She paused, and her attention seemed to be distracted by the spectacle of an old woman in black who was trying to catch three brown chickens in the long grasses near the temple.

"And so you went to Paris?" the professor prompted.

"I went to Paris, yes." She turned to him with a quick smile.

"I arrived there on my nineteenth birthday. It seemed a wonderful thing to be doing."

"I imagine it probably was." He returned her smile. "And you wanted to study art, no doubt."

"Yes."

"I'm glad of that. I would hate to have thought that your Dr. Marlowe's efforts had been entirely fruitless. And, if I may continue my own interpolations, it was in this world of Parisian art students, at the Café Deux Magots, perhaps, or the Club Colombier, that you once again met the young man who, a year or so before, had captured your heart at Montignac."

"No," said Polly. "It was quite a long time before I met him again. And then it wasn't in Paris at all. But I did hear lots of stories about him, and I suppose it was because of the stories that I didn't go out of my way to try to meet him."

"What kind of stories?"

"The sort of stories that half attracted and half repelled; that is, if you happened to be a young girl who had just left school and who wasn't really very sure of herself in spite of an extremely expensive education."

"There was one half of you that remembered the night on the riverbank at Montignac, and the other half that could not forget the silly love letters you had written, nor the things you'd put down in your diary?"

She glanced at him quickly. "Yes, I suppose it was something like that," she said. "And besides that, he had become rather a celebrity in his own way. He was really a very brilliant artist, you know, although he was still only young, and he seemed to know everybody, and he was terribly extravagant. There were all sorts of stories about the parties he gave and his conquests of women. . . ." Again she paused and said, "He seemed to have drifted rather out of reach of a girl of nineteen."

"Did it never seem odd to you that he had so much money to throw around? To you or to the others? I mean, I had always understood that young artists were supposed to struggle in Paris, not to act in the manner of visiting rajahs."

Polly shrugged. "I don't believe that aspect was ever given much consideration. I suppose it was taken for granted he had private means. Or gambled. There was an American millionaire at the atelier I attended, and he wore the raggiest clothes I've ever seen in my life—he had one pair of bluejeans and a black sweater and he never changed them in a whole year—and he never ate anything but tinned beans and boiled cabbage. Where your money came from, or how you spent it, didn't seem very material."

"Then you never suspected that Grasset might have been involved in any shady business?"

"Not really. Well, not at that stage, anyway. Oh, one knew that he was a great intimate of people like Claude Fanlec, and Fanlec had something of a reputation for sailing close to the wind. But then he was a genuine dealer—" She broke off and smiled. "—even if there were people who did say that he maintained a secret workshop in Montmartre where three students who were called Fanlec's Gremlins produced Renoirs and Manets and Watteaus and Corots to order. Nobody that I knew ever saw the three students. One accepted it merely as one of those stories that got around. Most of the dealers in Paris are queer people in one way or another," she added simply.

"You never heard it suggested, even in idle rumors, that the Rocamadour Reliefs were fakes, that Grasset might have faked them?"

"Never."

"Now, may I cut right across what you have been saying and ask you if you knew Roach—his name may have been Rakmet then, according to Bimbo—while you were in Paris?"

"I knew him very vaguely, as an expert and a writer on art. Sometimes I would see him at exhibitions. Bimbo had known him much earlier, when he had been studying in Paris."

"Flett then?"

She shook her head. "I never met him until he came to London to take over Paul's house. That was after Paul had disappeared, of course."

"In fact, it was because of the disappearance that you struck up an acquaintance with him."

"Well, yes." She leant forward and plucked a stiff stalk of yellow grass and examined it thoughtfully. "You see, I had already met Paul's brother, Bimbo, and he was naturally rather worried and puzzled by his brother's disappearance, and we talked a lot about it and it seemed perfectly logical that this man who'd known Paul in New York and who had taken his house would have some information that might be helpful."

"But, in fact, Flett was not helpful at all, was he?"

"Not really, no. When I tried to ask him questions, it would always seem to twist around so that I would find myself being questioned."

"Perhaps if you had been more frank with him, you would have found him more responsive," the professor suggested mildly.

"I beg your pardon?"

"Well, I gather you were suspicious of him. You were not too sure why he was so anxious to locate Paul Grasset; you felt that he knew something he was not prepared to disclose. You cultivated his society in the hope that ultimately he may have divulged something to you, either willingly or inadvertently, but all the time you yourself were withholding very valuable information from him."

She looked at him steadily, the stalk of yellow grass rigid in her fingers. "Such as?" she said.

"Such as the fact that the picture of the girl above the chimney piece—the girl Flett always referred to as Jenny—was actually a portrait of your sister Helen."

Her gaze never wavered from his, and then, after a long moment of silence, "That's purely a guess on your part, isn't it?"

"It is. When people aren't frank with you, it is necessary to make guesses. Maybe Flett has made the same guess. A guess may be wrong and it may be right, but anybody is at liberty to make one. This one, I imagine, is right. There has to be some deep personal reason for *your* concern about Grasset's disappearance, something far more important than a schoolgirl crush on a young man who seems to have been the sort of person who would hardly justify or inspire such a degree of sentimental loyalty. Then look at Bimbo's case. He seems not to have been on particularly good terms with his brother: indeed, if I had been in his shoes, I think I should have been more pleased than otherwise about the disappearance. Therefore I feel there must be another reason for his disquietude. And my guess is that that reason is directly related to you."

Rather to his surprise, she smiled at him. "I did intend to tell you, you know," she said. "I wanted you to hear *all* the story."

"Then since your sister is now introduced, I take it this leads us to your second meeting with Paul Grasset." He paused, and when she nodded in affirmation he said, "It was not in Paris, I believe you said."

"It was in Marseilles. Helen and I had gone there to pick up a boat for Piraeus. We had planned to come back to Greece for Christmas and New Year's. But the ship we had booked our passages on came from New York, and there had been very bad December gales in the North Atlantic and it was delayed. We had five days to wait. Isn't it queer how everything can happen because of a little thing like that?"

"Chance is the true ruler of our lives, I suppose. Do go on."

"Well, on the first night we were there, Paul Grasset came into the restaurant where Helen and I were dining. That was the first time he had met Helen."

"There was no renewal of the little romance that you had begun in Montignac?" His eyes were kindly. "Or was there?"

She shook her head. "I'm afraid once the introduction was made, he didn't really pay very much attention to me. Helen was much more beautiful than I, and older, and more sophisticated. She belonged in his world, she was more of a challenge to him, I suppose." She paused, and in the professor's mind was a picture of the girl in the striped shirt and tight black trousers, so assured in the arrogance of her youth and beauty. Even knowing Polly, it was not difficult to imagine the effect her sister would have had on anyone as susceptible, as predatory in his search for beauty, as Paul Grasset.

"The next day," Polly went on, "she went with him down to Cassis, and she didn't come back that night, and the day after, she sent me a telegram asking me to cancel her passage on the ship. I came back to Greece on my own. I found out later that she went with him to the Gulf of Spezia." Her fingers had broken the brittle stalk of yellow grass into fragments, and now she scattered them at her feet and turned to him quickly. "I know it all sounds horribly sordid, but I don't think it *was* really, not if you understand it." Her dark eyes implored him to understand it. "They loved each other. I'm sure they did. Even with what happened later, I'm sure they did. The following year I returned to France, but this time I took a studio apartment on my own, and I only saw Helen every now and then. She and Paul were still together."

"Were they happy?"

"I believe they were, but—" She shrugged. "In places like Paris, how can you ever tell? Anyway, then this other thing came up."

For a moment or two he waited, and then asked, "What other thing?"

She stared at her finger tips and bit her lip thoughtfully. "Well, it isn't so easy now to explain it, because it isn't so much things I *know* as things I've had to piece together. I think Helen must have found out where Paul was getting his money, or perhaps there was some other thing she had discovered. I think it was to do with the money, but he didn't *have* to earn his money in any dishonest way. He was talented enough not to have to. And, besides, Helen had plenty for both of them."

"There are lots of men who wouldn't accept that as a valid argument, you know," he suggested gently.

"Yes, I realize that. Anyway, I suspect she tried to get him to stop whatever it was he was doing. . . . I don't know what went on between them at this stage. . . . Helen came to my studio one night very late and she was very pale and trembling, and I think she had been drinking, but she wouldn't tell me what was the matter, although I had the feeling that she desperately wanted to say something to somebody. Perhaps she thought I was too young to understand, or she might have thought that I would consider it all too sordid and shameful. I tried to persuade her to stay the night, but she went away about two in the morning. She wouldn't even let me call a taxi. It was not until later that I learnt she had had a most terrible row with Fanlec. Paul was in New York at the time, having the show, and when he came back, she went to meet him. I—I didn't know she'd gone until later. . . ." Her voice faltered and trailed off into silence.

"And where is Helen now?" he asked gently.

"I don't know," she said.

"You mean—"

"I mean I don't know. When Paul disappeared, she disappeared, too."

"I see." He looked at her thoughtfully. "But you sent a cable to Bimbo which suggested—"

"That Paul had been here in Greece, yes. About two months ago."

"And was Helen with him?"

"I don't know. I've not been able to find out."

The silence this time was a long one, for they were both concerned with their own thoughts. Finally it was the professor who broke it.

"I'm sorry we have to move the discussion now into a rather sinister field, but it is not inconceivable, you know, that Paul, for some reason of which we are not really aware, murdered Claude Fanlec. If, having done this, he fled into hiding, he may never have known that the inquest returned a finding of suicide. The case was, in any event, treated in rather summary fashion by the newspapers. Is it not reasonable, then, to assume that your sister Helen, being in love with the man, would have accompanied him into hiding? Always assuming also that you concede the possibility of murder, knowing the parties and relationships concerned. Do you concede that possibility?"

"Yes, I do," she said softly. "But not in the way you say."

"I don't think I quite understand."

"But can't you see that if Claude Fanlec was murdered—if somebody wanted to kill him—don't you realize that it wouldn't have been Paul at all? It would have been *Helen!*" She had clenched her hands together until the knuckles were almost bone-white in the olive skin. "Paul was never the sort of person to kill the goose that laid the golden eggs. At least, I don't think he was. But even if he did kill him, he wasn't the sort of man who would have run away. He had audacity and cunning and he had spent all his adult life in a world of deceit and cleverness, where half the fun of life was in proving how much smarter he was than the other man. He was conceited and he was clever, and in a queer, distorted sort of way he was brave, too. Well, I suppose that sort of thing isn't bravery so much as bravado. But I know he wouldn't have run away unless he had to protect somebody else, somebody who was very dear to him, somebody he loved."

Professor Challis placed his finger tips together and examined them thoughtfully. The mental picture he had of Paul Grasset was far from complete—it was a sort of sketch in the Pointillist method, little separate flecks of color placed in a patterned juxtaposition, so that if you stood well back and looked at it, you had the impression of a complete image: a picture assembled not from true knowledge of the man but from the opinions and inferences expressed or implied by others who had known him, but all subject to the fallibility of human prejudice and human emotion. Yet there was nothing in the picture to suggest that Grasset was capable of such unselfish devotion, such a sweeping sacrifice, as Polly's story implied. All the stories about Grasset at least agreed on one thing—the man's almost megalomaniacal vanity, an obsessive and selfish egotism which surely ruled out any possibility of his renouncing everything for the sake of somebody else. Paul Grasset used people: he was not one to be used *by* them, or *for* them. . . .

"Yes," he said reflectively, "it's all a good deal more complicated than I think we had realized." He turned to the girl sitting quietly beside him, and as he looked at her, there was a deep curiosity in his old, bird-bright eyes. "You never really asked me to help you, Polly," he said gently, "but I had always taken it that the request, even if unexpressed, was there. I had often meant to ask you why. Why you felt that *I* could help."

Her eyes were on the pale wall that rimmed the rock, the wall of Pericles, a gilded edging to the deep blue silence of the day. "It was just a feeling I had," she said quietly. "I think I felt it the moment I first saw you, that night when you came to the house. I'm not sure that I know how to explain it. It was seeing somebody who looked as if he might understand, and be kindly . . . somebody who was detached and—forgive me—and *old;* somebody who was not all tangled up in young, silly, *uncontrolled* things. I saw you standing there looking at the statues. Did you know that I was watching you for quite some time before I went up and spoke to you? And I had this odd feeling—" She smiled shyly. "You did look so strange standing there, you know. . . . I had this odd feeling that you had come there, into the garden, to help us work it out."

Professor Challis blinked and coughed and said, "Well, that's very nice of you, my dear," and then he smiled at her mischievously and added, "I gather the feeling must have passed away later, when I found you not being entirely frank with me, either."

"I think that was because I had formed a habit of deceit," she explained gravely. "Everything had grown too complicated for me to see it without some sort of need for caution and guile. There is still so much about it that I don't understand, things that can't be explained, things that frighten me."

"Well, at least now we know where we stand. Come." He rose briskly from the slab of marble. "It's time we were getting back." He touched her arm lightly with his hand. "I think you'll find, Polly, that we shall be able to work it all out in the end."

4

HE SAT on the edge of the bed and glanced once more at the headlines in the Paris edition of the *Herald Tribune,* and then for the third time he took the thick gold watch from his waistcoat pocket. Eight-thirty. They had promised to call for him at eight.

He adjusted his glasses carefully and turned to the inside pages to see what Art Buchwald had to say, but the bedside telephone rang before he had time to find the column.

"Hello, Professor." It was Bimbo's voice, gruff and deep and faintly metallic. "Polly isn't over there with you by any chance, is she?"

"Polly? No. I have been waiting for the two of you to call. You did say eight, didn't you?"

"That's right. I'm sorry." There was a silence and then, "She was supposed to come here for me first. She must have been held up somewhere." Another silence. "I'll call you back." The phone clicked.

But he didn't take up the newspaper again. Instead, his thoughts wandered to the telephone call he'd received several hours ago.

"Professor Challis? This is Flett," the voice had said. "Brandon Flett. I'm sorry not to have answered your note before this, but I've been visiting with a party around Olympia and Bassae and we just got back to town an hour ago. Could you by any chance make it for dinner this evening?"

The professor had thanked him, but mentioned other plans. "Tomorrow?"

"If that would suit you, yes."

"Splendid. Shall I call you around eleven and name a time? Either lunch or dinner, whichever is best for you."

The professor had agreed, and after the exchange of a few amenities, hung up.

And now it was five minutes to nine and the telephone was ringing again. It was Bimbo, and there was an edge of strain to his voice.

"Polly?" he asked, and in the single word there was a sharp inflection of anxiety.

"I haven't seen her. Do you think—"

"You stay there, in case she comes. I'd better come right over. I can leave a message here at the desk." Again there was a long heavy silence, taut with meaning.

"Hello, hello, are you still there?" asked the professor.

"Sorry. I was thinking." Another pause, and then, "Did you see today's *Athens News?*"

"No."

"I'll bring one over. Don't go away, will you, just in case Polly calls."

But Polly had not called by the time Bimbo arrived, his face grave.

"We'd better give her ten minutes or so in case she phones through here," he said awkwardly. "I left a message. I—I just don't understand it."

"I shouldn't worry too much. Unpunctuality is not an uncommon failing with women."

"Not Polly. As a rule, she's always on time." He took a folded newspaper from his pocket and tossed it on the bed. "I think you'd better read that paragraph I've marked there," he said somberly.

There was a three-inch story on the front page, ringed with blue ink, under a single-column heading. Professor Challis folded the newspaper carefully and put on his glasses. He read:

VISITOR'S BODY FOUND

British embassy officials have been consulted by Athens police concerning the discovery early this morning of the body of an English visitor in the area known as the Limnae, between the Acropolis and the Pnyx.

It is believed the man stumbled and fell while exploring this area of the ancient city. His body was found in one of the disused archaic wells which are numerous in the vicinity. It was discovered by two stonemasons, Vassilis Kratsis and Stephanos Carayiannis, who were taking a short cut through the Limnae on the way to their place of employment at the Agora Reconstruction Project.

Police say there is no suspicion of foul play.

The dead man carried no passport, but from papers in his possession embassy officials, pending formal identification, believe him to be Stephen John Roach, aged about thirty-eight years, commission agent, of Maida Vale, London.

Professor Challis lowered the newspaper carefully and stared at Bimbo. "Hmmm," he murmured thoughtfully. "What do you think?"

The big man shrugged. "That's the way it happens, I suppose. In the midst of life. . . ." He took out a cigarette and tapped it slowly against his thumbnail. "Something starts out in Beirut and goes around through Paris and London, and ends up here with a paragraph in a four-page newspaper. I don't feel we owe him terribly much sympathy."

"Do you know what surprises me?"

"What?"

"The fact of his not having his passport with him. He always gave me the impression of being such a neat, tidy man, the sort of man who would always carry his passport with him."

"Maybe it's another Roach," Bimbo said rather disinterestedly. "The name is common enough."

"It would be rather too much of a coincidence, though. The name. And being about the same age. And a commission agent as well." He tapped the newspaper with his finger. "They suggest here that the identification is tentative." He paused and stared at Bimbo thoughtfully. "Do you know what I think I might do tomorrow? I might call at the embassy and offer my services on the matter of identification."

"Good God, why? They're perfectly capable—"

"I think it would be interesting to establish the thing conclusively. If it is *our* Roach, then we know where we stand. It's one fewer problem to consider."

"But they'll take you around to the morgue, and you'll have to inspect the corpse," Bimbo protested distastefully. "Why bother with all that grisly business?"

"I don't know. You could, I suppose, call it a hunch."

"Well, I wish to God you'd have a hunch about Polly! Do you realize it's twenty past nine?" He frowned and pushed his fingers through his hair. "Look, would you mind if I put a call through on your phone? I think I'd better ring her house."

Professor Challis watched Bimbo's face as he made the call. He grunted once or twice and said, "Yes, I see. Thank you very much." And then he dropped the telephone into its cradle and stared down at it for a moment before he turned to the professor.

"She left her home at ten past seven," he said. "That's more than two hours ago. She got a taxi from her door. It shouldn't have taken fifteen minutes to get in."

"She may have met somebody."

"Who? Who would she meet?"

"Brandon Flett? He is back in town. He rang me earlier in the evening."

Bimbo grunted. "There could have been an accident," he said darkly. "The way these bloody Athenian cabdrivers handle those cars. Should I ring the police, do you think?"

"You could, yes. I don't know whether they would be of much help, but there is no harm in trying."

Bimbo pulled at his lower lip thoughtfully. "That's right, there's no harm in trying," he said, but even as he glanced toward the telephone, it began to ring.

"Shall I take it, or you?" the professor asked.

"Go ahead," said Bimbo gruffly.

The professor lifted the instrument and a voice asked for him by name, a foreign voice speaking English with not too much accent.

"Yes, this is Challis," he said.

"Good evening, sir," said the voice, with that special intonation that goes with professional servitude. "This is the Hotel Majestic. The message which Mr. Grasset was expecting has come through, sir. He is there with you?"

"He is, yes. Do you wish to speak to him? He is here right beside me."

"It is not necessary, sir. I was asked to transmit the message either to you or to Mr. Grasset. Miss Sorelle asks that you and Mr. Grasset go on to dinner without her. She will not be joining you, as she has been called out of the city on an urgent matter."

"What sort of urgent matter?"

"That, I am afraid, was not specified, sir."

"How long ago did she ring?"

"The message came just now, sir. Miss Sorelle did not telephone herself. The message was given by a man who telephoned on her behalf. He did not give his name, sir."

"I see." He was silent for a moment. "Was the man English? American?"

"A foreigner of some sort, sir. I am never sure about accents."

"Yes, well thank you very much for calling us."

"By the way, sir, there is one other thing. I wonder would you be so good as to inform Mr. Grasset that his laundry has come back. It arrived just after he left the hotel."

"Yes, I'll tell him."

"Thank you, sir. I think he was anxious about his shirts."

Professor Challis put down the receiver and turned to Bimbo. He told him what the hotel clerk had said, and added, "It seems curious that Polly didn't telephone herself."

"Bloody curious." Bimbo clenched his fist and began to gnaw at his thumbnail. "I don't think I care for it."

"I believe I would still settle for my earlier suggestion, that she encountered Flett."

"Why?"

"Well, it had to be somebody to whom she could speak reasonably freely about having dinner with us, and where you were staying. And then there is the fact of Flett telephoning me. This is not much more than intuition, but I had the feeling there was something *pointed* about it."

Bimbo studied him uneasily. "I don't give a damn who it was," he said angrily, "there's something about it I just don't like." He flung himself into the chair, fidgeted uncomfortably for a moment, rose again, and said, "Look, would you mind very much if I begged out of having dinner with you?"

"Why, of course not. But I can ring for something to be sent up, if you'd like that."

"Just for yourself then. I'm not hungry. I really think I'd rather go out and walk around a bit. If I take a stroll, maybe I can think something out."

"I shall come with you, if you—"

"I'd rather be alone, I think—if you don't mind."

After the door had closed behind the big, anxious figure, Professor Challis went to the window of his room and waited. He saw Bimbo emerge from the hotel. For a few moments he stood uncertainly, staring up and down the street, and then he crossed over to the square behind a stationary grey taxi. He stopped to light a cigarette, then strode off diagonally across the square. Watching the big figure in the duffel coat, the professor could not help reflecting that, for a man taking a stroll, there was a re-markable air of purpose about him.

The headlights of the grey taxi flicked on, and it cruised slowly down to the corner of the square and turned left.

Professor Challis stared after the slowly dwindling glow of its rear light until he lost it among the lamps and braziers and neon signs. Above the theater by the corner where Bimbo had disap-peared, an electric sign blinked on and off, spelling out the name of Gregory Peck. ΓΚΡΕΓΟΡΥ ΠΕΚ, it said, ΓΚΡΕΓΟΡΥ ΠΕΚ.

5

"If it's all the same to you, Professor," said the man from the em-bassy as they approached police headquarters, "I think I shall take you in, explain the matter, and leave you to it." The man's name was Cyril Bloom, a name that the professor found strangely inappropriate. With a nose so aristocratically thin, a brow so noble, eyes so palely and superciliously patrician, with so languid and studied a politeness, and such an easy (and, the professor sus-pected, expensive) informality of dress, a name like Peregrine Fortinbras was surely demanded to set the whole thing off. Cyril Bloom was not good enough!

"I shall wait outside for your report," said Mr. Bloom urbanely, "although of course these chaps will be on the blower to the em-bassy like a shot. You don't mind about this, do you? I mean, it's not altogether that I'm squeamish—I was in Combined Ops in the war, you know—but I simply cannot bear the gruesome when it is contained within four walls. Particularly walls painted that beastly putty color."

It was almost half an hour before the professor emerged from the silent, almost empty room, with the police captain and the two corporals in grey uniforms. Bloom was still waiting for him, seated beside a small table sipping coffee with a lost, faraway expression in his blue eyes. Doubtless, by some curious focal magic known only to the British, he had been able to remove from the periphery of his being the portentous surroundings of Athens Police Headquarters, all Greece and its people, and the entire continent of Europe, so that he might establish private visual communion with a grouse moor in Scotland or a point-to-point in Cambridgeshire.

At the professor's return, however, his eyes gradually returned to a more immediate focus, and he smiled quickly as he said, "Your man?" in much the same way he might have said, "Your bird?"

Professor Challis shook his head. "A stranger to me," he said. "It wasn't the Roach I knew. The captain tells me they shan't want any papers signed."

"Capital!" said Bloom. "Tickety-boo, as we say."

"I gather it would have been necessary only had he been the man I knew."

"Good show," said Bloom. "Nothing to keep us here then, I suppose. Shall we trot off and have a glass of beer somewhere?"

"Well, I should be getting back to my hotel," said the professor doubtfully. "I am expecting a telephone call around eleven."

"Stacks of time," said Bloom cheerfully. "Let's press on to Zonar's."

When the beer came, Bloom said, "This cadaver you've been checking on, it couldn't by any stretch of the imagination be the chap you knew?"

The professor shook his head. "Not by any stretch," he said. "This man was big, fair-complexioned, inclined to stoutness; my man was short, rather compactly built, very swarthy—and, I would guess, a year or two younger."

"Pity," said Bloom. "It means this ghastly business of checking all the hotels, and so forth. And we're not awfully popular now over this Cyprus business."

"You don't have any record of English visitors who come here?"

"Heavens, no! Oh, some check in with us, of course: they're the types who have a sort of nanny complex about the embassy—a frightful trial many of them are, too; they seem to think every consular official is a sort of wet nurse plenipotentiary—but generally the tourists or businessmen on some brief visit, they simply don't bother. Why should they?"

"But these papers that were found with the dead man, would they not be accepted as reasonable proof of identity?"

"Not without the passport, I'm afraid. Without his passport an Englishman on foreign soil has no official existence, certainly no identity whatsoever. I mean to say, after all, it would be perfectly simple for somebody else to whisk his passport away and plant a bunch of letters in his pocket, and before you knew where you were, you would be intimating the death of some poor chap who, at that very moment, was walking in the door of his cottage in Stepney expecting to have his slippers put out. And then there'd be horrid things in the newspapers and questions in the Commons and filthy memoranda from the F.O."

"F.O.?"

"Foreign Office. Auntie Flo to those of us who have suffered." Bloom studied his glass of beer with morose suspicion, as if he expected to find there a filthy memorandum from Auntie Flo.

"When you do establish the identity of this man I have just been looking at, would it be too much to ask that you call me and let me have the details?" asked the professor. "I am naturally rather intrigued by the coincidence."

"Bob's your uncle," said Bloom.

"I beg your pardon?"

"I mean, I should be delighted, of course."

"You have been stationed here in Greece for some time, Mr. Bloom?" the professor asked, feeling that the official matter could now be set aside and some civil small talk indulged in.

"Eleven blissful years," said Bloom. "Since the war ended, in point of fact."

"You must know quite a good many people here in Athens." Bloom shuddered delicately. "Oceans," he said.

"I have been trying to locate the whereabouts of some friends of mine who were out this way some little time back—two months or so." He paused. This was the technique that Bimbo had defined with the quotation: *I shot an arrow into the air, it fell to earth I knew not where.* Well, at least Bimbo had conceded the point that there was no harm in trying. "They were not English," he explained, "and so would hardly have come within the orbit of your official concerns. At the same time, I thought perhaps so- cially . . ."

"Officially one tries to forget," said Bloom. "Socially one hopes to remember." He smiled invitingly.

"There was a French sculptor named Grasset. Paul Grasset. A man in his middle thirties."

"Grasset? Grasset?" Bloom repeated the name slowly and closed his eyes. There was a noticeable interval before he shook his head, still with his eyes closed, and said, "Doesn't mean a thing, I fear."

"Sorelle then? A young woman named Sorelle?"

The embassy man opened his eyes again, very blue and inter- ested. "Sorelle," he said. "The shipping Sorelles?"

"Yes," said Professor Challis quickly.

"You can't be thinking of Helen Sorelle?"

"That's exactly who I mean. You know her?"

"*Know* her?" Bloom smiled quietly. "My dear Professor, back in the good old days—oh, ages and ages ago—Helen Sorelle and I used to dance the minuet together."

"The minuet?"

Bloom smiled again. "A figure of speech. An allegory, as it were. No doubt you know what I mean. As I say, that was quite some time back, before she choofed off to Paris."

"A very lovely girl," said the professor.

"Ah, *that* you can say again," said Bloom fervently, and for a moment or two he was silent, lost in a warm reverie, hearing per- haps the tinkling music of his private minuet. And then, "And yet, shall I tell you something?" His voice was reflective, as if past thoughts still held him, hampering the brittle crispness of his speech. "I think something happened to the poor darling in Paris, something beastly. When she came back to Greece, it seemed to me there was a quality that was lacking. Something had been drained out of her, some vital spark, as it were. Oh, she was still quite lovely—that one couldn't possibly deny—and yet somehow she just wasn't the Helen Sorelle *I* had known."

"You have seen her then, since she came back." The professor succeeded in keeping his voice flat and casual.

"Oh, yes. Not all that long ago, if it comes to that. Possibly six weeks—two months—I can't quite remember. It was quite the briefest of reunions, you understand. Now, let me see. . . ." He paused for a moment. "Yes, it was on the wharf at Piraeus. She was about to embark on one of the Dodecanese ships. The *Miaoulis*? The *Kyklades*? I simply cannot remember. No matter. . . . Anyway, I was down that way trying to shepherd some diplomatic rum through the customs, that I *do* recall. And there was Helen standing by a great truck laden with galvanized drainpipes. There was no time for anything but chitchat—you've seen those Piraeus embarkations—all very brisk and staccato and skimming along above the surface of things, of things like the minuet we had danced together long, long ago. In a way, rather Noel Cowardish —I remember thinking that going back in the jeep with the rum. Bitter-sweet, shall we say. I kept trying to work out what there was about her that had changed. All very sad and nostalgic. At the club that evening I'm afraid I got frightfully high." He drained his beer and leant back in his chair. "Well now, so you know Helen Sorelle!" he said, and beamed. "Quite a girl, don't you think so?"

"Quite," said Professor Challis. "You don't know where she was going on that ship? Or where she is now?"

Bloom spread his hands helplessly. "Rhodes?" he suggested. "Kos? I mean, where *would* one be going, barging off in that direction?"

"That is what I was hopeful you might be able to tell me."

The Englishman shook his head vaguely. "I seem to recall she had a maiden aunt or somebody like that in Rhodes. Possibly it was there." He shrugged. "I could initiate some inquiries, if you would like me to."

"That would be very kind of you, Mr. Bloom." The professor took out his watch. "I am afraid I really must get back to my hotel now, lest I miss that telephone call I am expecting. Thank you very much for all your help. I've enjoyed this meeting more than I can say. You'll not forget to call me when you have something definite on that man?"

"The corpse?" Bloom grinned and raised his hand in a three-finger salute. "Scout's honor!" he said.

At the hotel the desk clerk handed a message to the professor. It was quite brief and obviously hurriedly penned:

Sorry again. Must go out of town on unavoidable business. Can we take a rain check for next week sometime?

—B. G. Flett.

"He gave you this message himself?" he asked.

"Mr. Flett? Yes, sir."

Professor Challis folded the note carefully and slipped it into his pocket. He realized that he had more than half expected it to be this way.

"There was no message from a Miss Sorelle?" he said.

"None, sir."

"Nor from a Mr. Grasset?"

The clerk shook his head. "Mr. Flett's was the only one, sir. There have been no others this morning."

Upstairs in his room he telephoned the Hotel Majestic, but Bimbo was not there. This time it was a girl on the switchboard. Mr. Grasset had not, she said rather stiffly, returned to his room during the night.

"He may have gone out of town," the professor suggested.

"It's quite likely," said the girl. "If you see him, sir, would you please tell him his shirts are here, waiting for him." She sounded faintly aggrieved.

"Yes, I shall tell him," said Professor Challis.

He put his head down on the pillow and closed his eyes. What was the use of trying to work anything out, he reflected tiredly, when *everybody* kept disappearing?

four: THE VENETIAN HOUSE

⟫⟪

I

When Polly came from the door of her house, she was pleased to find a vacant taxi waiting by the curb on the opposite side of the street. It did not occur to her to wonder why it should be idling there, so far from the beaten track of casual plying-for-hire. Obviously, it could not be the cab that Calliope had telephoned the garage to send around: there had not been time for it to make the journey, and it was clearly not one of Dimitri's conservative cars. Nevertheless, in her anxiety to join Bimbo as quickly as possible, because of what she had to tell him, there was something pleasingly propitious in the fact of the cab being there, and she turned in the doorway and called, "There is one here now, Calliope. Ring Dimitri, please, and tell him not to bother."

As she went down the steps, drawing on her gloves, the cab started and circled slowly across to draw into the curb beside her. It was a grey car, shiny-new, and of that extreme design that made it appear more like a projectile built for interstellar space than for the terrestrial hazards of the Athens streets.

The night was clear, and scattered with enough stars to challenge the imaginations of all the designers of projectiles in the world, but it had grown cold, with a damp dew wetting the pavement. The moon had not yet risen.

The driver of the cab was a young man, as flashily assembled as his vehicle—he would have an electric razor, she reflected, and drive always with the radio on—and he possessed the self-assured, rather mocking air which, at least in Athens, had become almost the mark of his calling. As he thumbed the door open—even the gesture was flashy—he looked at Polly in insolent appraisal, and grinned.

"Hotel Majestic," she said, and he nodded, and the cab took off with a hissing swoop which for a moment or two created the illusion that it really was a projectile rushing away from the mundane curve of the earth.

"I'll take the outer way to dodge the traffic," he said casually.

Polly nodded. The man drove with one hand on the wheel, leaning back with studied negligence, and for a time she was fascinated by the way they snaked through the dark streets, the black blots of the trees swinging by interspersed with the flash and flicker of bright open doorways inside which men were sitting around coffee tables. But after a time she became preoccupied by her thoughts, and with what she had to tell Bimbo; and it was with a sense of sudden misgiving that she realized a good deal of time had passed and they were still not in the city.

They were, in fact, rushing up a long, dark, tree-lined tunnel of a road that climbed a curving hill, and the tree trunks, bone-white in the glare of the headlights, seemed as if they were being mowed down, toppling toward them as they rushed past.

She leant forward in quick alarm and tapped the driver's shoulder. "The Majestic," she said sharply. "In Venizelous."

The man nodded slightly but said nothing. The grey projectile stormed on through the avalanche of flaring trees falling through the darkness.

"But you must have gone too far!" she protested. "Why, this is getting out towards Kifissia!"

Again he nodded, and began to whistle "Pepini" through his teeth.

"Please stop at once and turn back," said Polly stiffly. "This is taking me hours out of my way." She paused and took a deep breath, trying to control an inexplicable sense of panic that was rising within her. "I am already late for an appointment," she said coldly.

He braked for a corner, touching the wheel with his finger tips, went around it with a squeal of tires, and said, "You leave it to me, miss. I know where we're going. Back the other way they're working on roads."

Polly sat back suspiciously, the little knot of fear tightening in her chest. What if she opened her bag and took out a pencil and told him she was making a note of his number to report him to the police? The police were very severe with taxi drivers who behaved badly. And yet sometimes there were stories one read in the newspapers, terrible stories. . . . There was certainly something very unpleasant about this particular driver, something vaguely sinister and threatening . . . and then there was that impudent look he had given her when she had got into the cab. . . .

The streets in this part of the town were dark and lonely. It appeared to be a secluded and rather shabby area of decayed old houses with crumbling walls and tangled gardens, a place from which life seemed to have slipped away. Few windows were lighted and all the gateways were dark caves of shadow from which sometimes she would see the eyes of cats gleaming balefully. In the stories in the newspapers the taxi drivers always tried to put the blame on the girls, saying they had led them on, that they'd been provocative. . . .

"If you don't stop this car immediately and let me out, I shall report you to the police," she said angrily.

The man laughed softly. "If I did, you'd report me anyway," he said impudently. "And anyway we're there now."

She could feel herself trembling as the cab slowed down. The driver swung it in between two overhanging plane trees and brought it to a standstill outside a house with a beam of light in the doorway. It was an old dilapidated stone house of Venetian design, standing in an unkempt garden behind a high stone wall. On the top of the wall jagged pieces of glass and fragments of broken bottles had been set into the cement.

"Here we are," said the driver, and reached back to open the door. "Sorry we took so long."

"This is not the Hotel Majestic!" said Polly furiously.

"I wasn't hired to take you to the Hotel Majestic," he retorted coolly. "I was hired to bring you here."

"Why you—you—I hired you to—"

"Listen, *you* didn't hire me, lady," he said with weary patience. "I was hired by someone else to pick you up and bring you here. Now that's all I know."

"Then you'll take me right back to Athens, or—"

"Polly!"

The voice, gruff and heavy, came from the gateway behind her. She turned swiftly, shaking with anger.

"Polly, I'm sorry, but—"

The huge, square figure came slowly from the gateway, hand outstretched, either to placate her or to greet her.

"Ben Flett!" she exclaimed. "What are *you* doing here? And what is the meaning of all this? Look, I want you instantly to tell this man to take me back to Athens. He says—"

"I know, Polly. It isn't anything to do with him. He's just doing what I told him to do. I'm sorry it had to be this way, Polly, but I *had* to talk to you tonight. It's very important. If you'll just come inside I will try to explain."

"*Inside!*" She took a deep, outraged breath. "I shall do nothing of the sort. I have an appointment at a quarter to eight, and it is that already. Now, will you please tell this man to drive me straight back to the Hotel Majestic."

"Is that where he's staying?"

"Where who is staying?"

"Grasset?"

"Yes," she said coldly.

"I'll see that he gets a message. Were you having dinner with him and the old man?"

Polly glared at him wordlessly.

"Challis told me he was dining out with friends, so I guess you were," he said patiently. "Well, I'll see they get a message, just to tell them to go on without you." He sighed wearily. "Now, would you like to come inside for a bit?"

"I most certainly will *not* come inside."

"I think you will, Polly," he said quietly. "If you don't, I've an idea things might go pretty badly for your sister Helen."

2

IT WAS an oddly unrelated sort of room, as if its obviously alien occupancy had never had time to scratch off the surface of earlier local tenures. It gave the impression that if you went upstairs you would find, hidden away in a small back room, some solitary survivor of the original residence who had been there for years, bedridden and neglected.

A few photographs of stiff, poker-faced Greek family groups remained on the walls, and behind the ill-fitting glass door of a high cabinet, half a dozen icons were gathering dust. In back of the couch was a picture of donkeys and cactus worked in cotton embroidery. To these fragments from an earlier life the sideboard was unrelated, with its bottles of Seagram's V.O. and White Rock and gin and Rose's lime juice, and a box of pretzels and a big can of coffee from the American commissariat; and there were stacks of American magazines littered around the room: *The New Yorker* and *Holiday* and the *Saturday Evening Post,* magazines that had a smell of nostalgia about them, and one or two old copies of the *National Geographic Magazine.* Next to the whiskey bottle was a chessboard with the pieces spilt across it, and a deck of playing cards laid out for a game of solitaire that had never been completed. To Polly it had the appearance of a bachelor establishment that had grown very tired of itself.

"Whose place is this?" she asked suspiciously. "Is it yours? I thought—"

"No." Flett shook his head and glanced around the room indifferently. "It belongs to a friend of mine, a fellow named Brown.

He's in the Information Service. We've been buddies a long time; we were together in Korea. He's in Patras at the moment, something to do with that Cyprus rioting. He lets me use the place when I want. Occasionally it's handy to have some place outside the hotel. . . ."

"I suppose it is," she said frigidly. If only they could stop hedging with each other, and come to the point. "That horrible man in the taxi," she said suddenly, and shuddered. "I tell you, if I could find some way—"

"That's Charlie, "said Flett with the same indifference he had given to his survey of the room. "He's not all that bad when you get to know him. Sure, he's a little tough, but sometimes he gets saddled with jobs that have to be done and aren't very pleasant to do."

"Such as bringing me here against my will?"

"Well, I *was* thinking of other things. Not often that sort of thing." He smiled slightly. "He can do a lot worse than that, if he's put to it. That doesn't necessarily mean he's a no-good." He picked up one of the magazines from the side table and glanced at it portentously. "He does jobs for me," he said. "In a way he's pretty reliable."

He looked at Polly carefully, but there was no mistaking the hostility in her eyes. He put down the magazine and said, very seriously, "Polly, sometimes things have to be done that look pretty terrible on the face of it, but maybe in the long run those things turn out for the best. Like getting you to come here tonight; bringing you, as you say, against your will."

"I quite fail to see—" she began, but his upraised hand restrained her.

"Listen to me for just a few minutes, please. Hear what I have to say and then you can roast me all you like. Bringing you here like this is one of the things that all my experience tells me is a damn silly thing to do. Yet if I don't do it, if I let things run on the way they have been running on, then I think you're going to get hurt—maybe you'll get hurt badly—and—" He hesitated awkwardly and frowned. There was a sympathy and sincerity in his manner, a suggestion of warmth and softness that she had never seen before. "Well, let's just say it isn't the way I'd like to see it happen," he said, with something that almost sounded like irritation.

For some reason, against her will, she found herself wanting to listen to him. "If you would be more explicit," she said, "perhaps you could tell me what you have to say quickly, and then I can find my way back to Athens."

He stared at her thoughtfully. "All right, then let's stop beating around the bush. We've been stalling for a long time, Polly. And I don't think you understand what deep water you're getting into —or how rough it is, not only for you but for others, too."

"How rough what is?"

"I waste my time, don't I? You're still stalling." He seemed about to say something more, then hesitated and took a tangent. "Polly, do you know what a P.I. is?"

"A what?"

"A P.I. A private investigator."

"A detective, you mean?"

"Sort of, yes." He stared at his hands broodingly, as if he were studying the word to see what connotation he could give it. "When there are certain things that have to be found out, and you don't want other people to find out you're trying to find out—that's when you call in a P.I."

"You mean divorce, and things like that?"

"Sometimes." He shrugged. "Not me, though. I wasn't thinking of that sort of keyhole peeping."

"You mean that's what *you* are? One of these—these investigators?"

"No." He shook his head and smiled. "Well, if I am, it's only in an amateur sense. I don't carry a badge or a license card." He took a seat, straddling the chair facing her with his thick arms resting across the back. "Polly," he said, "have you ever heard of Curtis J. Grantheim, Jr.?"

"I don't know. I don't think so."

"That may be lucky or it may be a pity, I don't know. But

Curtis J. Grantheim, Jr., is a big man. A *very* big man. I don't know how much bigger he has to get to drop that Junior. He owns most of Pittsburgh. But he owns lots of other things, too—mines and oil and rubber and tenement blocks and islands and people and lakes and mountains. I guess they fought the Peloponnesian Wars for just about the equivalent of the things and places and people that old Grantheim finds on top of his executive desk each morning."

"I asked you to be explicit, and you're wandering off onto some other subject altogether," she said impatiently.

"I don't think I am, Polly. You just sit there like a good girl, and listen. This man Grantheim wasn't rich when he started out. I know that because my father was his partner years ago in Milwaukee when neither of them had a second suit of clothes. They had a little baker's shop in Milwaukee—Fletzenheimer and Grantheim, they called it. . . . My father came from Bavaria, you see, and nobody could say the name the way he liked to hear it said, and that's why he changed it from Fletzenheimer to Flett. Well, he died, but by that time Grantheim was getting on into big business. Now he's very big business indeed, and in business as big as his is, you can't afford to be made a monkey of. You can make a fool of yourself a thousand different ways and you can get the whole world to turn its head away with the wave of a high-denomination bill. If you've got money, people will condone a lot. You can keep a penthouse for the girl at your reception desk, and you can run over slaves in your chariot, and you can make damn-fool political speeches, and you can even have native kids dying of tuberculosis on the island you get your rubber from. You can buy your way out of all this, if the dollar bills you wave around have big enough numbers on them. Cruelty, murder, sex, selfishness—they're all other things. But you can't afford to make a fool of yourself where culture is concerned, Polly. Because then they start laughing at you, and when they start laughing at you *that* way, it's a big laugh. It's a laugh that carries an echo that never dies away."

"I haven't the least idea what you're talking about."

"I think if you listen long enough you will, though." He smiled. "You see, Polly, you make a big fuss about Beethoven and then find out it was Brahms all the time—maybe it wasn't even Brahms—maybe it was just a kid student in the next block playing 'chopsticks.' And then your face is really red. You can have all the millions in the world, Polly, but you just can't afford to get out of your depth so far as culture is concerned. Because even very poor people can know all the time that it *wasn't* Beethoven." He rose from the chair and said, "Look, I'll fix you a drink."

He walked across to the sideboard and took down the glasses, and while he measured out the drinks he continued to talk, with his back turned to her.

"Coming back to what I was saying about the P.I., there was a continental operator I knew called Joe Kelly. That was a pretty ordinary sort of a name for a guy who was anything but ordinary. I think you would have liked Joe. He had his own little inquiry agency in Paris, but he often did jobs for clients in Brussels or Marseilles or places like that where Joe knew the names of the alleyways. He set up this agency of his after the war. He went to France by way of Omaha Beach, which is the hard way to go, but he liked it when he got there, even with a couple of shell splinters in his leg, and after the armistice he liked it still more when he met a girl called Franquin. They got married and had five nice kids and a year or two ago they were able to buy a pretty little house out near Le Bourget." He paused and turned to her with the two glasses in his hand. "This morning," he said quietly, "Joe Kelly was murdered, and his business doesn't allow for pensions."

He came across to the armchair and handed the drink to her. "The funny thing," he said, "is that Joe wasn't anywhere near as directly involved in this matter as you are. Oh, he knew the trail was getting hot. When we had dinner together last night he—"

"You mean . . . you mean it was *here* that he was murdered?"

"Right here in Athens." Flett nodded. "Do you know *why* he was murdered, Polly?"

She stared at him dumbly.

"At dinner last night Joe told me he expected to have some information for me today, and—"

"What sort of information?" she whispered.

"I gather he was planning to tell me where Paul Grasset was hiding out," he said evenly. "Well, that was what I was paying him to find out. You see, in Joe's business he knew lots of people around Paris. He knew Grasset. That's why I got him to come down this way. It seems he knew your sister Helen, too, although not as well as he knew Grasset." He paused as if he were waiting for her to say something, but she was staring at the wall, her eyes empty and faraway. "It's a pity he couldn't have told me last night where they were," he said quietly. "I guess he still had something he wanted to check. . . ." He broke off and smiled at her. "You're not drinking," he said.

"No."

"Are you beginning to see why I had to talk to you tonight?" She nodded and glanced away.

"You see, Polly," he said patiently, "the situation is something like this. Somewhere here in Greece—maybe you know where, maybe you don't—Paul Grasset is tucked away, and your sister is with him. For various reasons, several independent parties are trying to get to him—to get to him *first*. It's in the very special interest of each one of these parties to get there first. Now, the trouble is that for some reason best known to you this old fellow Professor Challis has been called in. And he's begun to stir up the broth too much. It was better when it was thick. Things move slower in a thick solution, but they don't get lost altogether the way they do in a saturated solution. What I'm trying to say is that everyone was nice and relaxed and easy, and suddenly this dear old professor of yours comes in blinking with curiosity, and all the parties begin to get edgy. In some ways I suppose he's smart enough, but he just doesn't understand the tempo of things like these. You see, Polly, he's not dealing here with a bunch of kids in from the campus or with a college faculty. He's walked right into the jungle. And the jungle isn't a place to go around clucking your tongue and murmuring, 'Dear me, curiouser and curiouser!' like Alice in Wonderland." He frowned and said, "I'll freshen up that drink of yours, if you like."

Polly shook her head.

He went slowly across to the sideboard and poured himself another whiskey, and then brought it back to the chair and sat down heavily. He leaned forward, his arms across his knees.

"Now, get this," he said quietly. "Paul Grasset is damn near as contemptible as people can get. He's a heel who isn't worth five minutes of anybody's time. But because of him two men have been killed already. And these two men—in this sort of deal and in their own way—were pretty smart operators. Now, what chance do you think there is for you? Or for your funny old professor friend? I don't want to see anybody else get hurt. In particular, I don't want to see *you* get hurt."

He drained the liquor and put the glass on the arm of the chair. "Now, let's talk this thing out."

3

"THE NEWSPAPERS reported that Grantheim paid around a hundred and fifty thousand dollars for the Rocamadour Reliefs," said Flett. "I happen to know it wasn't that much. But it is usual to name a larger sum to cushion the bargaining in case of a resale. At the same time, my guess is that there was very little change from a hundred thousand. I am sure that the whole transaction cost him at least a quarter of a million, because it wasn't only the reliefs he bought on that little shopping excursion. There was a stack of other art work all of it medieval French—stained glass, illuminated manuscripts, odd fragments of sculpture, screens, chests, and so on.

"Old Grantheim was smart, you see—or that's what he thought. You know how it is. If the other millionaire wants Van Goghs and Cezannes, you take on something else to convey how passé and vulgar it is to collect Van Goghs and Cezannes. So you buy up Han jades or Persian manuscripts or T'ang figurines or Greek bronzes. In Grantheim's case somebody sold him on early Romanesque while he was making a visit to France, and that's how the story begins."

"But surely a man like that, with all that money, would have somebody to advise him, some expert who—"

"Of course he did. The expert got fired a couple of years back. He got fired because Grantheim—who, in spite of that Junior on the end of his name, is pushing the late sixties—had one of those sudden sharp stabbing pains in the heart. Or maybe there was some other small reminder of man's mortality. Anyway, what happened was that the old man decided to make one of those big, expansive gestures. The priceless Grantheim Collection should be made over *in toto* as a gift to the nation. In addition, he decided that a foundation of a million dollars should go with it, as a fund for future acquisitions and the building of a special wing on the National Museum, if necessary, to house it."

Flett grinned. "Now, I don't know whether you realize it, Polly, but the nation is a pretty funny customer to deal with. It didn't beam and touch its forelock and say 'thank you very much, sir,' like one of Grantheim's employees getting a raise in salary. Instead it sent around a shy, funny-looking old man, rather nondescript-looking, with a hoarse voice and a face jumping with nervous twitches. He was the museum's expert, sent along to give the Grantheim Collection the once-over. I met him several times. He was a nice enough fellow, once you got used to those nerves jumping all over his face. But after a while—not too soon, either— a formal letter arrived from the museum politely thanking old Grantheim for his offer and regretting that it did not see its way clear to accepting it. No reason was given, although there was a paragraph in the letter—thrown in to save his face, I guess—to the effect that the museum, because of insufficient space, was unable even to display fully the treasures it already possessed. In the circumstances, Mr. Grantheim would doubtless understand its reluctance to add further embarrassment to the situation, and so on and so on. . . .

"Now, as you can imagine, Grantheim didn't come anywhere near understanding. To a character like that, who'd had his own way for a good many years, this sort of reaction was like a red rag to a bull. And he stormed right around to the museum demanding to know why his good gift horse had been looked in the mouth. At first the curator tried to stall him off with polite evasions. But he wouldn't have any of that, and finally the curator got a bit sore himself and gave it to him straight. The substance of it was that, while they didn't doubt for one moment the genuineness of his suggested million-dollar endowment, nor indeed the value of some of the pieces in his collection—there were several small exhibits they would be most happy to accept—they regretted to say that some of the things, which had cost him an extraordinary sum to buy, were fakes.

"Well, to Grantheim that was using a very dirty word, and he called the curator a liar to his face. The curator's retort to this was to bring out the expert's report and to quote a few examples which the little man with the twitch had classified as phony. The first of the examples given was the Rocamadour Reliefs. At this, Grantheim blew his top entirely and stormed and ranted around until the curator became quite chilly, politely warned his visitor against being taken on any future antiquarian rides, and gently but firmly showed him the door. As you can understand, it was about this time that Grantheim's own personal expert adviser got the bum's rush."

He stared at her meaningly. "And now, Polly," he said, "shall I tell you a very curious and funny thing?"

He had her attention now, and a faint smile touched his mouth.

"When they picked up Joe Kelly's body this morning, they found in his pocket some letters addressed to a man called Stephen Roach." He saw the quick flicker in her dark eyes, and he said, "I see you know him—or *of* him." He paused, and suddenly his own eyes were grave. "Maybe you also know that Steve Roach is the expert whom Grantheim fired a couple of years back—the expert who talked him into buying the Rocamadour Reliefs. What you probably don't know, however, is that this man Roach is a killer. He killed Claude Fanlec. He killed Joe Kelly. And if he can get to him first, he's going to kill Paul Grasset."

"You . . . you mean—"

"I mean I want to get to Paul Grasset before he does. And as it's quite likely that someone might get killed, or badly hurt anyway, I just can't afford for anyone to get in the way."

"But if Paul is in danger it means that Helen—"

"I know what it means better than you do, Polly," he said patiently, and she realized that it was this sense of patience he possessed that made him so infuriating. There was something quiescent about him and yet something motive. His was a huge and seemingly inert mass slowly and implacably moving, like the tongue of a glacier imperceptibly lapping at the rocks; it was something you could not oppose; you could only run away from it.

"It isn't knowing, it's *feeling*," she said fiercely. "But that's something you wouldn't possibly know about."

"Maybe," he said noncommittally.

"You can't understand what it is to be a woman in this sort of thing, and to be hunted and—"

"Steve Roach is a little bit more than halfway toward being a homicidal maniac," said Flett quietly, almost absently, as if he were talking to himself. "If he gets there first, he'll kill Grasset and he'll kill your sister, too, because he's the sort of tidy little man who likes a clean blotter on his desk. I'm not interested in your sister Helen—except she doesn't figure in the case and doesn't have to be hurt, and I'm not altogether sure that Grasset *has* to be killed—there might be other ways of squaring things—but if he does. . . ." He paused and looked at her intently. "If he does, Polly, I'd like to be the one to do it."

For a long time she stared at him, her eyes dilated with shock and unbelief. In the deep silence of the room she could hear her own breathing, the pounding rhythm of her heart. "You . . . you can sit there like that," she said at last, "and cold-bloodedly tell me that—"

He lifted his hand and said quietly, "Maybe I'd better try to ex-

plain exactly how I figure in this setup. I don't say it will necessarily make you understand, but at least it will prove that I'm no
longer stalling with you." He moved slowly across to the sideboard
and poured himself another drink. "It comes back to old Grantheim," he said, returning to the chair with the glass cupped in
his big hands.

"In lots of ways he's all sorts of a scoundrel," he said, "and most
things about him aren't ones that I go for. Money has a way of
putting the milk of human kindness in a Deepfreeze: I guess that's
why it's never easy to get to like a rich man just for himself. But
in an odd sort of way there are parts of him I like, and I'm under
a kind of obligation to him. You see, after my father died, it was
Grantheim who looked after me and put me through college and
gave me the means of doing what I wanted to do—which was to
study architecture—and in many ways he was kind to me, perhaps because he never had children of his own. His wife divorced
him years and years ago. The story goes that he was so busy making money he didn't even notice she'd gone; and even before that,
it wasn't that he didn't notice what clothes his wife was wearing—
he wouldn't have known whether she was wearing any at all!
She filed her suit on the ground of mental cruelty, but she used
to say afterwards that she could have filed it on adultery and
cited the Chase National Bank as corespondent.

"Anyway, that's a long time ago, and now Grantheim is an old
man getting close to the end of the road, and he's a pretty sad
figure, and lonely, and I think he sort of half-realizes that he's
walked right through his life and come out into a desert. It might
be decorated with Aubusson rugs and Gobelin tapestries and have
liqueur Scotch in the decanters, but it's a desert just the same.

"Well, that brings us to this business of his failure to get the
museum to accept his collection. That hurt him a lot. It was as if
he had had a smell of immortality—of something that would have
made his life worthwhile, in a way—and then it had been whisked
away from him. It hurt and it rankled. He used to brood about it
for weeks at a time. The thing that stuck in his craw more than
anything else, I gathered, was the Rocamadour Reliefs—maybe

because that was the first thing the museum curator had cited as phony—and he used to say that he was prepared to spend the whole of the million dollars he'd intended giving to the museum on making the people who'd duped him pay for it."

"So just because a greedy old man is cheated—a greedy, ambitious old man, and stupid too—you think it perfectly right that Paul Grasset should be murdered!" Polly was indignant.

"Just a minute. You haven't heard all the story. However, Grasset is the cue for what we come to next. I met him when he brought his first exhibition to New York three or four years ago. Since I was studying architecture, I never missed a show of sculpture, and Grasset's was pretty good sculpture, and we became friendly—Grasset and I and the girl I was engaged to at the time. She was a girl I'd known at college and hadn't seen for a long time and we met again when I came back from Korea. I suppose I'm sort of dull-witted in a way, because it took me a long time to realize that Grasset was friendly to me only because he wanted to *use* me—to use me as a way of getting into the good graces of Grantheim most of all, but also to use me in another way. I found out about the other way through one of those kind friends who always run fastest with bad news. It seems Grasset and the girl I was engaged to were spending week ends at Lake Placid or in a nice cozy log cabin in the Adirondacks. The bastard certainly had charm, and a special sort of way with women—with nice women, too. Nice at first, that is. They only became ruined *after* he'd touched them."

Watching him, Polly saw that his knuckles were white around the glass he was holding. He had not touched his drink. His gaze met hers slowly, and in his eyes was a curious expression, a sort of bruised compassion.

"You knew him when you were very young, Polly," he said quietly. "When you were *too* young. You were lucky, because you escaped." He lowered his eyes, and for a long time he was silent. "Well, let's cut a long story short," he said. "My engagement was terminated, and not long after, the girl sailed for Europe. Except for just once, in Paris, along the Place Pigalle one night, I never saw her again. I allowed Grasset to think I took it all in a tolerant, broad-minded, man-of-the-world way—it wasn't at all hard to convince him that even *I* could understand his charm was irresistible —and I did that because I'm patient and I've learned to wait, and I'd begun to get suspicious of him in another direction. And so had old Grantheim.

"You see, Grantheim is no man's fool, and he's just as smart at smelling a rat as the next man, maybe smarter, because that sort of man has always got his nostrils set for the smell of rats. And Grasset . . ." He shrugged. "Well, he was clever, too, but did you ever hear that saying of La Rochefoucald? *C'est une grande habileté que de savoir cacher son habileté.* The height of cleverness is to be able to conceal it. Well, in that respect, Grasset wasn't clever at all. And bit by bit that rat smell got stronger, and the stronger it got, the more cunning old Grantheim grew. He used to take Grasset out to his place on Long Island—sometimes I'd go along, too—and he even advanced him a sizable lump of money with which Grasset was supposed to buy up genuine antique sculptures for the old man in Europe. They used to come back, crated up in London by Joákimos, *and every one of them was genuine.* My guess is that Grasset was working it through his buddies, Joákimos and Roach and Fanlec, but mostly Joákimos at this stage, and that baby is an old, old hand in this racket. It's like a game of poker, anyway, and Joákimos knew how to play it like a Mississippi cardsharp. What he was doing was playing it along for a really big advance and a really big killing."

He broke off and smiled wryly and drained his whiskey at a gulp. "The trouble was," he continued, "that Grasset didn't have the training for that sort of technique. He lacked patience. Whatever it was with him—women, or work, or money—he was always one for a quick turnover. He needed money to spend and he wanted more immediate results. So around this time we began to get a hint of an ugly word, and that ugly word was blackmail. Not blackmail itself at this stage, but the threat of its possibility. Then suddenly, before you could count ten, the quartet of operators became a very muted duet. Fanlec was dead and Grasset had disappeared."

He stopped and looked across at her. "I think the rest of it you know, Polly," he said. "I'd planned coming across to Europe anyway to study—that's partly the reason I took Grasset's house, although not the whole reason, because I thought it might be a good base to begin making some inquiries, to find out things. You see, it seemed to me that old Grantheim had spent so much time and energy and money on this rat-hunt of his that the least I could do was to try to finish it off for him. That's all," he said.

"I see," she said musingly. "And that's the story?"

"That's the story up to now—or as much of it as matters."

"And what do you want me to do?"

"If you know where your sister is, I'd like you to tell me, but I guess even if you knew you wouldn't do that, would you?"

"No."

"Then I'd like you and Grasset's brother and that professor friend of yours to keep out of this thing. What I would suggest is that the three of you take a trip up to Delphi or somewhere, take a look at some old ruins." He smiled quietly. "Challis could explain it all to you. Give me just three days, Polly, and I believe I can iron the whole thing out—without Helen getting hurt."

"And if we don't choose to go looking at old ruins?"

"Then it might be necessary to take some steps to see that the three of you don't get in my way."

"That sounds almost like a threat."

"That's the way it's meant to sound, I'm afraid," he said coolly, and then his inflection hardened. "You see, in this affair I'm working for Mr. Grantheim, Jr., and he's a big man and a tough one. You don't build a seven-figure bank account unless you're ruthless, and unless you've got people working for you who are prepared to be ruthless, too."

"And you really believe that by using all these silly, melodramatic threats you can bluff me into some form of acquiescence with—"

"I don't believe anything one way or the other," he cut in. "I just don't want to have to go back to those methods you don't approve of."

He stared down at his fingers, and the silence that hung between them seemed to gather a tangible substance of weight and portent. It was broken finally by the faint ringing of the doorbell.

"Ah, that'll be Charlie coming back," Flett said, and lifted himself from the chair and walked slowly to the door. "You'd better think about it, Polly," he said. The door closed softly behind him.

What followed seemed as isolated from the quiet room as the room itself was isolated from the reality of her waiting there. It was a thing, a series of things happening, out of the same silence that had stirred so ominously between them. The silence had crept out beneath the closed door, following him, and now on the slow ratchet of this silence the sounds moved, distinct and yet isolated also: the faint click of the door latch, Flett's heavy footfalls receding down the narrow passageway, a second peremptory peal of the doorbell, the slow, mouselike squeak of an unoiled hinge, the quick start of a raised voice, a shout choked off, and then quick scuffling and the thud of something falling.

And even as she began to move toward the door, the shouting split the silence into a million fragments. It was a cry half-exultant and half-fearful, and three times it called her name, "Polly! Polly! *Polly!*" The third cry seemed to be cut off short, and there was another crash, louder than before, and the tinkling spatter of breaking glass.

She wrenched the door open, and, in the dim light of a single electric bulb, the shaft of faded red wallpaper and the checkerboard squares of the tiled floor seemed as unreal as a stage set. To the right of her there was the tumult of conflict, a sound like the impact of wood against stone, a man's stifled groan, gasping and shuffling, and as she turned she could see them struggling in the passageway near the open door, beside the overturned hall table: Flett and Bimbo locked together, like a tableau of giants in battle from an ancient frieze.

And across the threshold, as if he were kneeling on the outside steps and reaching one arm inside to touch the edge of the hall carpet, was the crumpled figure of the taxi driver Charlie. In the dim light it was impossible to know whether he was dead or unconscious. There was blood on the side of his face.

Except for the gasping of their breath, there was no sound as the two men grappled with each other: two huge, strong men, each of a size, locked together in this almost motionless, heavy-breathing grip, reaching for each other's throats.

Polly could feel her own breath choking in her throat as she watched them. In the gloomy hallway there was something elemental and terrible in the spectacle, something that existed outside time and the cannons of humanity. They were huge figures from a nightmare, less men than animals, cruel and strong, breathing the fiery heat of hatred into each other's faces as they struggled; two great bulls locked together. . . .

And imperceptibly there *was* movement, because suddenly Bimbo stumbled backward over the leg of the broken table and lost his grip, and Flett was at him, pouncing on him with a speed that was astonishing in a man so thick and big, punching him back against the wall with both fists, hitting at his face, hitting, hitting, hitting, with great cruel blows. Bimbo's head crashed back against the faded wallpaper, the blood spilling from his mouth.

Flett seemed to come back half a step, deliberately, and pause for a moment to size up the man who stood facing him, the man with the glazing eyes and bloody face and the head lolling sideways against a white doorframe spattered with drops of blood. . . . He drew his right arm back behind his shoulder, the fist bunched like the knotted end of a club.

But even as Polly began to feel the sickness uncontrollably filling her stomach, Flett hesitated and turned his head away and looked down at the figure in the doorway and shouted, "Put that goddam thing away, you fool! Put it away!"

It was only then that she saw that the taxi driver had crawled into the hall, and he was crouching like an animal on the rumpled carpet, his face working, a gun in his hand.

"You keep out of this!" Flett ordered.

He took half a step sideways and kicked, and there was a

whimpering scream from the taxi driver as the boot smashed into his wrist.

Flett turned again, but his head jerked backward as the fist took him square in the face, and Polly saw that Bimbo had come away from the wall, and his broken face was screwed up into a grimacing mask, his teeth clenched between lips parted like an animal's, and he was battering Flett along the passageway with terrible ramrod punches, left and right, one after the other, and Flett was reeling back, stumbling, trying to twist his head away, gasping and weaving as he attempted to get his hands up.

Yet even as Bimbo moved in, square-footed, to plant the final punch, Flett twisted to one side and turned, and again with that astonishing speed, jerked his knee up into the other man's groin. Bimbo groaned and buckled up, and, as he began to slump, Flett moved in and hit with all his strength.

Bimbo went to the floor and lay there without a sound, and the blood began to ooze slowly across the checked tiles.

For what seemed a long time Flett stared down at him, and then he shook his head slowly and turned to where Polly stood cowering in the doorway.

He took a deep breath and said, "There are some angles in this business that aren't all that pretty."

She stared at him without a word, seeing the big, loose figure standing there with its arms swinging, seeing the blood that trickled from his nose and mouth and the corner of one eye, hearing the deep, convulsed rasping of his breath.

And suddenly a sob choked out of her and she turned into the room and slammed the door behind her.

Flett looked down at Bimbo again and almost absently dabbed his fingers at his own face and slowly brought his hand down in front of his eyes to examine it. Then he turned again toward the closed door, and in his eyes was a curious expression, as if he realized that all the pain was there in the closed room and not in his face at all. He turned to the man still crouched whimpering in the entrance hall.

"Okay, chum," he said curtly. "Put your playthings away, and get this one into a room before he wakes up. Otherwise he might hit you again." He touched his face tenderly. "You take care of them, Charlie," he said. "I won't be back tonight. I want to go down to the hotel Joe Kelly was staying at, and see what I can find."

He glanced at the closed door again, then walked very slowly down to the bathroom.

4

PROFESSOR CHALLIS had barely finished his breakfast when Bloom telephoned him from the embassy.

"That corpse of yours, Professor," he said brightly. "Not our pigeon, I'm happy to say. Man by the name of Kelly. Heaven knows what the blighter was doing with somebody else's mail. However, the main thing is he's not *our* responsibility. Joseph Parnell Kelly. American passport issued by your consulate people in Paris."

"Thank you very much, Mr. Bloom," said the professor. "It's very kind of you to let me know."

"Not at all, I dare say your own embassy here will be able to supply you with more information if you want it. If you ring Toby Jacobs—he's second secretary—I always find him absolutely the most helpful of bods."

"Thank you."

"Oh, there *is* another thing. You were asking about Helen Sorelle. Well, there was a bit of a consular do last night and I was nattering to Bunty Williams. Now, I feel I must warn you that Bunty is quite the most charming of girls, but rather . . . well, rather *unreliable*. What she says may be true. It may equally be something that came to her mind as she was talking and have no basis of reality whatsoever. An absolute charmer, Bunty, but hardly the most stable of informants. Still, for what it's worth, she claims to have seen Helen Sorelle in Kos last month. They have a little hospital there, and it seems Helen had gone there to make arrangements for the whatever you call it—she's expecting a baby, it seems. Or so Bunty says. Can't vouch for it, sir, but it may possibly be a clue."

"Yes, it may well be. . . . I'm very grateful to you. If she was living with her aunt on Rhodes, she would hardly go to Kos to have a baby, would she?"

"Good grief, no! There's a first-class maternity hospital at Rhodes, whereas Kos—I mean, after all, it's perfectly sanitary, I suppose, but it's rather page sixty-four of *The Golden Bough* and three spits for the evil eye. Hardly Helen Sorelle's dish of tea, I should have thought."

"Yes, well thanks again, Mr. Bloom. It's something to think about, isn't it?"

"I suppose it is, yes. Qualified, I need hardly add, by the warning that dear old Bunty may have been merely mixing persiflage with her gimlets."

During the morning the professor spent a more or less unrewarding hour with Toby Jacobs—he was a good-natured Californian and, as Bloom had said, very helpful in his attitude: the trouble was that what information he had on Joseph Parnell Kelly was extremely meager—and then took an early luncheon at a small *estiatórion* near the Omonia Station. The food was good enough, but the professor found himself with little appetite for it. A day and a night had passed, and he had still heard nothing of either Polly or Bimbo.

He sighed and pushed his plate back, the *kalamáre* scarcely touched, and signaled to the waiter. After he had paid the bill, he walked across the Plateia Omonia to Athinais Street and climbed aboard a No. 9 tram which, with considerable clatter and confusion, finally jolted him down to the Theseum and deposited him beneath the eucalypts. He dispersed two small boys anxious to sell postcards of the temple, and walked slowly around the edge of the ancient Agora toward the scrubby wilderness which was the Limnae.

For all the shabby, squalid suburbanism of its surroundings, it was a part of Athens he had always liked, for on the far slopes of the Pnyx you could still find herds of goats pasturing beneath the olives, or an encampment of gypsies down from Thessaly, and there were lonely thickets where you could wander through the fresh fragrance of the pines. And even the marvelously reconstructed Agora could never compete with that which stood so majestically behind it: the bold grey rock of the Hill of Mars, where Theseus had sat and St. Paul had preached and Orestes had stood trial, and the cave where the Furies had lived, and rearing above it all like a final consummation of human striving, the great crag of the Acropolis with all its temples defined in airy clarity against the pure sky.

He had looked at it a thousand times, and yet each time it seemed an experience completely fresh and new, moving him to wonder and amazement, an experience that was at the same time purifying and humbling.

As he pushed at the iron gate leading into the tangle of the Limnae, the hinges whined in stiff protest, as if what lay inside was the private and secret part of a long-dead, antique world, resenting intrusion.

For a little time he walked around slowly, almost aimlessly, assembling his own pictures from the chaotic piles of rubble and broken walls and overgrown tumuli. The sacred way was still there where the great processions had come in ritual, pagan progress to the Acropolis, with youths and maidens singing and animals garlanded for the sacrifice. It was odd that the tourists so seldom came here to the Limnae, for here were the most human remains of Ancient Greece: the old houses crumbling away, the broken sacrificial altars toppled among weeds and thistles, the hardy cactus and aloe thriving in the hollow shells where men once had thrived and since had withered, the strangled wells from which cool water had been drawn to slake the thirst of those journeying to some holocaust at the altar of Athena or walking in argumentative groups to hear Demosthenes addressing the people on the Pnyx. . . .

Two ragged derelicts were sleeping in the sun beside a broken wall and a small girl with a dirty face was searching for wild narcissus among the rank weeds. Life had not retreated altogether from the area but it had reached its ultimate stage of quietness.

And death, too. Death still crept in here and touched it again with cold fingers. In which of the ruined wells, he wondered, had they found the body of Joseph Parnell Kelly? And who *was* Joseph Parnell Kelly? And what was his link with the quiet, secret man called Roach?

The same questions were back in his mind, little gnats of persistent irritation, slapped at and driven away and always returning to torment and sting.

This was the queer thing about the human mind: its willingness to submit like the most miserable slave to the tyranny of trivia. All of life and death had been met and answered here in the slumbering secrecy of the Limnae, and all its mystery and struggle and futility added up to two bums sleeping on the ground and a little girl picking wild flowers and an old man wandering idly among the stones. Yet the thing that had brought the old man here was this stubborn, illogical preoccupation with questions which in the broad, historical view of intelligent scholarship were not of the least importance. He had been drawn here, against all the canons of his reason, simply out of curiosity concerning the death of a man of whom he knew absolutely nothing—a man whose very name until this morning had been unknown to him.

He stared thoughtfully down at the broken lip of an old well alongside the dilapidated wall of what once must have been a great house. Most of the coping had fallen away and it was now no more than a stone-lined shaft, roughly circular in shape, falling away to a depth of some twenty feet and choked at the bottom with thistles and rubble.

"It wasn't this one," said a voice from behind him. "It was up the slope there, near the trees."

Professor Challis swung around, to see Brandon Flett smiling at him across the broken wall.

"Good heavens, Flett!" he cried, with a surprise he had no need to simulate. "What on earth are you doing here?"

"Pretty much the same as you, I guess," said the big man casually. "Just poking around trying to piece things together. Things like how Joe Kelly died—and why."

For a moment Professor Challis stared at him, and then he nodded quickly and smiled.

He could not delude himself that the answer had been one he had expected. Far from it! In its very casualness so much was tacitly admitted, so much more inferred: it was as if Flett had set out deliberately to bridge the gap between their last meeting in the house in Tite Street and this unplanned reunion among the forlorn debris of the Limnae. And in bridging that gap to make it perfectly clear that in accepting a mutual interest in the death of Kelly they automatically shared an interest in all matters related to it. There was no need, for the moment, to be more specific than this. But if this was the way that Flett wanted to play it, then this was the way he would have it played.

"Yes, and how Roach's letters got into his pocket," said the professor.

"Quite," said Flett evenly. "Although that angle isn't as troublesome as it looks on the face of it. Would you like me to show you the place where it happened?"

"I would very much, yes."

As they climbed across the rough tangle of weeds and rubble the professor looked curiously at his companion's face and clucked. "My goodness, you've cut yourself quite badly, haven't you?"

"Shaving," said Flett. "New razor."

The professor could not repress a faint smile and Flett, catching the expression, grinned wryly.

"Come to think of it," he said, "I've never known a razor, new or old, that could give you a black eye as well."

"You had an accident then?"

"I was just romping around, playing it for laughs," said Flett, and went ahead up a broken pathway of stones. He stopped when he came to a ridge of shattered masonry beneath a thick hedge of brambles. Beneath the ridge the ground sloped away, littered with grey boulders, to the edge of a deep, stone-lined cavity, more a cistern than a well, floored with shattered blocks of marble. There was a drop of some thirty feet between the lip of the well and the fractured stone at the bottom. Flett picked his way carefully down the slope and sat on the lichened coping with his long legs dangling. The professor joined him.

"This is the place then?" he said, peering curiously into the shaft as if he might see there the crumpled shape of the man whose stiff, cold body he had examined on the mortuary slab.

"This is it," Flett said, with a sigh. "It happened in the dark. I had dinner with Kelly that night, and they dragged him out of here soon after dawn."

"Who *was* Kelly?"

"He was a guy doing some work for me."

Professor Challis waited, but when it became evident that his companion had no intention of elaborating on the statement, he said, "I gather you're not altogether satisfied it was an accident."

"I'm damned sure it wasn't an accident," Flett said morosely. "You've got to explain first how or why anyone would get himself into a godforsaken place like this at night." He stared thoughtfully into the pit. "It wouldn't be at all difficult," he said, "to give a guy a smack over the head or a push, and make it *look* like an accident—not in this place. It's pretty lonely even in broad daylight. It'd be like the grave at night. But first of all you have to get him here."

"Yes, I follow. The potential victim, in other words, has to be enticed."

Flett glanced at him quickly. "That's exactly the word. He has to be enticed by the promise of being told something or shown something."

"Or of meeting somebody?"

The big man nodded and swung his legs. "Or of meeting somebody. He wasn't any man's fool, Kelly, not by a long shot, but even the smartest fellows sometimes make mistakes. Besides that, he was on to something hot and maybe he got excited and a bit reckless."

"What do you mean by something hot?" asked the professor. It was very queer sitting here on this ledge of ancient stone, the two of them together with their legs dangling over the place where Joseph Parnell Kelly had died, talking together as if all the gaps had been filled in, as if each knew what the other knew, as if all the motives of their separate curiosities were completely understood.

"Well, for one thing, he'd come across Roach here in Athens," said Flett, his voice rather detached, as if he were reviewing his thoughts more for the elucidation of problems in his own mind than to impart information to his companion—although he seemed to take it quite for granted that the professor would know about Roach. "And he'd known Roach and something about his activities in Paris. I gather he'd been tailing Roach around for a day or two, and maybe while he was out eating or buying some souvenirs Kelly slipped into his hotel room to have a frisk around—that was an angle Joe was very good at, and that was when he picked up the letters."

"Why did he do that?"

"The letters? Because I told him to."

"Was there something in them of special significance?"

"I thought there just might have been, but in fact there wasn't. The embassy will let you look at them if you're interested. There's nothing in them."

"What did you think *might* have been in them? Baseball scores?"

Flett grinned. "Maybe I just thought they'd be handy things to carry around. They were dated. They carried the post-office stamp showing the date they were received in Athens. I just thought it might be well to have in hand some little proof that Roach was around these parts."

"To show somebody, shall we say, like Paul Grasset?"

"Sure, somebody like that," Flett said evenly.

"Perhaps Kelly believed he was coming here for a rendezvous with Grasset—or at least with somebody whom he expected would have specific information about him."

"Perhaps."

Professor Challis took a pebble from the ground beside him and dropped it into the well. It tinkled sharply against a fragment of marble and rolled away beneath the thistles.

"Do you think it was Roach who enticed him here and killed him?" he asked, his eyes searching for the pebble.

Flett frowned and pursed his lips. "They knew each other. And I guess if Kelly had found a coincidental significance in the fact of Roach being down in these parts—knowing what he knew about Roach in Paris—I don't suppose there was anything to stop Roach from drawing his own conclusions, too." He took out a pack of cigarettes and lit one. "Joe had the feeling that things were getting hot," he said slowly. "Maybe that was the feeling Roach had, too." He seemed to consider the thought for a moment, and then he asked, "Would you say Roach was a killer?"

Professor Challis hesitated a moment, recalling the two images he had of Roach: the quiet man in the doorway of Joákimos' shop with the pistol in his hand; the strangely menacing figure in the gabardine raincoat standing by the open door of the Orient Express. He smiled quickly and said, "I am afraid my experience in such matters is strictly limited. To be perfectly candid, Flett, I doubt if I should recognize a killer when I saw one. At the same time, I must admit that, to me, the man has an oddly disturbing quality—one might almost say sinister. As for being a murderer . . ." He shrugged. "Well, I simply don't know."

Flett nodded, as if he had not really expected a definite answer to his question. "Do you know anything about a man named Fanlec?" he said.

"Yes, I've heard about Fanlec," the professor admitted guardedly.

"Fanlec was a pretty shrewd operator by all accounts. And Joe Kelly was a pretty shrewd operator. And now they're both dead. Two smart guys get killed, and in the first case they say it's suicide and in the second it's an accident. It's a screwy setup, when you come to think of it."

The professor nodded. If Bimbo had not been there, that night on the train in the rush of the Yugoslavian night, if Bimbo had not been there and Roach had completed that step forward and pushed, that would have been an accident, too. The old man stared at the stones in the bottom of the well, the stones across which Joe Kelly's body had been broken.

"When we met the last time at your house in London," the professor said interestedly, "most of what we are talking about now was known to you, was it not? Your feelings about this man Roach, your suspicion that Fanlec's death had not been all it seemed, your awareness that these two men had been involved with Paul Grasset in certain rather dubious enterprises."

"I was beginning to put things together," Flett admitted. "I didn't know all I know now, but the picture was beginning to take on a sort of shape."

"Why did you never take Polly into your confidence?"

Flett turned slowly and stared at him, and then a slow smile touched his mouth. "For a whole lot of reasons—the main one being that Polly was hardly the girl from *True Confessions* herself. She didn't want anyone else to inquire too deeply into the matter of Grasset's disappearance because she was scared her sister Helen might get involved."

"So you knew about *that*, too?"

"Paul Grasset's girl friend in Paris had the same name as Polly. Sorelle isn't a common name. Polly herself is friendly with Grasset's brother. You don't even have to put two and two together. It adds itself up."

"And then there was that portrait of—of Jenny."

To the professor's surprise this remark seemed to have a marked effect on his companion. "Of Jenny, yes," he said slowly, and turned to the professor a face that was dark and bitter, and with something smoldering in his eyes that could have been hatred. "I knew all along the picture was of Helen Sorelle, but I used to call her Jenny, didn't I? Do you know *why* I used to call her Jenny, Professor?"

"I've no idea. I simply assumed . . ." He allowed his assumption to peter away into nothing. Flett had locked his big, bruised hands together and was staring at them fixedly. "Maybe if I told you why, it might explain something," he said in a low, musing voice, as if he had not even heard the professor's words. There was a long silence before he continued with what for a few moments seemed a remote irrelevance.

"In Korea," he said, "there was a fellow I knew in a field hospital behind Seoul—he'd got all mashed up by mortar fire, and he was in a terrible state because he used to tear the dressings off and work away at the wounds with his knuckles until he screamed with the pain of it. It went on and on and finally they had to strap the poor bastard's hands behind his head. One of the unit doctors explained to me that sometimes there was a reaction to shock that filled a man with this uncontrollable desire to feel pain. Maybe it's true. Maybe there's a medical word for it. I don't know. Maybe it's just an extreme example, in a way, of why I used to call that girl in the picture Jenny. You see, there was a girl in the States I knew once and I called her Jenny, too. I knew her in college and I knew her when I got back from the East. What I didn't know until I took Grasset's house was that Jenny was one of the girls in that garden of his. You didn't know that, did you? You didn't know Jenny was there with all the others?"

He paused, but Professor Challis waited, tense and silent, knowing that it was a question that asked for no answer. Flett unlocked his hands and turned to the professor. His eyes contained only a somber bitterness.

"Do you know the way the French pronounce Jenny?" he said. "They don't say Jenny, they say Giji. That's what it becomes in Paris, anyway—in the back streets and the bright streets, around the Place Pigalle and the sleazy joints in the dark blocks behind. I don't know whether you're acquainted with that district of Paris, but around those parts everyone knows Giji. That's what they say to you. 'Everyone knows Giji!'—that's what they tell you."

He broke off and looked away, and while the professor waited for him to resume, a vivid image took possession of his mind—an image of Polly in the house in Tite Street, seated cross-legged on the hearthrug beneath the portrait of the girl in the striped shirt, trying to overcome her disgust as she said, "Everyone knows Giji."

"I saw her once on the Place Pigalle," Flett went on. "She was in a café next to one of those nude-show night clubs, trying to bum the price of a drink off two sailors. Giji doesn't have anything left any longer—pride or beauty or self-respect—and the sailors wouldn't give her money but they gave her a cigarette, and they were killing themselves laughing at her when she left them and went out into the street. Sure, around those parts everyone knows Giji. She's rotten, and she's stiff with drugs more often than not, and there's nothing much left of her except a big laugh for those who appreciate that sort of comedy. She's at the end of the road —except it's more like a sewer than a road—and do you know, she won't be thirty until the year after next. That's Giji. Just one of the girls from Paul Grasset's garden. . . ." He flipped his cigarette away and said, "Skip it. What were we talking about?"

"Joe Kelly," said the professor quietly. "We were discussing Joe Kelly."

"That's right. There's that, too."

5

To Bimbo it seemed to come out of the air, spinning slowly, forming itself out of a circling pattern of lights which kept changing color from yellow to green to violet to red. It was hard to understand how the lights could suddenly become quite still and solid and transformed into a thick wooden icon of St. Demetrios in a dusty glass case. He closed his eyes tightly and then blinked several times to try to start the colored lights circling again.

When he blinked, the pain stabbed through the back of his skull and he groaned softly.

"If you could try to drink a little water," the voice said.

He kept his eyes tightly closed so that he should not see the icon of St. Demetrios talking to him, and now the colored lights were revolving again, but much more slowly than before . . . barely moving at all, in fact. . . .

He opened his eyes. The icon which had been created out of the revolving globes of light had unaccountably passed through another transformation and had become the face of Polly Sorelle, and even though the face was strained and anxious, it provided a deeper sense of security than the dusty icon had given. Her face was pale and her eyes swollen. She had been crying.

"What's the matter?" he said.

"Try and drink some of this water," she said.

He closed his eyes. "What happened?"

"You were fighting. You were hurt in a fight with Flett."

"Yes." He tried to smile, but there was something wrong with his mouth, as if someone had been stitching his lips up and had left the needles there, jabbing at him. When he tried to smile, the pain in his mouth was deeper and sharper than the pain in the back of his head. "Flett got hurt, too, I remember that," he said.

"Yes." She bent over and held the glass of water to his lips. "Just try to sip it," she said. "It probably hurts because he hit you in the mouth."

He lowered his hands and felt the springs of the couch beneath him, and then his eyes wandered curiously around the room. His gaze finally came to rest on the sideboard. "There's liquor there," he said. "Is there brandy?"

"I think there is. I'll look." She went to the sideboard. "There is."

"That would be nice."

The brandy was much more successful than the water had been. After he had drunk it, he felt a good deal better, and he was able to lift himself slowly into a sitting position. For a moment or two his head hurt more than ever, but then the pain began to ease. He looked at Polly ruefully.

"They've locked the door," she said. "That horrible creature who drove the taxi dragged you in here and then they locked the door. That was some time ago, an hour or more. But we've got to get out of here. We've *got* to!"

"Of course we have, yes." He looked around the room carefully. The single door was of that thick, old-fashioned pattern which could hardly be forced by anything less powerful than a battering-ram. The solitary window, like all Greek houses on the ground level, had a grille of thick iron bars beyond the glass. The house was silent as the grave.

"I think they might have gone," she said urgently. "Some time ago I heard the front door close, and a car started up and went away."

There was a squeal and splutter of static from somewhere outside the room, and a radio started.

"Well, they haven't *both* gone, that's certain," said Bimbo.

"We *must* get out of here!" There was something trembling at the edge of her insistence that caused him to look at her sharply. Clearly, she was not very far from the point of losing control of herself. "I know where Helen is," she said. "I know where to find her. And I know what they're going to do to him. To Paul—perhaps to Helen, too. They're going to kill him, Bimbo, *kill him!* He talks about it cold-bloodedly, as if Paul weren't a human being at all—as if . . . as if he were some sort of animal to be destroyed!"

"Listen, Polly, stop a minute." He began to raise himself from the couch, reaching for her arms, as much to steady himself as to pacify her. "Polly, you *must* be calm and tell me about it quietly."

"Oh God, it's all so brutal and callous," she said. "You didn't hear the way he talks about it. There are two of them who want to kill him, and the other one is mad! Flett told me he was a maniac. Bimbo—can't you understand?—they're going down there *to kill him!* He's your brother, and they're going to kill him!"

"Polly . . . darling . . . whatever they're going to do we can't help having time to talk about it. They've shut us in here. We can't get out. We will, yes, but we can't for the moment. Now, you must sit down, Polly, and take it easy, and tell me about it—tell me quietly." He had risen to take her arms as one would take a child's to shake her or restrain her, but now in some unaccountable way his arms were tightly around her and her small, dark head was pressed to his breast as she clung to him, trembling. "Come now," he said quietly, "let's have the first thing first." He waited, and the trembling of her body seemed to subside, and he pulled her gently down to the couch beside him. "You say you know where they are," he prompted quietly. "Where?"

"Astypalaia," she said.

"Where's that?"

"It's a little island in the Aegean. It's the last island of the Cyclades, at the edge of the Dodecanese."

He smiled slightly. He was strange in her native country, and she was his mentor; the little geographical explanation indicated that she was regaining control of herself. "Who told you this?" he asked. "Did Flett tell you?"

"Flett doesn't know. At least I don't think—no, I'm sure he doesn't. You know that for months I've been writing letter after letter to people I knew, trying to find out if they'd heard any-thing about Helen, or had seen her. Well, a woman in Piraeus who used to work in our house before she was married apparently talked about it to an old sailor called Vassilis Klonaris. Years ago, before he went into the oil trade, Daddy used to own a fleet of small coastal ships here, and Vassilis was the captain of a little steamer we had called the *Phryne*. It used to run between here and Ydra, and we often went down on it as children. . . ." She paused, but he was aware that she was talking like this to steady herself and he did not interrupt. "Then later," she went on, "when Daddy sold out his coasting interests, he gave Vassilis the money to buy his own boat, a big *caïque*, and ever since then Vassilis has been sailing it around the more remote islands, taking freight down from Piraeus. Well, in this letter that arrived this after-noon—" She broke off. "You'd better read it," she said, and then, "but you can't, of course. It's in Greek." From the pocket of her skirt she took a single, rumpled sheet of notepaper.

"Don't read it," he said, "just tell me."

"Well, it seems Vassilis had taken his boat to Astypalaia to pick up a cargo of asbestos, and he met Helen there. He was talking to her."

"When? When was this?"

"Only four days ago. Vassilis went from Astypalaia to Naxos and then sailed straight back to Piraeus."

He stared down at her. "And you think Flett doesn't know?"

"I'm sure he doesn't. He wanted to know if I knew, and I didn't tell him, of course. And . . . and there's something else . . . something that makes it worse. Vassilis says that Helen is about to have a baby."

"I see," he said thoughtfully. "But if Flett doesn't know, and we do, we can get down there first and warn them, and then—"

"But how *can* we if we can't get out of this house?" she said desperately. "And how do we know that this other man Roach hasn't found out? Besides, Flett had this man Kelly working for him, and he *had* found out something, but he was killed last night, and—" She turned her face to him imploringly. "That's . . . that's what's so horrible about it. Everything that happens makes it *more* horrible. It's . . . it's like a nightmare, darling. All these dark, shadowy things moving around us, and we don't know what it means or what they're doing. We only know they want to kill Paul."

She was trembling again, and her fingers were clutching at his shoulders, and as he looked down he found that his own fingers were gently stroking her hair.

"You still love him, do you, Polly?" he said.

Her fingers were suddenly still, and she lay for a moment stiff and silent in his arms. "Love who?" she whispered.

"Paul."

"I don't love him," she said. "I never loved him, not after that silly schoolgirl thing. Sometimes I think I hate him—hate him for the things he's done to people . . . for the things he's done to you. And in the end I . . . I don't think he was good for Helen, either. But that doesn't mean one can stand aside and . . . and see him murdered like an animal. And besides that, there's Helen. . . ."

"Yes," he said softly, but with a queer exultance rising within him, queer because it was a mixture of pain and joy. "It will be all right, darling," he said gently. "It will be all right." He bent his head and kissed her, and he could feel her face warm and

wet against his, and her fingers were clutching at him again, but
in a different way. It was a long time before either of them spoke,
and then it was Polly who said,

"I still don't understand how you discovered where I was. Or
how you got here."

"Oh, I knew about this place before I went down to Ydra to
meet you. I've never trusted Flett, as you know, and so I did a
little bit of quiet investigation on my own account, and I discovered that he used this place sometimes. Then tonight, when
you didn't arrive, and that suspicious telephone message came
through, old Challis had the idea you must have met Flett. So I
thought I'd come out and have a look. I didn't tell the professor
because I thought there might be trouble, and he's an old man.
While I was nosing around outside, this taxi came along, so I hid
behind the wall of the steps and waited until the driver came up
onto the porch and rang the doorbell. And then I crept up behind,
swung him around, and caught him the most terrific wallop on
the face. Just then the door opened, and as soon as I saw Flett
standing there, I knew my idea was right. And besides that, I
saw your gloves and bag on the side table. That's when I yelled
out to you. And then Flett grabbed me, and the fun began." He
touched his face with tender fingers. "Up until then it had been
fairly easy."

"To get in, yes," she said, "but how are we going to get out?"

"Well, they can't keep us here forever."

"No, but we should be in Piraeus *now*," she said urgently. "Vassilis' *caïque* is still there. We could see him and talk to him; perhaps there's more he can tell us. We could even get him to take
us in his boat to Astypalaia."

"Yes," he said, and frowned. Piraeus was not more than ten or
twelve miles away, yet it might as well have been in another continent. As for Astypalaia—well, that was on the other side of the
moon!

His eyes moved unhappily from the barred window to the icon
of St. Demetrios in the dusty cabinet. The saint sat stiffly in his
saddle on the rearing horse, his sword raised above a mortally

stricken Turk, and in the background flame and smoke rose from a burning city.

For quite a long time he stared at the icon, and then his eyes wandered back to the wide, thick window ledge with the bars behind it, and a slow smile touched his lips.

"Polly," he said thoughtfully, "there *is* a chance, I think—just a chance. It might not work, but it's worth trying. Now, you must listen to what I say, and do exactly as I tell you. . . ."

6

THE TAXI DRIVER whom Flett called Charlie (but whose name, in fact, was Constantinos) had hardly become conscious of the fact that in the air there was the smell of something burning, when the girl began to scream.

Since he was seated in the kitchen with the radio turned on to a program of *bouzoukia* music, amid the litter of a late night meal he had prepared for himself, he had at first been inclined to attribute the odor to something smoldering in the charcoal grate over which he had cooked his macaroni and potatoes.

In any case, he had been sunk in a mood of such gloom and resentment and self-pity that it would have taken an outside circumstance of considerable force to penetrate his preoccupation with his own misery.

He had had an unpleasant evening and an even more unpleasant night. He would have caressed his smarting jaw but for the fact that his left hand was picking over the remains of the cold potatoes and his right hand still ached severely where Flett had kicked it. He resented the fact that Flett had kicked him, but not as much as he resented being left in the house alone all night while the American enjoyed the liberty of the town.

Enviously he considered the picture of Flett, standing at the bar in the Grande Bretagne, with the lights glinting on all the bottles and the waiters getting big tips and good-looking women

smoking cigarettes and laughing. That was the world that Charlie
enjoyed—the big, wild, handsome, outside world: the smell of
women all mixed up with the leathery smell of a car's upholstery,
and the rush of the cab through the darkness, and the soft, muffled, tempting laughter of women in the back seat. That sort of
thing, and lights flicking past, and the knowing faces of men in
doorways, and the excitement of taking people to queer places
and bringing them back and guessing what had happened. Sometimes the people would get gay and generous, and they would
take him in with them and there would be lots of fun for
everybody. . . .

The nights Charlie liked best of all, but if you were out and
about, the days were all right, too: meeting the ships at Piraeus
and taking the gamblers and their women down to Phaleron,
and even waiting around in the rank with the other drivers, polishing up the cars and comparing gadgets and radiator grilles and
things like that. One way or another, Charlie spent a good deal of
his money on automobile gadgets, flashing lights and indicators
and a new radio and a whole set of white-walled tires; even a
sterling silver vase for the dash, to keep paper roses in.

These were the things he liked, being out and about and looking at life, and to him there was nothing worse than the stillness
of a confined room: worst of all when it was late at night—just
about the time the night clubs were emptying out—and there
was nothing but a porcelain clock ticking on the wall, and his jaw
still smarted from that punch, and his wrist ached as if the bone
had been broken. . . .

This was the nature of Charlie's introspection as he sulked in
the kitchen, and consequently, it was some time before he realized
that the smell of something burning was growing stronger, and
seemed to have a source other than a few potatoes fallen into the
charcoal embers of the kitchen grate.

He sat up stiffly and looked carefully around the room and began to sniff the air, and it was exactly at this moment that the
girl in the room along the corridor began to scream.

Remembering the contempt in her eyes, his first impulse was

to let her scream herself into hysterics. He conceded to any woman the right *not* to fall for him—he would have conceded it, however, with a faint measure of surprise, because Charlie found his own personality captivating and had had the experience, on a number of enjoyable occasions, of finding that women agreed with his self-estimation—because there was no accounting for women's tastes, but he was damned if he would allow them the privilege of looking at him as if he were something the dog had dragged in.

He accordingly allowed her to scream three times before he responded, and he reacted then only because he realized that she was screaming something about fire, and there was some significant link between this word and the fact that the smell of burning was now very distinct and acrid in his nostrils.

When he opened the kitchen door, he was startled to see that the corridor was misted with smoke, like the beginnings of a sea fog coming in.

Charlie paused, suspicion and some unexplained sense of misgiving wrestling in his mind with a more natural sense of alarm. The girl screamed again, and he hurried down the passageway to the locked room.

"What's happening in there?" he called sharply.

"Open the door quickly!" came the reply, imperative and fearful. "Open the door! The place is on fire!"

She choked on another cry, and he could hear a paroxysm of coughing, and then a clatter like a chair overturning, and the thud of something or somebody falling. From beneath the doorjamb soft little curls of smoke crept like stealthy, furry creatures. Beneath the lintel there was a soft, thin, fuzzy growth, grey and woolly and exactly like the mold that grows on a neglected bowl of food, except that it seemed to have thin tentacles, fanning slowly outward and waving in the air.

"What the hell's going on in there?" he growled suspiciously. There was another burst of coughing from the girl, and he could hear fists drumming against the locked door.

"Let me out! For heaven's sake let me—" The words were lost in a harsh, choking gasp.

He turned the key in the lock and pushed the door open, and a billow of foul-smelling smoke rolled out at him and thinned away, and he could see the shadowy figure of the girl staggering to one side and then groping toward the open door. He had no time to wonder why the lights in the room were out, nor why smoke so thick and choking should thin so quickly, for out of the corner of his eye he had glimpsed the other figure, big and menacing, which was moving toward him from the shadows behind the door. He began to turn to meet it, but he had only instinctively measured the threat of it, when the fist struck him full in the face. For a moment he was aware of small blue flames dancing on the window ledge, then the flames exploded into twisted tubes of colored light, like the signs above the Phaleron night clubs, and vanished into a gulf of blackness. . . .

When consciousness returned to him, he was aware that his jaw hurt more than ever, and his eyes were hot and stinging with the smoke, although there was not much of it in the room now, no more than a drift of haze. Slowly and painfully he lifted himself and rubbed his eyes and staggered across to the open window. The breeze blowing in through the grille still drifted wisps of smoke from the blackened heap of embers and soot and ash on the wide window ledge—the charred remains of some old wooden icon and on top of them the stinking, smoldering remains of the stuffing from a cushion.

Charlie turned and staggered from the room. The front door was open, and the draft had dispersed the smoke from the corridor. As he walked slowly to the door, he had that sick-headache feeling that goes with a bad hang-over.

The grey taxicab was not parked beneath the plane tree where he had left it. The grey taxicab was gone!

He went inside to telephone the Grande Bretagne, but Flett was not there. The taxi had gone and Flett was not there and his jaw hurt worse than ever.

In the kitchen he sat by the littered table for a long time, hearing the small secret sounds that stirred within the confines of the greater silence, and finally he was aware of the clock on the wall, ticking, ticking, ticking—as if it were laughing at him.

He rose from the chair very deliberately and took the frying pan from the stove and then flourished it once and swung it flat into the face of the clock. The oil splashed across the wallpaper and the clock fell to the floor, but Charlie went down on his hands and knees and kept hammering at it with the flat of the big black skillet, until there was nothing much left of it save broken glass and twisted metal and powdered fragments of porcelain.

Then he went back to the chair and put his head down on the kitchen table and began to weep.

7

OUTSIDE THE GATE of the Limnae they found a cruising taxi, and as he hailed it Flett said to the professor, "I'm going back to the hotel. Is that where you're going?"

"Yes," said the professor. They exchanged no other words as the cab maneuvered them back through the traffic to the Grande Bretagne.

The clerk at the inquiry desk greeted Flett with what seemed to be considerable relief. "Ah, Mr. Flett, there is a man over there in the lounge waiting to see you. He has been waiting for quite some time, sir. He called last night and kept telephoning through the morning, and finally I suggested he should come here and wait for you. I trust that was all right, sir?"

"Sure, that's all right," said Flett, but there was a frown on his face as he looked across the crowded lounge to the man waiting beside the statue of Artemis. "You'll excuse me, Professor," he said. "I guess you're going up to your room, anyway."

"Yes, I am." The professor took his key and his letters—he was delighted to see that Mr. Valentine had finally written—but he made no immediate move to leave the lounge. Instead he watched

with great interest as Flett walked across to his visitor, a somewhat overdressed young man with brown-and-white shoes, a singularly blatant tie, and a suit that was extravagant in both cut
and material. He gave the impression of having dressed with a
flamboyance deliberately designed to distract attention from his
face. The professor found it difficult to repress a smile. Quite a
few people, it seemed, were having trouble with new razors! Or,
as Flett would say, romping around, playing it for laughs! On the
whole, the desk clerk's obvious relief at Flett's arrival was perfectly understandable.

The big American did not invite his visitor to sit down, but
stood with him beneath the marble statue. They talked for some
minutes and, although they kept their voices low, it was perfectly
clear that whatever they had to discuss was exceedingly displeas-
ing to both of them. Finally Flett escorted the flashy young man
angrily to an armchair in the most obscure corner of the lounge,
left him there, and returned thoughtfully to the inquiry desk. He
seemed surprised to find the professor still waiting there.

"I thought you'd gone up," he said.

"I'm just going now." The professor smiled pleasantly. "I thought
I'd remind you about that luncheon."

"I'll let you know," said Flett curtly. He began to turn to the
desk clerk, but hesitated and turned back to the professor. "If you
see Polly," he said, "you might tell her she left her handbag and
gloves."

"Did she really? Yes, I'll tell her. She is quite probably wondering where they are. Good-by, Mr. Flett." He smiled and shook
hands and set off briskly toward the elevator, only to be intercepted by a man hailing him from a corner table of the lounge.
He was a tall, thin man with stooped shoulders and features as
undeniably English as the front page of *The Times*. He was drinking beer with a raw-complexioned woman in tweeds, who looked
as if she had just given her horse into the care of an ostler.

Flett watched the professor shake hands with the man and give
his quick, birdlike little bow to the woman, and take a seat at their
table. He turned back to the inquiry desk, frowning, and took

from his pocket the envelope that Charlie had given him: a crumpled envelope bearing a two-drachmae Greek stamp and still smelling faintly of the face powder and scent which inevitably linger in a woman's handbag. It was an envelope addressed to Miss Polyxéna Sorelle, and on the back of it, in the Greek fashion, the sender had written his own address:

> Vassilis Klonaris,
> c/o K. Kareglis & Co.,
> Nikita Street, 37,
> PIRAEUS.

He looked at the desk clerk. "Do you have a business directory that lists commercial houses in Piraeus?" he asked.

"It all depends, sir. There are so many small businesses in the port, and of course not all of them are listed. If you could tell me the nature of your inquiry, Mr. Flett, possibly I could help."

"Thanks. I'm trying to locate a man—" He glanced down at the envelope. "—by the name of Vassilis Klonaris. He gives it here as care of K. Kareglis and Company." He slid the envelope across the counter. "There's the full address."

The clerk took the envelope, glanced at it, and pulled at his lower lip. "Ah, yes," he said, "but it depends when the letter was written. Often people give an in-care address when—"

"He was there yesterday morning. The date's on the postmark."

"Then the company is sure to know. Shall I ring them and make the inquiry for you, Mr. Flett?"

"I'd appreciate it if you would. I'd also like to know what sort of business this Kareglis Company handles, if you can find out." He took a twenty-drachmae bill from his pocket and placed it on top of the envelope. "I'll be waiting over there in the lounge with my friend."

He was drinking his second whiskey by the time the desk clerk came to him. "I'm sorry to have been so long, Mr. Flett," he said apologetically. "Those Piraeus telephones!" He sighed. "However, I did get on to them finally. It seems the man you were inquiring about is no longer there. He sailed from Piraeus early this afternoon."

"Sailed?" Flett looked up at him sharply. "Sailed where?"

The sudden asperity of his tone seemed to take the edge off the clerk's urbanity, and he looked rather crestfallen as he replied, "I am afraid that is a point I neglected to inquire about, Mr. Flett. This man Klonaris, you see, is the captain of a boat—Kareglis and Company is a shipping agency handling Aegean freight and trans-shipment and—" He paused and then his face brightened. "I *did* ascertain the name of his boat. The *Barbara*." He referred to a scratch-pad in his hand and nodded. "That's perfectly correct—the *Barbara*. I dare say the port officials at Piraeus would be able to supply the necessary information as to the ship's destination, and so on." He paused. "I could call the company again, although I think they were just closing when I rang. Shall I try?"

"No, don't bother, thanks. I have to go to Piraeus anyway. I can check down there. Thanks a lot for the information."

"Not at all, sir." He bowed himself away.

"Why Piraeus?" Charlie asked. "Why do you have to go there?"

"I have a hunch that's where we might find your cab," Flett said thoughtfully. He stared at the crumpled envelope resting on the flat brass tray beside his whiskey glass. "My feeling is this is the time when you might as well play a hunch as anything else," he said. The observation was made to himself rather than to Charlie, and as he spoke he looked down to the far end of the lounge. Professor Challis was engrossed in conversation with the tall Englishman and his tweedy lady. He turned back to Charlie. "Okay, let's go," he said brusquely.

Night had fallen by the time they reached Piraeus. Nikita Street had been abandoned to prowling cats and an old man clearing cabbage leaves from the gutter and a girl and two sailors in a dark doorway lost in some teasing, sniggering byplay. The offices of Kareglis and Company, a small and narrow building with a cobbler's shop at ground level, were dark and shuttered.

"If you look around these side streets," Flett said, "you'll probably find that cab of yours. Not *now!*" he added sharply. "You come along with me. I might need you to interpret."

As it turned out, he had no need for Charlie, because one of the officers in the Port Authority spoke excellent English. Most of the building was in darkness, and there were only two officers and a sailor on duty. The sailor was heating a pan of beans over a paraffin cooker, and the two officers were playing a desultory game of backgammon beneath a large wall chart of the Saronic Gulf. They seemed glad of the distraction occasioned by Flett's arrival, and even gladder of the distraction when he insisted on each of them having a pack of Lucky Strikes.

They offered no objection whatever to undertaking an examination of the port log to find the information that their visitor sought.

It was the younger of the two who spoke English, and he lit his cigarette from Flett's lighter and went across to the duty book beside the telephones. It was not many moments later that he looked across at Flett and said, "Here is what you want." He put his forefinger down on the page and began to read. "*Barbara*. Single-screw diesel auxiliary schooner, 260 tons, V. T. Klonaris, master. Outward at *pharos* 2:07 P.M. Explosives or inflammable cargo, none. Cleared in ballast on private charter." He glanced up. "That's the one, is it? The one you wanted?"

Flett nodded. "It was the destination I was mostly interested in," he said.

The officer shrugged good-naturedly. "Not allowed to give that out when it's private charter, not unless it's foreign clearance. There's no foreign clearance here. That means Greek waters. It's up to the charterer to give information on where the vessel is bound, that is if he wants to."

"I see. And who is the charterer?"

The officer gave his attention once more to the book, running his finger along the entries.

"Sorelle and International Lines," he said, and frowned. "That can't be right, can it? Well, that's what it says." He began to smile and said something in Greek and his older colleague laughed. "I was just saying," the younger man explained to Flett, "that the

Sorelle Line must have come down in the world, chartering an old scow like that. Next week they'll be hiring dinghies to take parties out fishing! The Sorelle Line has an office in Churchill Street. They'll let you know."

"But they won't be open now. I'd have to wait until tomorrow and I'm rather anxious to find out tonight."

The officer glanced at the pack of cigarettes on the table and grinned and went back to the book.

"Astypalaia," he said, and laughed suddenly. "That makes it funnier than ever!"

Outside the Port Authority Building the bright, raucous world of nighttime Piraeus rushed at Flett, a surrealistic world of lights and noises and smells churning together above the rutted asphalt. A big white liner with a blue Maltese cross on its funnel was warping in behind the concrete piles. An old dredge clattered its buckets. Garbage drifted on the still, oily water in the form of a French curve. A floating crane swam in a flare of arc lamps, dropping its red steel grab into the mud like the snout of a prehistoric monster, and the grab came rearing up again into the flaring silver air with a flood of salt saliva dripping from its jaws. Flett could smell mud and rotting fish and carbide lamps and the cheap scent of women.

He turned to Charlie.

"You better take a walk around," he said. "See if you can find that cab of yours. I've got things to do."

five: THE ISLAND

I

DURING a comparatively long and, in its particular field, useful life, Professor Challis had known a number of occasions when he had been given cause to reflect upon the prominent role that pure chance so often plays in human affairs. "Fortune," he had once written in the solitary poetic passage in an otherwise rather dull and technical monograph on the Gournian carvings, "is sometimes a fellow wayfarer who springs unbeckoned from the wayside to lead us along pathways which, but for this chance encounter, we might never have reason to explore."

This sentence was apropos the fact that his spectacular discovery of the great Minoan treasury outside Gournia had arisen in the first instance from the pure chance of having been let down by an irresponsible Cretan muleteer who had failed to bring three promised donkeys for a hard journey across the mountains to Kritsa: the professor had set out to walk the first six miles or so, and in doing this had inadvertently stumbled onto both the remains of an ancient wall and everlasting archaeological fame.

Indeed, the very fact of his having become an archaeologist at all had been in itself fortuitous, arising solely from the blind chance of his having wandered into the Metropolitan Museum on a rainy April day in New York. He had been at Harvard at the time, which was 1915, with every intention of ultimately embracing a career in the law. On this particular April day a young lady from Vassar, who had suddenly become more interested in the new phenomenon of Dadaism than in Challis' rather immature observations on constitutional law, had failed to keep a tryst with him in the lobby of the Algonquin: in the museum he found himself attending a lecture on the Mycenean excavations, and was promptly lost both to matrimony and the legal profession.

Consequently, the professor was not greatly surprised when at a later date, reviewing what had come to pass, he was able to attach a rather special significance to this utterly fortuitous meeting in the lounge of the Grande Bretagne Hotel with his old friend Mr. Cyril Bloom, of Her Britannic Majesty's Embassy to the Kingdom of Greece, and, through him, with the rather intimidating woman who was introduced to him as Mrs. Williams.

As it usually is, the significance was at first concealed. In fact as he shook hands, accepting Bloom's invitation to a chair and an *apéritif*, he was conscious of a faint sense of irritation that the social conventions interrupted and delayed his pursuit of the matter which had so promisingly begun in the Limnae with Brandon Flett.

"We met, you might almost say literally," Bloom said, by way of explanation to his lady companion, "over the body of a man."

"Really!" She looked at the professor without much interest, and grunted. She had a heavily veined face, a small wart on her chin, and a rather disturbingly masculine habit of uttering a noncommittal grunt whenever she was addressed. There was an unresponsive and uncommunicative quality about her which did nothing to lessen the professor's impatience. She would, he reflected, be good with horses and splendid with dogs: it was clear that she considered Homo sapiens an unfortunate but unimportant mischance in the progress of the animal kingdom from the slime to the sublime.

Bloom, on the other hand, was full of his customary bright and brittle patter, but at about the same time as the professor realized that Flett and his flashy young companion had disappeared from the lounge, he also sensed that the Englishman's invitation to drink with him may have been based on something more than a mere social obligation.

Professor Challis had, in fact, finished his *ouzo* and was mentally framing some polite remark upon which he might take his leave, when Bloom said, "Coming back to that point about the dead chap you were looking at, I thought you might be interested in learning that this morning I ran into the actual fellow you went down to identify."

"Roach?"

Bloom nodded. "He trotted into our office this morning, not two hours after I phoned you. Well, I'm presuming it *is* the same bod as you had in mind. Slight, quietly dressed chap, not a great deal to say for himself, rather dark-complexioned for an Englishman. . . ."

"That sounds like Roach."

"In fact, of course, he *isn't* English, which explains that swarthy look. I was looking at his passport. Born in Syria. Naturalized some years back as a British subject. He'd trotted along to us to see whether he required a visa to go directly across from Rhodes to Izmir. He has a branch of his business there, I gather."

"So I understand. He was going first to Rhodes, you say?"

"That was the impression I had. A little *peripató* around the Dodecanese. He wanted some information on interisland ships and so forth. He seemed particularly interested in Astypalaia."

"Astypalaia?"

"Yes, that's what struck me as odd, in a way, because nobody's ever frightfully interested in Astypalaia. His interest, I gather, was knives."

"Knives?"

"There's a sort of folk industry they have there," Bloom explained with a smile, "for making rather charming knives and forks. Roach evidently feels he can make something of them commercially in London. I seem to remember they're made of goathorn or something. Isn't that so, Bunty?" He addressed the question to the woman, but she merely grunted.

"Bunty does *know* Astypalaia," Bloom explained benevolently, and turned to her again. "Don't you, Bunty, darling?"

Mrs. Williams grunted and nodded, and proceeded to a moody examination of the olive in her Martini.

"Well, that's about all there is to it, Professor," Bloom said cheerfully. "I just thought you might be interested to know that your acquaintance is still very much alive and kicking, as it were."

"Thank you," said the professor.

"Astypalaia," said Mrs. Williams suddenly.

They both turned to her.

"Astypalaia," she repeated, exposing some rather large, yellowish teeth in what might have been a smile, but which left the professor with the feeling that her own link with the animal kingdom was more toward the equine than the human branch. "Yes, that is it," she said.

"That is *what*, Bunty, dear?" Bloom asked patiently.

"Oh, heavens, Chick, why can't you *follow!*" she snapped. "You perfectly well remember that absolutely frightful party last night at the Egyptians. You were asking me about that Sorelle girl. It was on the tip of my tongue at the time, but I simply could *not* remember. Astypalaia, of course." She favored him with a glance of triumphant disdain.

"I'm very much afraid, my dear, you're absolutely right in your judgment. *This*, I don't follow at all." He flashed a quick glance of amused commiseration at the professor and resumed his patient expression.

"Damn it, Chick, you simply have no memory at all!" she retorted with some asperity. "You ask me an interminable series of idiotic questions when I have a migraine coming on, at a perfectly foul, dull party simply swimming with saris and men in those horrible red *taboosh* things—and then you promptly forget all about it." She glowered at him, took a deep breath of resignation, and went on, "You were interrogating me about the Sorelle girl, were you not? And I told you she was having a baby under simply barbaric conditions at Kos, and—"

"Oh, come now, Bunty, she was not *having* the baby, she was *expecting* it, as I understood," Bloom interpolated mildly. "And in a perfectly efficient hospital. One can hardly define as barbaric—"

"And," Mrs. Williams swept on, "now I have just remembered it was Astypalaia."

"Where she's having the baby? Ah well, that's quite different. Now that *could* be barbaric, I do agree, but—"

"Don't be such a fool! You really can be an obtuse man when you choose to be! *Not* where she is having her baby—that is arranged for in Kos, as I told you. Astypalaia was where she was living."

"You are quite sure of this, Bunty?" Bloom asked carefully.

"I am not in the habit of fabricating information merely for the purpose of keeping the ball of conversation rolling," said Mrs. Williams tartly, grunted heavily, and lapsed into a brooding silence from which she emerged finally to say, "I am now going to powder my nose." She rose to her feet gauntly, and with dignity. Her nose, the professor observed, was already quite freely powdered, and for some absurd reason he was reminded of the line: *You have baked me too brown, I must sugar my hair.* . . .

When she had gone, Bloom said, "Another drink?"

"I think I'd like one, yes."

"I warned you before, you may remember. Awfully good value, Bunty, but rather unstable. On the other hand, of course, she may be perfectly right." The professor was aware that Bloom's attitude had changed subtly. He was leaning toward him, his thin, pointed elbows on the table, and suddenly all the rather ridiculous superficiality of the man had been shed: his voice was serious, his eyes thoughtful. There was about him a quality of awareness and competence which the professor had not noticed before.

"She is also rather a fearful old gossip," Bloom said, "so I think I had better tell you this now, while she is away." He paused. "I had Toby Jacobs from your embassy in for a chat with me this afternoon," he said quietly. "That dead man you went in to see— Kelly—it appears now that there may be rather more to the case than meets the eye. It seems he was a private inquiry agent doing some sort of investigation work here for another American, and there is—well, this is Toby's opinion, for what it's worth—more than a breath of suspicion that it might, after all, have been foul play." He looked at the professor meaningly. "I take it from what Toby told me about your talk with him that all this won't seem entirely double Dutch to you?"

"No, not entirely," said the professor, after a momentary hesitation. "Do the Greek authorities also subscribe to this?"

"My dear Professor Challis, one seldom ever knows *what* they subscribe to. By the same token, they are very far from inefficient. Let me put it this way—they offered no objection at all to your embassy's request for a full and formal inquest. No doubt it will all come out in the wash."

The professor nodded thoughtfully and stared at the empty glass on the table before him. "How long would it take to get to Astypalaia?" he asked at length.

Bloom locked his thin fingers together, studied them for a moment, and closed his eyes, as if he might find a list of steamer sailings printed on the inside of his eyelids.

"It all depends," he said. "There's no regular winter service. In the summer a ship calls there once or twice a week, but at this time of year everything's rather up in the air. Your best plan, I would suggest, would be to fly to Rhodes and get a boat across. A good boat shouldn't take more than five or six hours." He opened his eyes, smiled, and signaled to a waiter. After he had ordered the drinks, he leaned back in his chair, crossed one grey-flanneled leg over the other, and studied the professor with eyes that were shrewdly inquisitive.

"I am not quite sure what is in your mind, Professor," he said. "I am simply putting two and two together and probably making the most ghastly mathematical mess. I may be quite mistaken in thinking that the questions people keep asking me—people like you and this fellow Roach, for instance—are in any way related to the questions they keep asking Toby Jacobs. I may be even wider of the mark when I relate these questions to what Toby was telling me this afternoon." He glanced across with a small, deprecating smile. "So I am at the stage where I must rather put myself in your hands, you see." He paused. "Would you say, Professor Challis, that this is essentially a matter at which we, as officials, would be wise to wink the blind eye?"

Again the professor hesitated, and then he said, "In a way I think it probably is."

Bloom nodded, and looked down at his sleeve to adjust his cuff link. "I always feel it sound to get these preliminary understandings straight," he said. "Now, what I think I should do is scribble you a note on one of my cards to a chap I know in Rhodes. You will find him absolutely reliable. He has a sturdy little boat, and I am sure he will be most happy to run you across to Astypalaia. If you get the morning plane, you should be on the island by to-morrow evening. Weather permitting, that is." He lifted the glass which the waiter had brought and said, "Chin-chin!"

The professor was about to say something, but he saw that his companion's attention had already wandered. He was looking across the lounge and the bright, inane smile had returned to his face as if a switch had flicked it on.

"Ah, here's to the charmer whose dimples we prize," he murmured, and rose to his feet. "Darling Bunty," he said effusively. "All well, I trust."

Mrs. Williams grunted and sat down. The professor was rather surprised that there was no sound of saddle leather creaking, nor clink of stirrup irons. A streak of powder clung to the craggy, roughened promontory of her nose.

"We were remarking," said Bloom, "on how well you carry yourself."

2

THE LAUNCH that had brought him from Rhodes gave three farewell squeaks of its siren as it bucked out past the breakwater, and the professor stood on the quayside and waved until it disappeared behind the lighthouse. He saw it again for a moment, lifting against the dim blue outline of Syrina, and then it was gone.

He had a queer, momentary twinge of loneliness, the sense of being a man marooned, as he turned to look at Astypalaia—or, rather, to look at such of it as was represented by the tiny, pretty seaport of Pera-yalo.

He saw a speckle of small white houses, square and clean, against a roll of soft hills folded away like a rumpled green blanket toward a misty line of hills. To the left a dramatic ridge of red earth and stone climbed steeply above the sea to a big monastery that had the appearance of a medieval castle, and surmounting the ridge was a line of bare-armed windmills standing above stunted, wind-twisted pines. A priest with three donkeys was slowly climbing the ridge. The pastel-tinted domes of many tiny churches were scattered everywhere through the village and the fields.

Since no boat had been expected, the port was almost empty. Beneath a clump of mulberry trees four men were unloading sacks of lime from a string of donkeys. Two fishermen in a red boat by the quay had stopped folding their nets and were studying him curiously. Three small barefoot boys stood some six paces away, watching the professor with eyes that were wide with a patient expectancy.

Professor Challis was an old hand in the Aegean, and, although he had never before visited Astypalaia, he knew that the oracular center of any island seaport is the coffeehouse nearest the landing steps, and across from the wharf he could see four tables set out in the early December sunshine and the sign above an open door saying *Kafenéion—Theódoros Milos.*

Instructing one of the boys to follow with his bag, he walked across. There was a pepper tree overhanging the door of the coffeehouse, a row of geraniums in old paraffin cans painted pink, a good many speckled brown hens picking in the dirt. An octopus was hanging to dry on the lower branch of the tree.

Theódoros Milos proved to be a big man in a brown and white striped undershirt and patched dungarees washed out to the color of the sky. He had a scarred chin, very light and timid eyes, and the ferocious mustache of a Cretan bandit. When the professor took a chair at one of the outside tables, he came across with a sponge and carefully wiped from the table top the few rose-pink pellets which had fallen from the overhanging tree. The professor's invitation to take a glass of *retzina* with him he accepted with a shy smile. As they sat together at the table in the milky, wintry sunshine, Professor Challis sipped his wine and began to make his inquiries.

It appeared that there was no hotel: visitors could be accommodated in any one of a number of private houses—the warmth, hospitality, and cleanliness of which the proprietor himself would vouch for—or, if one were more spiritually inclined, the monks in the big monastery astride the ridge would provide a welcome for as long as he chose to stay. On the other hand, Milos suggested with a deprecating gesture clearly meant to offset the offense of personal soliciting, there was an excellent clean room available in his own *kafenéion*, if the professor desired it.

As the professor had more than half suspected, the names of Grasset and Sorelle meant nothing to the Greek.

"The man is French, I believe," he said in further explanation. "His wife is a Greek girl. I understand she is expecting a baby."

"Ah!" The big man's eyes brightened. "I know. I think he is an artist, the man. They have the big farmhouse of Costas Lobas, past the church of St. Nicholas. They stay very much to themselves. We see them seldom."

"I must go to their house to see them," said the professor.

"Now?" Milos pursed his lips dubiously. "It is seven kilometers."

"As soon as possible, I think."

Milos shrugged and stared at the sky. The sun had already begun to dip below the craggy monastery. The sea was darkening. The air suddenly was chill.

"I think it would be better for you to go in the morning," said Milos seriously. "We have had much rain here in the last few days, and when the rain is heavy, the earth washes down from the cliffs. The roads become mud, and where they run above the sea cliffs they are very soft and dangerous."

Professor Challis nodded. The man's warning was obviously sound. In little more than an hour it would be dark; the very wildness of the setting in the immediate environment of the town made it easy to imagine what conditions would be like seven kilometers over the hills. To anyone who knew the Greek islands there was an undeniable wisdom in the man's suggestion to wait until morning. And yet . . .

He stared at his wineglass and frowned, trying to analyze the impulses that tugged at him, urging him to start now; to rise from the table beneath the pepper tree this very minute and begin trudging the seven muddy kilometers through the night's blackness to the house where Paul Grasset had hidden himself away from all the world except that personal fragment of the world which he had chosen to retain.

By the extraordinary fortune of his chance encounter with Cyril Bloom, it had fallen on him to discover Grasset's place of self-exile. But how long would this advantage remain with him? Time so fortuitously gained should not rashly be squandered.

And, more positive in its insistence, there was his own insatiable sense of curiosity to be considered. For weeks now this image had persisted in his mind of a man he had never seen, an image that had become queerly symbolic not only of a mystery that was deep and diffuse, but also in some significant way of a truth that had not yet been stated. The thread that was knotted at one end to the quiet house in Chelsea led all the way to this remote Greek island, and now no more than four miles separated him from the knot that tied the other end of the thread.

What should he say when he finally confronted Grasset? What *was* there to say? And how should he be received—he, the first intruder from that outside world which the Frenchman had deliberately renounced?

The sun had slid behind the gaunt, rocky crag; in five or ten minutes it would be gone beneath the sea line. Already the mountains were harboring the dusk in their crevices, and beginning to come forward in that eerie, overhanging movement that is the harbinger of a Grecian nightfall. There would be no twilight, merely a quick shadowing, then total darkness. All things considered, the coffeehouse man was probably right. After all, he told himself dryly, Grasset would not be expecting him: the morning would serve as well.

"Can you get someone to take my bag inside?" said the professor. The decision made, he had a warm feeling of contentment. The long journey by plane and boat had tired him: in the morning his wits would be sharper. He would have a leisurely meal in a cozy, smoky room with a charcoal brazier beside the table, and a half oka of wine, and a good sleep in a quiet room.

Milos had taken the bag himself, and the professor followed him into the dusky interior of the coffeehouse.

"The room is upstairs," said the Greek. "I shall fetch a lamp for you." He set the bag down at the foot of the staircase and vanished through a low door.

Professor Challis walked slowly toward the staircase, his gaze fixed on the two pieces of luggage that stood against the wall beside his own—a plastic overnight bag and a small, neat attaché case.

Milos emerged from the other room carrying a square oil lantern, and the beam of light picked out the small gilt letters stamped into the leather of the attaché case. S.J.R. Stephen John Roach! Then he was not the first. . . .

"There is somebody else's baggage here," he said sharply, turning to Milos.

"Ah, yes, but it does not matter," said the Greek anxiously. "I have more than one room, and the room you will have—"

"This other man," the professor cut in impatiently, "when did he come?"

"This morning, just before noon—in a boat from Rhodes."

"But how could he, when—" He broke off. Roach had called on Bloom during the morning of the day before: there was nothing to have prevented him flying down on the afternoon plane. "Where is he now?" he said.

Milos spread his hands and shrugged. He seemed bewildered by the professor's manner, as if he sensed an accusation which he could not understand. "He talked to me, but I did not know what he said," he explained guiltily. "He speaks no Greek. He had some food here in the middle of the day, and then he went away somewhere." He gestured vaguely. "He has not come back yet."

Professor Challis took a chair and sat down and for some moments he was lost in thought, while the Greek stood stiffly at the foot of the staircase, lantern in hand, watching him with puzzled concern.

"There will be a moon tonight," the professor said finally, making it a statement rather than a question.

"A moon, yes," said Milos gravely.

"And perhaps there is someone from whom I can hire a mule?"

"There are several men here who have mules. I have mules."

"Then I think perhaps I shall go now. If perhaps you could arrange . . ." He smiled. "You must forgive me if I seemed sharp with you. I had not expected this other man to be here. The fact that he is makes it imperative that I visit the Frenchman and his wife tonight, and not in the morning."

"I shall bring two mules," said Milos. "It is almost dark, and I must go with you to show you the way. Besides, the road is very bad. It will take us three hours, I think, even with the mules."

The first half hour was reasonable enough, for the lamplight from the cottages spilled out across the cobbles, and even where there were no lights the whitewashed walls of houses gave a certain luminosity to the scene, and usually a chasm of darkness had a light beyond to guide them on. But then there was an hour beyond the houses when the moon had not risen, and the hour was spent in negotiating a rocky saddle which stood between the harbor and the enclosing barrier of mountains. What Milos had called a road was no more than a goat trail cutting around the sea cliffs, zigzagging higher and higher until the surge and rush of the sea against the unseen rocks below was no more than a faint sighing in the night, the uneasy stirring of some remote yet menacing thing that lurked in the darkness far beneath the slow, nervous tread of the mules.

Milos took the lead, walking by the rump of his own mule, guiding the animals with a series of curious muleteer's cries—harsh, coughing grunts and a sort of rhythmic blubbering sound made through loose lips—which, the professor suspected, were meant more to give reassurance to the stranger than to encourage the animals.

Twice, when his mule stumbled, the professor was sickeningly conscious of the black abyss at his side, the slow churn of the sea over the jagged rocks, but each time the beast recovered its footing and went on, trembling a little, and on each of these occasions Milos had mumbled some inarticulate encouragement—to himself perhaps, or the mules, or the professor—and laughed softly as if some joke had been made which only he could understand.

A three-quarter moon rose above the sea as they reached the crest of the saddle, and struck the mud washed down from the cliffs on the left of the trail. Far below them and about a mile offshore a triangle of lights—red and green below and white above—was moving in toward the harbor.

"What boat would that be down there?" the professor called, but Milos merely shrugged without answering. His attention, in any case, was concentrated on the mules. In the mud they were less sure-footed than they had been on the slippery rocks during the long climb from the port. They slipped and plunged and frequently went to their knees, and sometimes, as they floundered at the edge of a deep gorge, the professor had to fight to control an almost overwhelming impulse to fling himself out of the lurching saddle into the comparative safety of the clinging mud.

The moonlight, in making the danger more visible, acutely sharpened the sensation of fear.

They struggled ahead, laboriously and without words, for a long time before Milos suddenly turned and shouted, "There! The church!" After the animal cries and incoherent mumblings with which he had punctuated the journey, the very clarity of his words seemed a measure of his relief. Behind the man's bulky silhouette the professor could make out the slender pencils of five cypresses against the sky and the squat, moon-pale bulk of a small domed church.

They left it on their right and took a narrow earthen road, wheel-rutted and overgrown, which seemed to lead through a grove of olives and thence to an area cultivated for vines. The nubbly, spiky roots, cut back almost to the level of the soil, looked like an army of small goblin creatures doing some strange ritual dance in the moonlight.

On the far side of the clearing was a single cypress and beside it a low white farmhouse with two lighted windows. A dog began to bark, a deep, throaty bay, and from inside the house came the muted yelping of a smaller dog. A terrier, perhaps, the professor thought nervously, remembering what somebody had once told him: that when there are two dogs and one is large, it is always the small one that is more ferocious.

Milos waited for him to come alongside him and said, "The farm of Costas Lobas. It is here that the Frenchman lives."

The door of the farmhouse opened in a sudden oblong of yellow light, and the yapping of the small dog grew shriller. Professor Challis could see the figure of a man in the doorway holding a kerosene lantern at shoulder height.

"Who is it there?" he called suspiciously, leaning forward to peer into the darkness.

"Ah, it is only Milos. Milos from the port. And a friend who has come to visit you."

His voice set the dogs into a greater clamor than ever, while Professor Challis wondered if the man in the doorway would agree with Milos' definition of him as a friend. But the man had left the doorway now and was coming slowly down a roughly flagged path toward them, the lamp held high above his head. Stabbing, jagged shadows moved among the cropped vines on either side, and the goblins danced more frenziedly than ever. Stiffly the professor dismounted from his mule.

The man with the lamp moved past Milos without a word of greeting and stopped in front of the professor, the lamp still held high and a little behind his head so that his own face was in shadow and that of the professor fully illuminated.

"Who are you?" he said.

"I must apologize for calling like this, and so late, but—"

"Who are you?" the man repeated, quietly but with a particular insistence.

"My name is Challis. We've not met. I am a friend of your brother's. Of Charles Grasset."

The silence hung between them for what seemed like many seconds, a silence with something of solidity to it, as if it were the dark cement holding in absolute rigidity the man in the night with the lamp in his hand. The wind stirred the vines with tiny crackling noises, and in some distant corner of the night a cock improbably crowed. The big dog had stopped its barking. Milos was stooping beside his mule to pat a small mongrel terrier and he was crooning in the same incoherent way he had used to the mules on the trail from the port.

"Why have you come here?" the man asked.

"I am not sure. I think to help you."

"You think to help me?" The words were softly inflected, as if the statement had amused him. "I was not aware that I needed help," he said.

"I think it is because you are not aware of it that I have come," the professor said quietly.

"You mean—"

"I mean there are others coming, others beside me. When they come perhaps you *will* need help."

"I see," said the man, and lowered the lamp to his side. "Who are these . . . these '*others*' of whom you speak?"

"Flett. Brandon Flett. You know Flett?"

"I have never heard of him. Who else?"

"A man called Roach."

There was a pause. "Yes, I know Roach," he said finally.

"He is already here. He came this morning. And then I think your brother will be coming also, and your wife's sister."

"They are coming to find Paul Grasset?"

"Yes."

"Why?"

"I think they have various reasons."

"Very compelling reasons, surely, to bring them this far."

"I think they consider them compelling, yes."

"How sad, then, that they will be disappointed, having journeyed so far. Come," he said, and turned on his heel.

Professor Challis followed him into the house.

3

HAVING SHOWN HIM into a big, low-ceilinged room where a log fire was burning in an open hearth, the man with the lamp had promptly excused himself and gone upstairs, heavy-footed in his thick farm boots of rough leather soled with many layers of rubber cut from old automobile tires and studded with hobnails. Faintly from an upstairs room voices were rising and falling. Whatever was being discussed seemed to be taking a long time, and every now and then the voices seemed to be raised as if in dispute.

Professor Challis shrugged, lowered himself into an old-fashioned rocking chair beside the fire, and looked about him.

A meager collection of books on a makeshift shelf, a small crayon drawing of a market place in Britanny, two colored prints cut from continental art magazines and set behind rather clumsy frames which probably had once contained family photographs or icons: these few intrusive details did little to diminish the frugal farmhouse character of the room.

Beneath a low ceiling of bamboo canes laid across heavy beams of walnut, two kerosene lamps with painted porcelain bases burnt in wall brackets, throwing light and shadow in dramatic upward scoops against the whitewashed walls. A third lamp, of more elaborate design and with an inverted bowl of opaque white glass, stood in the center of a round table beside a pen and inkwell and an untidy scatter of foolscap sheets of paper covered with writing. The chairs were for the most part high-backed, solid, un-compromising, and black with age. The walls revealed their astonishing thickness in the deep, arched tunnels of doorways and windows, and beyond the glass the windows were so heavily barred that the professor could not decide whether he was reminded of a fortress or of a prison. On a roughly hewn marble *lavabo,* nicked sepia with the marks of the chipping hammer, soiled dishes were piled beside an earthenware bowl and pitcher.

At one end of the room the floor level was raised to the white-washed platform of the water cistern, and from this rose the stone cylinder of the well shaft, capped by a flat cover of chipped wood supporting a galvanized-iron bucket with a rope tied to the handle.

Although there was some intuitive harmony of proportion in the house, and the big hearth gave out a comforting warmth, it was on the whole a somewhat intimidating room, as if its values were placed on a harsh indifference rather than a protective se-curity. It was a far remove, he reflected, from the gracious little Georgian house in Tite Street.

From upstairs the voices continued. Professor Challis glanced curiously at the sheets of paper on the table. He hesitated for only a moment, then rose quietly from the rocking chair, went across to the table and took the top sheet from the stack. What he read caused an immediate raising of his eyebrows:

"What van Meegeren had early discovered," the first sentence read, "was the vital principle that, in simulating any work of art from an earlier century, the establishment of receptiveness in the minds of both experts and connoisseurs might well be of far greater account than the most gifted knowledge of early pig-ments, canvas weaves, or brush techniques. . . ."

He returned the sheet of paper thoughtfully to the table and went back to the rocking chair. He stooped forward and picked up a pair of crudely forged iron tongs, tapped the burning logs into a shower of sparks, and carefully arranged the coals. Outside the wind appeared to be rising: he could hear it moaning through the trees and around the walls; leaves rustled against the windows, and sometimes a shutter would rattle uneasily. The darkness seemed to stir with a multitude of small, secret sounds.

Where was Roach? Already he had been on the island ten hours or more. He was somewhere outside there in the restless darkness —but *where?* And what was the boat he had seen from the muddy spur above the cliffs?

He was staring into the fire, an anxious frown on his face, when the voice came to him from the doorway:

"Helen, this is a friend of Polyxéna's come to call on us. His name is Challis. . . ."

The professor turned swiftly.

They stood side by side in the wide doorway, the two of them together: a dark, graceful man and the girl from the portrait above the chimney piece. A brown, smocklike garment falling loosely from her shoulders completely concealed her pregnancy. Her face and poise were exactly as he had remembered them. She looked older, and her complexion was pale, but the same arrogance and hauteur were there as she stared across at the old, white-headed man struggling to rise from the rocking chair. Against the bleak, austere background of the frugal room, in the dramatically subdued lighting from the simple oil lamps, there was something about her that was startlingly inappropriate—except that the man who stood beside her shared her alienness equally. The crude farm boots he was wearing, the thick serge trousers, the loose shirt woven of some coarse, dark material, emphasized his inappropriateness rather than distracted from it. In his dark, good-looking face there was a mocking, supercilious quality, almost of contempt, that gave to his arrogance a deeper force and an older character than the girl's.

Standing at last, and with his hand grasping the curved back of the rocking chair, Professor Challis could not help feeling that the couple in the doorway looked less like fugitives from a world they had rejected—or which had rejected them—than some royal pair exiled against their will, and sublimely confident of the inevitable summons that would recall them to a rightful sphere of majesty. Indeed, in their faces—and particularly in the man's—

there was an aloof, disdainful nobility that seemed to put the simple Astypalaian farmhouse behind them, less as something strange and unsuitable than as a setting that had no true reality at all, a thing of paint and canvas to be removed at the right moment by workmen in dirty overalls.

"My husband tells me that you know my sister," said the woman, walking across the room toward him. Her voice, musical but cool, was as withdrawn and proud as her manner. There was neither warmth nor welcome in her attitude. The man had entered the room behind her, more slowly, and now was leaning against the wall just beyond the scoop of light cast by the nearer lamp, leaning with a sort of studied negligence, like an actor who has for the moment relinquished the front of the stage to another player. His dark, shrewd eyes watched the professor with an expression of guarded cynicism. It was the face of the French aristocrat—fine-boned, narrow-browed, deep-eyed, sensitive, intelligent, intolerant—a face with that special combination of delicacy and force that one sees so frequently in early Flemish portraits.

The professor turned his attention to Helen Sorelle. "I know your sister, yes," he said simply.

"Where is she?"

"She is in Athens. That is to say, she was in Athens yesterday, I believe. She has been trying to find you. Perhaps she is on her way here now."

"I do not wish to see her."

Professor Challis stared at her for a moment and said, "It was my impression that she was most anxious to see you."

"Please don't misunderstand, Mr. Challis," said the man in the shadows. "Had my wife wished her sister to come she would naturally have invited her. But we have both come to place a high value on privacy, you see. We prefer not to be—er—to be intruded upon, by relatives or anybody else."

"I quite understand your point of view," said the professor politely. "At the same time, the desire for privacy is not altogether uncommon; the pity is that it is so often a fallible ambition, for there is always somebody who will pay no attention to our wishes. I am a total stranger, and yet *I* have intruded on your privacy."

"You were not to know, Mr. Challis," he replied urbanely.

"And Stephen Roach, who is *not* a stranger to you," continued the professor imperturbably, "has also come to the island, although I doubt he was invited. This matter of privacy, you see, is so often a thing quite beyond our control."

"Why has Roach come here?" the woman asked.

Professor Challis stared at her deliberately, and said, "According to the information I possess, he has the intention of killing your husband."

The remark had the effect he had intended: for a moment fear flickered across the woman's dark eyes, and she flashed a quick glance toward her husband. He came slowly into the light and took a chair by the fireside. The mongrel terrier followed him, circled the rug, sniffed, and settled itself at his feet.

"To kill my husband! Why should he want to do that, Mr. Challis?" She had almost recovered her composure, but not quite. The fear was still in her eyes. He had the feeling that it was always there, lurking behind the cold, studied arrogance of her beauty, rising like some loathsome and menacing creature from the depths of her self-control at the unexpected remark, the creaking of the gate, the sound of footfalls on the flagged path, the rustle of leaves in the night. His statement about Roach had not taken her by surprise: it had merely made visible for an instant the hidden terror that for so long had stalked her.

He was touched by a moment of compassion, and said, "The purpose of my call, however undesired it might be, was to warn you of this."

"Thank you, Mr. Challis," said the man by the fire. He was crouched forward in his chair, elbows on his knees, his chin in his hands. He did not turn his head, but continued to peer into the flames. "But you have still not answered my wife's question. Why should he want to kill *me?*"

"It's quite a long story, and rather complex," said the professor blandly. "However, I do assure you that the threat is very real.

You see, it seems that Roach has developed rather a habit of kill-ing. I gather he has already killed one man—possibly two—and once you begin these things . . ." He smiled. "No doubt in your French schools you were told the fable of St. Denis, who was said to have walked two leagues carrying his head in his hands. Somebody who was asked to comment on this very singular feat replied, 'Oh, the distance is nothing; it is only the first step that counts.'" He chuckled to himself and added, "I should tell you that Roach even tried to kill *me*, simply because he suspected I was coming here to warn you."

"I have already expressed my gratitude for your thoughtfulness, Mr. Challis. I am still waiting to hear your opinion of why he should want to come seeking me."

The professor leaned back in the rocking chair, linked his fin-gers behind his white hair, and said, "I find myself frequently saying this, but I think the Rocamadour Reliefs have something to do with it."

The thin, dark face turned slowly toward him. "They have found out, then," he said, and smiled slightly. "One always knew, of course, that they were bound to in the end. It was an approxi-mation of perfection, but it was not perfect. Then you think this is the reason why Roach is coming to kill me?"

"I think it may be *one* reason," said the professor guardedly.

"And what else?" He turned his head away, picked up the tongs and began rhythmically to tap one of the logs, and the sparks jetted upward and whirled away into the dark cavern of the chimney.

"I have an idea blackmail comes into it," said the professor quietly. "And the murder of a man in Dieppe."

The black tongs continued to tap at the fiery log in a slow, unflagging rhythm. Nobody spoke.

The silence was broken by the sudden deep baying of the dog outside. The terrier on the hearthrug leapt instantly to its feet, bristling for a moment before it began to yelp.

The woman had started up from her chair, and there was no concealment now of the terror in her eyes. Her husband was at the door, reaching for a double-barreled farm shotgun in a rack above the lintel.

As Professor Challis scrambled from the rocking chair to follow him, he found himself thinking that his warning had by no means been without its effect. At least when the barking dogs had heralded *him,* he had not been greeted with a gun!

He followed the Frenchman through the door into the night, and almost immediately the door was slammed behind them, and he heard the thud of the bolt ramming home into its socket, and the sound of the woman's sobbing.

There was a swift scud of cloud across the moon, and all the dark, secret world ran together in a queer mobile abstract of black and silver—shadow and moonshine, the pierced and jagged sky mirrored in shimmering water channels, cypress and olive and the goblin vines, everything alive and spiky and malevolent. . . .

To the left of them, across the vineyard, a dark shape seemed to be moving furtively toward a thick hedge of thorn, vanished in a gulf of shadow, reappeared momentarily like the blinking of an eyelid, and then was gone.

"Over there," whispered the professor. "There's something over there, near the hedge." It was the quality of the night that, in its apparent animation of dead things, it robbed living things of life. It was only *things* that stirred in the darkness, not persons.

The Frenchman grunted, half-leveled the shotgun, lowered it, then leapt down the steps and hurried across the vineyard toward the hedge.

Professor Challis made a move as if to follow him, then thought better of it. The terrain, after all, was strange to him, and quite possibly dangerous, and at the best he could be no more than a nuisance. And in any case the dark figure with the shotgun had already been swallowed in the thick shadows beyond the vines.

The dog still barked, although less frantically now, and from inside the farmhouse he could still hear the choked sobbing of Helen Sorelle. These, and the sighing of the wind in the cypress above him, were the night's only sounds.

He was about to turn and knock at the door—at least he could try to comfort the woman—when he saw the light bobbing toward him. It seemed to be coming toward the house along the trail that led through the olive grove, in the direction opposite from that which the Frenchman had taken.

Slowly and cautiously he went down the flagged path to meet it, and after a minute or two he could hear the soft, careful thud of mules' hooves and the queer blubbering noises which Milos had used to encourage his beasts. His confidence increased immediately and he quickened his pace, but the light of the hurricane lantern was still in his eyes, and nothing behind but the dim shapes of animals and people, when he heard the deep voice crying in astonishment,

"My God! How the hell did *you* get here?"

4

AFTERWARDS, Professor Challis was always inclined to regard that moment in the olive grove when he heard Bimbo's voice as the most pleasant of the whole adventure.

There was, in the first instance, his overwhelming relief that out of the strange and sinister forms of the night friendliness had come and not a deeper continuance of the menace which seemed to surround the white, moonlit farm. And he was vain enough to enjoy a deep and satisfying relish of the astonishment which his presence had occasioned. And the fact that Polly was there with Bimbo filled him with relief and gratitude. In the brief moment he had paused outside the locked door of the farmhouse, he had felt a profound concern for the woman inside. In her condition the sudden shock and fear she had so obviously suffered was not only dangerous: it posed a situation with which no man could easily cope.

"I'm so glad you've come, my dear," he said simply, giving his hand to help her from the saddle of the mule. "Helen is all right but she's rather upset. She might need careful handling. There has been a prowler. It could be Roach. He came this morning and is wandering around somewhere. Grasset's gone off with a gun, looking for him."

"Flett's come, too," said Bimbo gruffly. "We saw him at the quay as we were riding out of the town."

"I'm not so worried about Flett. I have a feeling he could be of advantage to us. It's Roach who is the problem at the moment. The thing I don't like is that your brother may be doing exactly what Roach hoped he would do. He could have deliberately roused the dogs as a way of luring Grasset from the house."

"Can't we talk about this later?" said Polly anxiously. "I must go to Helen."

"She's locked herself in," said the professor. "I suggest we leave it like that for a little while. If she hears voices outside she'll be more terrified than ever—and, besides, there are some things we must discuss before we go in. I must know—"

"But I have to go to her," Polly cut in desperately. "If she's inside there alone she may—"

"I think the professor's right, darling," Bimbo said gently. "A few minutes aren't going to make that much difference, and we should get things straight." He turned to the professor. "You're right about Roach," he said. "Evidently he's a homicidal maniac and he's got an obsession about Paul. He's always hated him, and I gather Paul was trying to blackmail him and he's terrified that if he doesn't kill Paul something pretty terrible will be exposed."

"I think the fear is mutual, then," said the professor. "They were both very shocked indeed when I told them Roach was here on the island." He paused. "They don't seem particularly interested in Flett," he added.

"Polly knows about Flett," said Bimbo. "She can tell you."

For some minutes the professor questioned her, and they were still talking together by the mules when the professor caught sight of the thin, dark figure emerging from the hedge beyond the vineyard. He saw him take a few paces toward the house, then hesitate, tense and rigid amid the cropped vines, staring toward the group around the hurricane lantern, and then he lifted the gun into both hands and began to walk slowly toward them.

"Ah, here comes Grasset now," said the professor. He turned to Polly. "I think it would be best if you took charge of your sister," he said. "I suggest you try to get her upstairs into her room, put her to bed, and then—" He stopped abruptly. The girl's mouth was open and her eyes dilated and filled with an expression of astonishment and terror. She was looking past his shoulder, staring at the approaching figure in the moonlight, and for a moment he thought she was about to faint. "What is it, Polly?" he said sharply, and swung around, and even as he turned, he was aware of Bimbo's figure frozen into the same horrified rigidity. "What is it?" he demanded.

The man with the gun emerged from the shadows into a pool of moonlight, stopped a few paces away from them, and lowered the shotgun slowly. There was a moment of silence, and then in a quiet voice he said,

"Hello, Polyxéna. Hello, Grasset."

The silence that followed seemed to last an eternity, seemed to scream with a million voices. It was Bimbo finally who broke it, speaking in a voice that seemed to come, labored and straining, from very far away.

"Where is Paul?" he said. "Where is my brother?"

The night moved with all the quiet, furtive sounds of its stirring, and a low, shuddering moan was forced from Polly's lips, before the man with the gun replied.

"I regret to say your brother is dead."

For what seemed a long time the professor was locked in the same still trance of unbelief, his eyes staring at the frozen tableau of the three figures in the checkered pattern of the moonlight.

"Then in God's name who are *you?*" he cried at last.

"My name is Fanlec," said the man with the gun. "Claude Fanlec." He turned on his heel and strode toward the house.

5

"Go AWAY," moaned the woman who was huddled into the corner on the bottom step of the staircase. "I don't want you to come near me. Please go away. Leave me alone."

"Helen, darling, you must listen to me, *please!*" Polly was on her knees in the flagged hall, her face white with shock and pain. "You must let me take you upstairs. You're not well and—"

"Why can't we be left alone? Why does everyone have to come hunting us down? Oh God! Go away! Go away, *all of you!*" She buried her head in her arms, her body convulsed by sobbing.

Fanlec moved across and put his arm around her shoulders. "Come, dear," he said gently. "You must do as your sister says. You must go up to bed, Helen. There is nothing to worry about now. It will be all right, you'll see. Now, come. Polyxéna and I will take you up."

It was half an hour before Fanlec left her and returned to the room below, but Polly stayed with her in the low, raftered bedroom. Two lamps were burning, and Fanlec had lit a fire in the small open grate, and the very calmness and warmth of the room gradually gave the overwrought woman peace and composure. It was a long time before either of the sisters spoke, and the silence itself must have acted as an unguent upon the hurts they shared, for when speech came it had that rare and intimate purity, an instinctive reliance on truth, which children share sometimes but adults seldom.

Indeed, in the calm, silent room, with the clock ticking on the wall and the fire spluttering, and occasionally the sighing fret of the wind outside or the almost inaudible spit of the lampwicks, it was difficult not to be sensible to the feeling that all intimacy and candor of thought had been sealed within these dusky, white-washed walls, as within a confessional, immune from the profane inquisitions of the outside world. Within this half-dusk and half-silence the things said were related only to the *now* and not to the past—although they were concerned with the past—as if the thick Astypalaian walls formed an impregnable bastion against the forces of yesterday and the threat of some unrevealed tomorrow.

"I wanted to explain it all to you in Paris," Helen was saying. "I tried to tell you several times, but somehow I couldn't do it. There was my own conscience to contend with: I had this feeling of guilt that I had taken him away from you . . . and I thought— I don't know what made me think it—I thought you still loved him, that you had some queer, stifled, romantic thing about him. You used to talk about him as if you did."

"It was you I was anxious about, not him," Polly said quietly. "I thought you were becoming involved in his dishonesties, that you might—"

"That was the least of it, Polly. You were too young to know what was behind it, too young to understand. You never *did* understand—you never could have—the intolerable viciousness of the man, the brutality of his mental cruelty, his eternal pursuit after women—in the end almost any woman would do—his cheap little lies and deceits and betrayals, his conceit . . . and the horror of seeing that everything he touched was smirched and tainted. You were young, Polly. You were too young to know."

"But you loved him at first. I *saw* you together. And I . . . I used to think—"

"Yes, I loved him. He was easy to love—at first. Any number of women will tell you that. But afterwards it was not the same. It wasn't until I began to know Claude Fanlec that I came to see what Paul was *doing* to me. He was tainting me, destroying me, as he had everybody else. And he *knew* he was doing it . . . he always knew. It was Claude who made me see that." She paused and smoothed her hands across the counterpane. She had regained complete control of herself, and her face against the two white pillows had come alive again and rich with beauty, and her eyes were warm and thoughtful. "Did you ever realize how oddly alike they were?" she said. "In appearance, I mean. I think that was what first attracted me to Claude. When you saw the two of them together they looked almost like brothers—and yet in temperament they were poles apart."

"You know that I never knew him well," said Polly. "Claude, I mean. And I never knew that you were—"

"Unlike Paul, he was never given very greatly to public appearances. I didn't get to know him for a long time, but as I began to get acquainted with him I grew to like him very much. After Paul's passions and tempests you could go to him and find quietness and understanding, and I suppose more and more I came to rely on him for support, to go to him when I was fearful or troubled, or when Paul had been particularly beastly."

"But the last time I saw you in Paris, the night you came to my studio—I found out later that you had had a violent quarrel with . . . with Claude."

"I know," Helen said quietly. "Paul was in New York at the time, and I'd gone to dinner with Claude at Ricci's. He seemed quite different from his normal self. He was nervous and irritable and anxious, and I put it down to the financial trouble he was in, and he didn't tell me until long afterwards that he had received a letter from Paul threatening him with blackmail. It wasn't our usual sort of dinner at all, and we both drank too much wine, and he grew more and more morose until finally he turned on me in an absolute fury and demanded to know why I continued to associate with Paul. And that made me angry, too, because his bad mood had spoilt our dinner, and because I was very young and stupid, and because I'd been drinking too much wine. I told him that if Paul was good enough for him to associate with in business, he was good enough for me to associate with in bed. He just looked at me. He didn't say anything; he just looked at me across the wineglasses, and his face was tense and pale, and I remember thinking that that was the way someone would look at you if he was going to kill you."

She stopped and lowered her eyes, and her fingers plucked at the hem of the counterpane. "And then, in a tone of absolute contempt," she went on softly, "he asked me to marry him. And suddenly I was out in the street, running away, crying. . . ." There was another long pause before she said, "That's when I went around to see you, but when I got there I found I couldn't say anything. It didn't seem worthwhile somehow. Nothing seemed worthwhile. That was when I realized that I had the taint, too—like all Paul's other women."

"And after that?"

"I saw Claude once or twice, but we were both deliberately very cool and polite, and then one day—it was in Ricci's again—I told him that Paul was on his way back from New York and that I was going to Dieppe to meet him. I didn't *want* to meet him . . . I never wanted to see him again. It was just that silly, young, cruel thing again. I wanted Claude to think I was still in love with Paul. I wanted to hurt him as much as he had hurt me. But he just smiled and said, 'Give him my best regards,' and turned on his heel and walked out of the restaurant."

"And you did go to meet Paul, didn't you? I was told you had."

"I went, yes. I hated myself for going—but I went. I waited three days in Dieppe and Paul didn't come. He had cabled me from the ship, telling me to meet him in Dieppe—but he didn't come. I had just checked out of my hotel when I met Claude. He had come up from Paris two days before and had been searching for me all over Dieppe. I didn't tell him what had happened. I didn't explain anything. We were walking back and suddenly we saw a bus standing there, ready to leave for Rouen, and we looked at it and looked at each other, and suddenly we were in the bus, side by side, running away together. Claude didn't even go back to his hotel to check out, or pay his bill, or to pick up his baggage. We were halfway to Rouen before I realized it, but when I reminded him of it he just shrugged his shoulders and laughed. He said he had only come to Dieppe with the intention of getting me and taking me back to Paris and so he hadn't brought anything with him of particular value. The following week we were married in Rouen." She put her head back on the pillow and closed her eyes wearily.

"You mustn't talk any more, Helen," said Polly anxiously. "You must rest now. You're exhausted. And you have to think of the baby. This isn't good for you."

"I have to tell you, Polly. I *want* to tell you. If I don't tell you, you can't understand. Sometimes I . . . I don't understand it myself. But I want to talk. I've been caged here for six months, Polly, wanting to talk, talk, *talk!*" She passed her hand across her eyes, and when she spoke again her voice was low and controlled.

"We had been in Rouen only two days when we saw this fantastic thing in the newspaper. It was only a little piece, no more than a couple of inches long, but I can read it now for you, word for word. It was an account of the death in Dieppe of Claude François Fanlec."

"But how could—"

"You mustn't interrupt, Polly. You must let me explain. The body of the man who had died in Dieppe was found floating beneath the concrete piles of the new pier, with a bullet wound in the head. The newspapers said it had been in the water for several days. What papers were in the man's pockets were illegible. The revolver which had killed him was found on the sea bed not far from where the body was floating. I think perhaps the police investigations were conducted a little carelessly, but anyway, in the course of these inquiries they learnt that a certain Claude Fanlec had disappeared from his hotel several days before, leaving all his clothing behind, and an unpaid hotel bill. The hotelier told the police that the man had seemed to be under considerable strain and was obviously greatly agitated."

"Yes, but surely that was because of *you*, not—"

"Shhh, dear. The police made other inquiries, too. They discovered that Fanlec was acutely worried by business matters, and that bankruptcy proceedings against him were pending. He had no booking for a Newhaven crossing, nor any apparent reason for being in Dieppe. And because he had no living relatives who could be found, the formal identification was made by the hotelier. The man whose body was found beneath the pier was Paul, of course. He and Claude were alike—sufficiently alike, at any rate, for the mistake to be made. The body had been in the water several days. A hotelier's image of his transient guests, even one who doesn't pay his bill, must be a sketchy one at best. Probably in the best of faith, he testified that the dead man was his missing guest.

"But the police were still cautious. They allowed three weeks to elapse before the inquest was held. During that period Claude Fanlec never returned to his apartment in Paris, nor to his business affairs. Claude Fanlec was never seen again. The inquest only lasted seven minutes, and the finding was of death by suicide while the balance of the mind was disturbed."

"But . . . but it's all too fantastic, too impossible!" Polly protested. "It's too much of a coincidence . . . it's—"

"There was no coincidence," said Helen calmly. "Paul had come there to meet me, as he had promised. So both he and Claude were there in Dieppe at the same time for a very definite reason —for the *same* reason. They were there because each of them knew that I was there."

"Then why should Paul commit suicide if he had gone there to meet you?"

"Paul didn't commit suicide. He was murdered. He was either followed to Dieppe, or intercepted there, and in some way he was lured to the end of the pier, probably at night, and he was shot and his body was thrown into the sea. If his body had been identified correctly, I imagine there would have been a much greater hue and cry, much more diligent inquiries—it would have been a matter for the Sûreté and not just a more or less routine inquiry by the provincial police—for while there was a perfectly plausible motive for the suicide of Claude Fanlec, there was no motive whatever for the suicide of Paul Grasset."

"Then . . . then supposing what you say is true—who would have wanted to murder him?"

"Quite a number of people, I imagine. But the person who *did* murder him was Stephen Roach. That's why he has come to this island, looking for us. Don't you see, Polly, that he wants to kill us, to kill Claude and me. He *has* to kill us, Polly, because we are the only two people on the face of the earth who know."

There was a long silence. The fire spat, and outside the big dog began to bark, and the deep bay faltered and growled into silence.

"You can run away from things, Polly, but you can only run away a certain distance," she said wearily. "Perhaps it's wrong to think you can run away at all, but at all events I think this is about as far as one can go. Then one has to stop and turn and look back to see what it was one was running from. Or perhaps it has caught up with you by then. I think we've run far enough, really." She closed her eyes. "I'm tired," she said, "very tired, Polly. I don't believe I want to talk any more."

She opened her eyes for a moment and smiled at her sister, then turned her face to the wall.

6

"You are not in any doubt at all that it *was* Roach then?" The professor sat at his ease in the rocking chair, watching Fanlec pace backward and forward in front of the whitewashed cylinder of the well.

In the constant movement of the man there was some terrible, tormented restlessness: the dark, fine-boned head lowered and thrust forward and moving from side to side, as if all the organs were questing for the causes of fear and torment . . . the strained eyes turned to the stairs, to door and windows, flicking to the dark-beamed ceiling through which the murmur of women's voices drifted . . . the ears cocked for every sound that crept in from the uneasy night . . . the nervous flexing of the soft, rather plump hands . . . the pad-pad-pad of the thick-soled boots. He was like some caged animal: passionate, proud, humiliated—and *trapped*.

Yet for all his fear and torment and anxiety for the woman in the room above, he was still formidably in control of himself, for when he answered it was with an arrogant indifference in startling contrast to the obvious state of his nerves.

"Doubt?" he said. "How can there be any doubt? It is perfectly clear, surely."

"Yes, but *why?*" Bimbo asked angrily. "You give us this long rigmarole about what happened in Dieppe, but you don't explain why." He stood before the fire, nervously tapping the iron fire tongs against his leg, a gigantic finger in the lamplight beneath a vast shadow that climbed the wall and was lost in the black gulf of the roof beams. It was obvious that he, too, was deeply affected by the pervasive atmosphere of shock and strain and tension. He looked baffled and angry. "It was my brother who was murdered," he said gruffly, "and I want to know *why.*"

Fanlec stopped, and rested his hand on the top of the well as he turned to Bimbo. Except for the restless drumming of his fingers on the well lid, he was quite motionless. His face was set and haughty, the face of the French aristocrat staring down at the canaille. "He was your brother, yes," he said coldly, "so I suppose I should apologize. Your brother was a wretched, contemptible little swine. He was—"

"He was not too contemptible for you to grab his woman and his name, and to scuttle away into hiding with both of them!" said Bimbo savagely.

"I did not take his name. My passport—"

"To hell with your passport! I'm not talking of your passport. I am talking of your tacit acceptance of another man's identity."

Professor Challis moved his chair gently on its rockers, backwards and forwards, soothingly.

"If you will allow me to continue," said Fanlec icily, "I was about to say that your brother was also a fool. And *that* is why he was killed." He turned to the professor, who was immediately very still and small in the chair, watching. "In New York," Fanlec went on, "Grasset had ingratiated himself with Grantheim to the point where he was receiving money for the purpose of buying European art works for the millionaire. These commissions he placed in the hands of Roach and Joákimos, and—"

"Why were the commissions not placed with you?" the professor asked patiently.

"At this stage my association with Grasset had been terminated."

"Can you tell me why?" The professor's voice was still very quiet and soothing. It was clear that Fanlec was deeply distressed and humiliated by the necessity for explanations. He was not the sort of man, the professor reflected, who normally would explain anything.

"I had come to dislike the man," Fanlec said coldly, "to dislike the whole association."

"Was this because of Helen?"

"Because of a number of things," said Fanlec shortly. He had resumed his pacing, backward and forward across the width of the room. "He had altered his connections," he went on, talking very rapidly as if he had an unpleasant duty to perform and was anxious to get it over and done with. "He always did have something of a genius for using people, so he was perfectly happy to allow Roach to do all the work while he sat back and picked the plums, even though he was well aware that Roach had picked the earlier crop—or some of it, anyway—in cheating his employer on the matter of the Rocamadour carvings."

"In that deal you'd done some cheating yourself, hadn't you?" said Bimbo roughly. "Or are you trying to claim a lily-white status now the money's spent?"

"My dear Grasset," he said contemptuously, "I have not the least feeling of guilt or repentance so far as the Rocamadour sculptures are concerned. May I remind you that it was Proud'hon who said—" He paused deliberately, as if to make it perfectly clear that he did not expect his listener to remember anything that Proud'hon had said. ". . . who said, 'Property is theft.' Grantheim had immense, incalculable property. I suggest to you that it could scarcely have been acquired without some considerable disregard for conventional morals. He was, moreover, a *nouveau riche* of the most abominable kind. It gave me some pleasure to take from him a little—such a very little—of what he had taken from others. As a rule, one does not repine one's pleasures." He turned his attention to the professor, as if it were to him that his explanations should be made. "What I took I put back into art," he said. "I helped a good many artists who otherwise might have received no encouragement at all, who would have perished creatively." A sudden gust of wind rattled the shutters, and he stopped abruptly, his body tense, his head cocked to one side, listening.

"The wind," said the professor mildly. "I believe it is strengthening." He smiled. "These artists you assisted—they were grateful, of course."

Fanlec made a small, wry grimace, as though he were eating a lemon: the professor was not sure whether the grimace pertained to what he had to say or was a device used deliberately to minimize the fear which had momentarily gripped him. "On the contrary," he said. "They hated me for it, and mistrusted me deeply. From that I derived some pleasure also. Unfortunately, it was a pleasure which finally reduced me to a condition of bankruptcy."

"Look, why don't we stop mincing words?" said Bimbo impatiently. "You had your fun, and you had your profit, and in making Grantheim pay for his particular form of snobbery you at least gratified your own. All right. Let's drop it at that and get back to the subject."

"Quite," said Fanlec loftily. "One finds it somewhat difficult to collect one's thoughts when one is subjected to constant interruption and cross-questioning." He turned his head away and resumed his nervous, heavy pacing.

Pad-pad-pad . . . up and down, up and down, up and down. . . . The thick, crudely cut layers of old automobile tires moved restlessly back and forth across the pink stone flags.

How he must hate it all, Professor Challis reflected—the unrefined frugality of this primitive environment which imprisoned him, the coarseness of his clothing, the remoteness from all the things he understood and held dear . . . from beauty and culture and tradition, from civilized things. . . . How tormented he must be by the unending strain of living always in fear of the unexpected knock on the door, the footstep on the path outside. . . . And how every fiber of his aloof, contemptuous, aristocratic person must loathe and resent this brutal and unsolicited intrusion from the outer world into his innermost privacies. . . .

"Yes, I was talking of Grasset," he said. "I was trying to explain to you that he was not altogether happy with the new arrangements he had undertaken with Roach and Joákimos. He did not, in fact, care very much for the tempo of these new activities. His mode of living had plunged him fairly deeply into debt. He could no longer afford to keep up his London house. He had come to a point where he was extremely anxious for results . . . for *money*. . . ."

"And so," said the professor, "he began to blackmail you?"

Fanlec stopped and turned, a thin, rigid figure against the white platform of the cistern. "That was his intention, yes." His eyes rested for a moment on Bimbo, and in them the hatred for the dead man who had persecuted him was transferred in some fashion to the big figure of the dead man's brother who stood watching him suspiciously from the fireside. "It is not a pleasant thing to find oneself threatened by a filthy little *petit bourgeois* trickster, by a conceited upstart from a graveyard in Cherbourg, and—"

"Nor very pleasant, I imagine," Bimbo cut in violently, "to have the shame of knowing that it was your own trickery that had got you into the position where you *could* be threatened by him. He was clever enough for you to use when it suited you, but—"

"Shhh, Bimbo," said the professor placatingly. "Let M. Fanlec say what he has to say."

"That is not the point anyway," said Fanlec tersely. "I was quite incapable of paying blackmail money, even had I succumbed to his threats. The vital thing is that he also began to threaten Roach and Joákimos. That was his mistake. That was where he proved himself a fool."

"Yes. . . ." said the professor thoughtfully. "But—"

"Indeed, he did more," said Fanlec. "He led Roach to believe that because of his dissatisfaction with the way the Grantheim commissions were being handled he was planning to resume his association with me. This must have been most disconcerting to Roach, who had spent much time and energy on what he had hoped would be a long-term project with very rich pickings at the end of it. Roach had already suffered considerable psychological injury at the hands of Grasset. His reputation was in jeopardy if Grasset fulfilled his threat—possibly you were not aware that Roach is the author of several creditable works on medieval and Byzantine antiquities—and he came to the conclusion that this troublesome person would have to be eliminated. The works of art which Roach had purchased and which had given Grantheim great satisfaction had all been sent to New York by Joákimos, and doubtless Roach felt that with Grasset out of the way Joákimos would have no great difficulty in convincing Grantheim that the good work could be carried on by the old, reliable firm." For the first time he smiled, but it was an ironic smile with no amusement in it.

"I see the motive now, yes," said Professor Challis thoughtfully.

"Exactly. Roach was entirely *au fait* with all Grasset's movements. He could not afford to allow him to return to Paris in case he resumed his association with me. He simply followed him to Dieppe, enticed him to the end of the pier at night, shot him, bundled the body into the sea, and tossed the gun in afterwards so that it might look like a case of suicide. The rest you know."

"Since when, of course, Roach has been vitally concerned that nobody should probe too deeply into the matter of Grasset's disappearance or Claude Fanlec's death."

"Quite."

"So concerned, in fact, that in Athens he has already killed one man who had begun to pick up the scent, and has now come to this island with the deliberate intention of killing you."

"Yes," said Fanlec calmly. "I think that sums it up."

"I see it all now," said the professor mildly. "Yes. Thank you, M. Fanlec."

Upstairs there was the sound of a door closing, and footsteps, and they waited in silence while Polly came down the stairs. She walked across the room slowly and stood beside Bimbo, and then she looked across to Fanlec and said, "She is all right now." On her face as she looked at the Frenchman was an expression of cautious wonder, and then she lowered her eyes. Bimbo reached awkwardly for her hand.

Fanlec seemed at a loss for the first time. He glanced at the ceiling, looked across at the professor, and then turned his head away as if he were unsure of what he should do.

"Go up to her," said Professor Challis gently. "Go on up."

The single chime of the clock marked the half-hour after midnight. The mongrel on the hearthrug opened one eye and cocked an ear to the sound, as if it had something to communicate to him, found that it was an echo of earlier and equally unimportant night noises, and returned to sleep.

Fanlec went slowly up the stairs, and each step of the coarse thick boots with the white lining frayed through the licorice-black strips of rubber brought a protesting creak from the planks. He would hate that, too . . . the creaking of the boards, the chiming of the clock . . . the noise of things, the feel of things, the look of things . . . hate every trivial flavor and fragment of the prison that walled him in.

The professor's face was very thoughtful as he watched the crude, homemade boots slowly climb the staircase and vanish.

He turned to the girl and said gently, "Polly, you must go to bed. You are exhausted."

"I'm all right," she said. "I'm tired, yes, but I don't imagine I should sleep."

"Nevertheless, I think it would be wise to try. And anyway I want Bimbo to take the mules and go with Milos or your man back to the town. I want him to try to find Flett."

"Flett!" Bimbo turned to him in astonishment. "Why the devil do we want *him?* I should have thought it was complicated enough without—"

"It will be more complicated still if this question of confused identity isn't cleared up. I have an idea it might save a lot of trouble if Flett knows. I suspect he will not be particularly interested in Fanlec." He did not express the other thought that was in his mind—that it might be safer not to have Bimbo and his brother's murderer together in the same house.

7

Professor Challis stretched his small body on the hard-padded wooden *kanapés*, lifted himself to his elbow, and looked at the gold watch lying on the chair beside him. Twenty minutes to three. Bimbo and the muleteer would be more than halfway down the mountain by now.

It was very quiet. The wind had dropped away, and the night was held in an absolute stillness which was somehow more ominous than the earlier stirrings and rustlings and sighings. Nobody seemed to be abroad in the darkness. . . . Had there been a prowler at all, or had the dogs been roused only by the approach of the mules bringing Bimbo and Polly? There was no sound from the room upstairs, where Polly slept with her sister. At the far end of the dusky room, motionless on one of the high-backed chairs, Claude Fanlec sat, his eyes closed, his hands folded in his lap. He had been sitting there without a sound ever since he had come down from the upstairs room, but the professor doubted that he slept.

All the lights had been extinguished except the one lamp on the table beside the written sheets of paper—the crammed and knowledgeable papers which represented a continuance of his identification with that world of culture from which he was separated: how ironic that it should take the form of a treatise on the techniques and practice of art forgeries. . . .

Had the man really believed that his story would be accepted? Here was a man, intelligent, proud, cultured, fastidious, the product of his country's best blood and brains, who asked you to believe that he would voluntarily submit to exile in what he must regard as a barbarian land simply to escape from his financial troubles and the sordid implications of bankruptcy—from which, in any event, Helen Sorelle's money could have saved him—or even so that this woman he loved could, as he had put it, "wash her hands in a clean stream somewhere." No, there had to be much stronger compulsions than these to force Claude Fanlec into a renunciation of all he held dear in life.

And how was it possible, knowing the pride of the man, to imagine that he could have accepted the fortuitous mistake in identity at Dieppe and have found his own salvation in the assumption, however tacit, of the name and personality of the very man whom he most hated and despised? And even apart from these considerations, his story itself would have condemned him in any court in the land. How plausible it had seemed on the surface; how full of weaknesses upon examination.

He had been so careful in explaining the motives of Stephen Roach—yet were not his own motives even stronger? Like Roach, he had been treated badly by the sculptor, he had suffered from his ingratitude, he had been threatened with blackmail, and he believed that Grasset was fattening up a goose to lay a golden egg which he was not going to be permitted to share. But, unlike Roach, he had a second and much more compelling motive for murder—the motive of jealousy. He had become deeply enamored of Helen Sorelle, and so far as he knew, the girl was rejecting his suit and planning to go back to her old lover. How could he have borne the thought that this woman whom he had come deeply to love, and whom he had rescued at the very brink of the pit of degradation, should once again become the tool of this contemptible upstart he despised? So he had hurried after her to Dieppe—by his own account, to save her and bring her back unsoiled. But he had moved with strange slowness for a Sir Lancelot hot with passion. He had been in Dieppe, alone, for nearly forty-eight hours before he had found her. The professor smiled to himself. He was an old man, and a sedentary one, but he did know Dieppe and he would guarantee to make a very thorough examination of every hotel register in the town—every hotel, that is, at which Helen Sorelle could possibly stay—in a single morning. In a court of law, Fanlec would not find it altogether easy to account for his actions during those forty-eight hours. . . .

And how could he possibly have known the *terms* in which

Grasset was attempting to blackmail Roach? If Grasset had been using him as a play-off to Roach, he would hardly have written to tell him. He could not have found out from Grasset personally because Grasset was dead. Roach or Joákimos would not have told him—and there was nobody else who knew; that is if the story were true, as Fanlec had told it.

And finally, there was the matter of the gun which had killed Grasset and which, according to Fanlec's account, was thrown into the sea after the body. The fact was perfectly true, as was revealed in the transcript of the inquest evidence which Jacques Monfreid had sent to him together with the rest of the press clippings on the matter. But it was a comparatively trivial detail, and in the scant reports on the case it happened to be a detail that was never mentioned. The story, in fact, had been covered by only two men: a Dieppe provincial reporter and a man from *Agence France Presse,* whose story had serviced all the Paris newspapers. If Fanlec's story were true, newspaper reports would have been his only source of information. There were only two versions of the story which had ever been printed. Neither of them mentioned the unimportant little detail upon which Fanlec was so singularly well-informed. . . .

Professor Challis arranged himself more comfortably on the hard couch and closed his eyes and began to think about the Duc de Fanlec, whom Mirabeau had criticized. What, he wondered, had been the reason for his attack? He would have to look it up one day, when he was once more within reach of a good library. . . . What a poor press the death of Fanlec had received . . . such a pathetic little epitaph for the termination of a noble line. . . .

The thought depressed him vaguely, and for some unaccountable reason he found himself thinking of Brandon Flett. In a curious way he felt more sorry for Flett than he did for Fanlec. Flett had yet to realize that the man whom he had pursued for so long, and with such patient implacability, was less than a shadow. His interest in Fanlec would be strictly limited. After all, the dealer's role in the hoaxing of Grantheim had been a not altogether uncommon one, and, in any case, it was likely that Flett had undertaken his mission in the first place more from a sense of obligation than of obsession. It had hardened into an unrelenting and vengeful hunt only after he had discovered the fate of the girl whom he had called Jenny; the girl who, under the dark alchemy of Paul Grasset's callous charm, had been transformed into the pitiable travesty of Giji, the woman of Montmartre, the girl everybody knew. . . .

Poor Flett! His fellow-American was not a particularly likable man—there always appeared to be something ruthless beneath the surface, a kind of buried brutality that gave the tone to his stubborn, ungracious character—and yet there was some quality in him that evoked a grudging admiration: a kind of honesty of purpose, and a deep awareness of injustice. Where an injustice was concerned he seemed incapable of tolerance or forgiveness. He was a sort of surly knight-at-arms, not palely loitering but obstinately pursuing his own strange, puritanical quest for a balance of righteousness—pursuing it in a world that no longer gave employment to the knight-errant. The Holy Grail was a cotton-wool wrapping for the vanities of the world's Grantheims, and damsels in distress were no longer rescued from fire-breathing dragons, but ended up instead on the Place Pigalle asking sailors for cigarettes.

A formidable figure in a way, Flett, yet sad and lost and lonely. But even now he would continue to pursue his own strange, intractable course. In his conflict with Paul Grasset he had been grappling with shadows, but that did not mean that his search for a righteous balance of things was over. The account still remained to be squared for Joseph Parnell Kelly. . . .

The heavy, dusky silence of the room settled on the professor's eyes, and he slept.

But it was Brandon Flett who was in his mind when he was awakened three-quarters of an hour later—awakened by the crash of breaking glass and the echoes of the pistol shot roaring through the room: the pistol shot that killed Claude Fanlec as he sat with closed eyes on the high-backed chair.

8

To FLETT, clambering down the steep goat path to its junction with the mule trail from the port, the sound of the shot was distant but unmistakable. The goatherd who had guided him over the short trail from the port heard it, too, and he began to scramble more quickly down the rocks. He was a lithe, agile man with an instinctive skill for picking the easiest path. Flett found himself almost as grateful for the man's experience as earlier in the night, during his long search of the port taverns, he had been grateful for the smattering of English he spoke.

He could see, about two hundred yards ahead, a small white church with five cypresses growing in the yard. The mule trail was just below them, chopped into a mess of soft mud by the hooves of animals, skirting the edge of a ravine so steep-walled and deep that it looked as if the skin of the earth had been gashed wide open.

They had scarcely reached the edge of the trail when the goatherd stiffened and said, "Look!" But Flett had seen it at the same time—the dark figure that had emerged into the dapple of moonlight from the deep bars of shadow cast by the cypresses. It ran a few yards along the trail toward them, then stopped, half-crouched, as if listening for something, and then it came running toward them, weaving and skipping from side to side, as if it were dodging the puddles and the slippery patches.

It had covered perhaps fifty yards when the second figure broke from the shadows—a very small figure, trotting briskly and waving its arms.

Flett grabbed the goatherd by the arm and dragged him in behind a big limestone boulder. "Keep quiet," he said softly, and waited.

It seemed a long time before he could hear the soft slap and slither of the man's feet in the squashy slush, and as the sound grew more distinct he could hear the man's panting and gasping.

He tensed himself behind the rock. A head and shoulders appeared, jerking forward against the shining steel sheet of the sky. Flett made his leap, a gigantic figure in the moonlight, and the other man started and reeled away. Flett could feel his feet sliding from under him as he grasped at the man's arm, and the whole weight of his falling body seemed to be in the clutch of his fingers feeling for the man's coat, feeling the polished grain of the gabardine like the rasp of a fine file. . . . And then he was flat in the mud, and the figure was away from him and a little below him . . . less a figure than a pair of hands scrabbling at a loose, oozing lip of mud and a terrified face turned up to him in the moonlight—the face of Stephen Roach.

It was an image of an instant, a flickering thing of a nightmare, and then it was gone. The mud moved as if it sighed, and a brown clot in which a white stone was embedded slid slowly over the edge and dropped away. Nothing was left in the night but a wild, choking scream that floated in the air a moment, then died abruptly.

Flett was still on his hands and knees in the mud, staring down into the blackness of the pit, when Professor Challis came panting to his side.

"It was Roach," Flett whispered.

"Roach, yes," said the professor.

"I thought it was Grasset," he said dully. "I don't know why, but I thought it was Grasset."

"You wanted to think it was Grasset, that's why."

"No. It seems a stupid thing to say, but it's the way I always thought I'd meet him—running toward me at night . . . at night in the moonlight. It was a night like this—just like this—the night he took Jenny away."

"That's what it is then; it's an association of ideas. It doesn't matter. Roach mistakenly killed Fanlec, thinking he was Grasset, too. He shot him through the window at the back of the house, away from where the dog was tethered. The room was almost dark, and they looked alike. He must have thought it was Grasset, sitting there in the chair." He reached his hand down. "Come on," he said. "Get up out of that mud."

Flett scrambled to his feet, and said, "That's a queer thing, thinking it was Grasset. I can't seem to get it out of my mind."

"Grasset is dead," said Professor Challis, and for a moment he was thoughtful. "Paul Grasset destroyed people. In a way he destroyed himself, as he destroyed almost everyone he touched. Even after he was dead, himself, this destructive thing of his lingered on. Now it's all finished. It's all cleaned up. Everything." He paused and added, "It's all cleaned up for Curtis Grantheim, too. That will please him, won't it?"

"I guess so," said Flett.

9

THERE WAS a fresh rhythm and sparkle to the sea, and the islands sliding by were a deep violet and as sharply edged as if they had been cut from colored paper. Vassilis Klonaris was singing at the wheel, and the spray from the *Barbara's* high, curving prow was making sunny rainbows above the deep blue sea.

Flett had gone below to see that Helen was as comfortable as possible in the captain's spotless little cabin. Bimbo, duffel-coated against the sharpness of the wind, stood in the curved wedge of the bow, his arm around Polly's waist. The wind had blown her short hair into curls and was streaming the red handkerchief from her neck.

Professor Challis settled himself more comfortably on the coil of thick Manila rope, and reached into his pocket for Mr. Valentine's letter. He was sure it would amuse Polly to hear about it.

"Polly!" he called, but the wind took the name and flung it away.

"Polly!" he shouted more loudly, but even as he did so he saw that she had turned her face to Bimbo, and the old man smiled. For the moment they were beyond distraction, beyond any necessity for amusement. He put on his spectacles and turned his attention to the letter, to read again what Mr. Valentine had to say:

I managed to get in through the pensioners' garden and climbed the side wall. The statues are there all right, so you must have been misinformed. I counted twelve of them. Very nice, I thought they were. One in particular took my fancy, that's the second one down from the pensioners' garden on the wall nearest the Embankment. I was wondering—I hope you don't mind—if you could find out if any of the statues are for sale. You remember that second floor landing of mine just down from the door of your room, where I used to keep the Tudor chest. Well, that would be a lovely place for that statue I fancy if they're willing to dispose of it. The price would have to be reasonable, of course. . . .

Professor Challis smiled and took off his spectacles and looked again toward the bow, but clearly it was less than ever a moment for interruption.

Well, he could find out later—although he felt reasonably sure that the girl in the garden who had taken his landlord's fancy was Polly.

Perhaps Mr. Valentine had a greater acumen than he had given him credit for. Polly *would* look lovely on the second floor landing. Any sort of landing, if it came to that. . . .